angement with Simon and Schuster, Inc.

003-9

anuary 1983
aneously in Canada

the United States of America
Madison Avenue, New York, New York 10016

Shulcross leaned forward. "I don't understand how Sutton was able to return from Cygni 61—the ports were broken, and that means he navigated eleven light-years exposed to space, without a suit. In addition, his ship is just a pile of junk. There are layers of rust on everything and the wiring is completely non-functional. There is no possible way he could have returned with that ship. But he did."

Clark added, quietly, "Besides, Sutton had no food or water."

"I don't think," said Anderson, "that the man is human. Oh, it's Sutton, all right. On the outside, or at least part of the same body. But he's a rebuilt job. . . ."

Other Ace Books by Clifford D. Simak

CITY
THE TROUBLE WITH TYCHO (coming in April)

CLIFFOR

TIME

AGA

TIME AND
Copyright ©
All rights res
any means,
permission

All characte
living or de

An Ace Bo

Published b

ISBN: 0-44

Third Print
Published s

Manufactu
Ace Books

SF
ACE BOOKS, N

FOR KAY
without whom I'd never have written a line

TIME AND AGAIN

THE MAN came out of the twilight when the greenish yellow of the sun's last light still lingered in the west. He paused at the edge of the patio and called.

"Mr. Adams, is that you?"

The chair creaked as Christopher Adams shifted his weight, startled by the voice. Then he remembered. A new neighbor had moved in across the meadow a day or two ago. Jonathon had told him . . . and Jonathon knew all the gossip within a hundred miles. Human gossip as well as android and robot gossip.

"Come on in," said Adams. "Glad you dropped around."

And he hoped his voice sounded as hearty and neighborly as he had tried to make it.

For he wasn't glad. He was a little nettled, upset by this sudden shadow that came out of the twilight and walked across the patio.

He passed a mental hand across his brow. This is my hour, he thought. The one hour I give myself. The hour that I forget . . . forget the thousand problems that have to do with other stars. Forget them and turn back to the green-blackness and the hush and the subtle sun-

1

set shadow-show that belong to my own planet.

For here, on this patio, there are no mentophone reports, no robot files, no galactic co-ordination conferences . . . no psychologic intrigue, no alien reaction charts. Nothing complicated or mysterious . . . although I may be wrong, for there is mystery here, but a soft, sure mystery that is understood and only remains a mystery because I want it so. The mystery of the nighthawk against a darkening sky, the puzzle of the firefly along the lilac hedge.

With half his mind he knew the stranger had come across the patio and was reaching out a hand for a chair to sit in, and with the other half once again he wondered about the blackened bodies lying on the riverbank on far-off Aldebaran XII and the twisted machine that was wrapped around the tree.

Three humans had died there . . . three humans and two androids, and androids were almost human. And humans must not die by violence unless it be by the violence of another human. Even then it was on the field of honor with all the formality and technicality of the *code duello* or in the less polished affairs of revenge or execution.

For human life was sacrosanct . . . it had to be or there'd be no human life. Man was so pitifully outnumbered.

Violence or accident?

And accident was ridiculous.

There were few accidents, almost none at all. The near-perfection of mechanical performance, the almost human intelligence and reactions of machines to any known danger, long ago had cut the incidence of accident to an almost non-existent figure.

No machine would be crude enough to slam into a

tree. A more subtle, less apparent danger, maybe. But never a tree.

So it must be violence.

And it could not be human violence, for human violence would have advertised the fact. Human violence had nothing to fear . . . there was no recourse to law, scarcely a moral code to which a human killer would be answerable.

Three humans dead.

Three humans dead fifty light-years distant and it became a thing of great importance to a man sitting on his patio on Earth. A thing of prime importance, for no human must die by other hands than human without a terrible vengeance. Human life must not be taken without a monstrous price anywhere in the galaxy or the human race would end forever and the great galactic brotherhood of intelligence would plummet down into the darkness and the distance that had scattered it before.

Adams slumped lower in his chair, forcing himself to relax, furious at himself for thinking . . . for it was his rule that in this time of twilight he thought of nothing . . . or as close to nothing as his mind could come.

The stranger's voice seemed to come from far away and yet Adams knew he was sitting at his side.

"Nice evening," the stranger said.

Adams chuckled. "The evenings are always nice. The Weather boys don't let it rain until later on, when everyone's asleep."

In a thicket down the hill a thrush struck up its evensong and the liquid notes ran like a quieting hand across a drowsing world. Along the creek a frog or two were trying out their throats. Far away, in some dim otherworld a whippoorwill began his chugging question. Across the meadow and up the climbing hills, the lights came on in houses here and there.

"This is the best part of the day," said Adams.

He dropped his hand into his pocket, brought out tobacco pouch and pipe.

"Smoke?" he asked.

The stranger shook his head.

"As a matter of fact, I am here on business."

Adam's voice turned crisp. "See me in the morning, then. I don't do business after hours."

The stranger said softly, "It's about Asher Sutton."

Adam's body tensed and his fingers shook so that he fumbled as he filled his pipe. He was glad that it was dark so the stranger could not see.

"Sutton will be coming back," the stranger said.

Adams shook his head. "I doubt it. He went out twenty years ago."

"You haven't crossed him out?"

"No," said Adams, slowly. "He still is on the payroll, if that is what you mean."

"Why?" asked the man. "Why do you keep him on?"

Adams tamped the tobacco in the bowl, considering. "Sentiment, I guess," he said. "Sentiment and faith. Faith in Asher Sutton. Although the faith is running out."

"Just five days from now," the stranger said, "Sutton will come back."

He paused a moment, then added, "Early in the morning."

"There's no way," said Adams, crisply, "you could know a thing like that."

"But I do. It's recorded fact."

Adams snorted. "It hasn't happened yet."

"In my time it has."

Adams jerked upright in his chair. "In your time!"

"Yes," said the stranger, quietly. "You see, Mr. Adams, I am your successor."

"Look here, young man . . ."

"Not young man," said the stranger. "I am half again your age. I am getting old."

"I have no successor," said Adams, coldly. "There's been no talk of one. I'm good for another hundred years. Maybe more than that."

"Yes," the stranger said, "for more than a hundred years. For much more than that."

Adams leaned back quietly in his chair. He put his pipe in his mouth and lit it with a hand that was steady as a rock.

"Let's take this easy," he said. "You say you are my successor . . . that you took over my job after I quit or died. That means you came out of the future. Not that I believe you for a moment, of course. But just for argument . . ."

"There was a news item the other day," the stranger said. "About a man named Michaelson who claimed he went into the future."

Adams snorted. "I read that. One second! How could a man know he went one second into time? How could he measure it and know? What difference would it make?"

"None, the stranger agreed. "Not the first time, of course. But the next time he will go into the future five seconds. Five seconds, Mr. Adams. Five tickings of the clock. The space of one short breath. There must be a starting point for all things."

"Time travel?"

The stranger nodded.

"I don't believe it," Adams said.

"I was afraid you wouldn't."

"In the last five thousand years," said Adams, "we have conquered the galaxy . . ."

" 'Conquer' is not the right word, Mr. Adams."

"Well, taken over, then. Moved in. However you may wish it. And we have found strange things. Stranger things than we ever dreamed. But never time travel."

He waved his hand at the stars.

"In all that space out there," he said, "no one had time travel. No one."

"You have it now," the stranger said. "Since two weeks ago. Michaelson went into time, one second into time. A start. That is all that's needed."

"All right, then," said Adams. "Let us say you are the man who in a hundred years or so will take my place. Let's pretend you traveled back in time. What about it?"

"To tell you that Sutton will return."

"I would know it when he came," said Adams. "Why must I know now?"

"When he returns," the stranger said, "Sutton must be killed."

II

THE TINY, battered ship sank lower, slowly, like a floating feather, drifting down toward the field in the slant of morning sun.

The bearded, ragged man in the pilot's chair sat tensed, straining every nerve.

Tricky, said his brain. Hard and tricky to handle so much weight, to judge the distance and the speed . . . hard to make the tons of metal float down against the savage pull of gravity. Harder even than the lifting of it when there had been no consideration but that it should rise and move out into space.

For a moment the ship wavered and he fought it, fought it with every shred of will and mind . . . and then it floated once again, hovering just a few feet above the surface of the field.

He let it down, gently, so that it scarcely clicked when it touched the ground.

He sat rigid in the seat, slowly going limp, relaxing by inches, first one muscle, then another. Tired, he told himself. The toughest job I've ever done. Another few miles and I would have let her crash.

Far down the field was a clump of buildings and a

ground car had swung away from them and was racing down the strip toward him.

A breeze curled in through the shattered vision port and touched his face, reminding him . . .

Breathe, he told himself. You must be breathing when they come. You must be breathing and you must walk out and you must smile at them. There must be nothing they will notice. Right away, at least. The beard and clothes will help some. They'll be so busy gaping at them that they will miss a little thing. But not breathing. They might notice if you weren't breathing.

Carefully, he pulled in a breath of air, felt the sting of it run along his nostrils and gush inside his throat, felt the fire of it when it reached his lungs.

Another breath and another one and the air had scent and life and a strange exhilaration. The blood throbbed in his throat and beat against his temples and he held his fingers to one wrist and felt it pulsing there.

Sickness came, a brief, stomach-retching sickness that he fought against, holding his body rigid, remembering all the things that he must do.

The power of will, he told himself, the power of mind . . . the power that no man uses to its full capacity. The will to tell a body the things that it must do, the power to start an engine turning after years of doing nothing.

One breath and then another. And the heart is beating now, steadier, steadier, throbbing like a pump.

Be quiet, stomach.

Get going, liver.

Keep on pumping, heart.

It isn't as if you were old and rusted, for you never were. The other system took care that you were kept in shape, that you were ready at an instant's notice on a stand-by basis.

But the switch-over was a shock. He had known that it would be. He had dreaded its coming, for he had known what it would mean. The agony of a new kind of life and metabolism.

In his mind he held a blueprint of his body and all its working parts . . . a shifting, wobbly picture that shivered and blurred and ran color into color.

But it steadied under the hardening of his mind, the driving of his will, and finally the blueprint was still and sharp and bright and he knew that the worst was over.

He clung to the ship's controls with hands clenched so fiercely they almost dented metal and perspiration poured down his body and he was limp and weak.

Nerves grew quiet and the blood pumped on and he knew that he was breathing without even thinking of it.

For a moment longer he sat quietly in the seat, relaxing. The breeze came in the shattered port and brushed against his cheek. The ground car was coming very close.

"Johnny," he whispered, "we are home. We made it. This is my home, Johnny. The place I talked about."

But there was no answer, just a stir of comfort deep inside his brain, a strange, nestling comfort such as one may know when one is eight years old and snuggles into bed.

"Johnny!" he cried.

And he felt the stir again . . . a self-assuring stir like the feel of a dog's muzzle against a held-down palm.

Someone was beating at the ship's door, beating with his fists and crying out.

"All right," said Asher Sutton, "I'm coming. I'll be right along."

He reached down and lifted the attaché case from beside the seat, tucked it underneath his arm. He went to the lock and twirled it open and stepped out on the ground.

There was only one man.

"Hello," said Asher Sutton.

"Welcome to Earth, sir," said the man, and the "sir" struck a chord of memory. His eyes went to the man's forehead and he saw the faint tattooing of the serial number.

He had forgotten about androids. Perhaps a lot of other things as well. Little habit patterns that had sloughed away with the span of twenty years.

He saw the android staring at him, at the naked knee showing through the worn cloth, at the lack of shoes.

"Where I've been," said Sutton, sharply, "you couldn't buy a new suit every day."

"No, sir," said the android.

"And the beard," said Sutton, "is because I couldn't shave."

"I've seen beards before," the android told him.

Sutton stood quietly and stared at the world before him . . . at the upthrust of towers shining in the morning sun, at the green of park and meadow, at the darker green of trees and the blue and scarlet splashes of flower gardens on sloping terraces.

He took a deep breath and felt the air flooding in his lungs, seeking out all the distant sacs that had been starved so long. And it was coming back to him, coming back again . . . the remembrance of life on Earth, of early morning sun and flaming sunsets, of deep blue sky and dew upon the grass, the swift blur of human talk and the lilt of human music, the friendliness of the birds and squirrels, and the peace and comfort.

"The car is waiting, sir," the android said. "I will take you to a human."

"I'd rather walk," said Sutton.

The android shook his head. "The human is waiting and he is most impatient."

"Oh, all right," said Sutton.

The seat was soft and he sank into it gradually, cradling the attaché case carefully in his lap.

The car was moving and he stared out of the window, fascinated by the green of Earth. "The green fields of Earth," he said. Or was it "the green vales"? No matter now. It was a song written long ago. In the time when there had been fields on Earth, fields instead of parks, when Man had turned the soil for more important things than flower beds. In the day, thousands of years before, when Man had just begun to feel the stir of space within his soul. Long years before Earth had become the capital and the center of galactic empire.

A great star ship was taking off at the far end of the field, sliding down the ice-smooth plastic skidway with the red-hot flare of booster jets frothing in its tubes. Its nose slammed into the upward curve of the take-off ramp and it was away, a rumbling streak of silver that shot into the blue. For a moment it flickered a golden red in the morning sunlight and then was swallowed in the azure mist of sky.

Sutton brought his gaze back to Earth again, sat soaking in the sight of it as a man soaks in the first strong sun of spring after months of winter.

Far to the north towered the twin spires of the Justice Bureau, Alien Branch. And to the east the pile of gleaming plastics and glass that was the University of North America. And other buildings that he had forgotten . . . buildings for which he found he had no name. But buildings that were miles apart, with parks and homesites in between. The homes were masked by trees and shrubbery

—none sat in barren loneliness—and through the green of the curving hills, Sutton caught the glints of color that betrayed where people lived.

The car slid to a stop before the administration building and the android opened the door.

"This way, sir," he said.

Only a few chairs in the lobby were occupied and most of those by humans. Humans or androids, thought Sutton. You can't tell the difference until you see their foreheads.

The sign upon the forehead, the brand of manufacture. The telltale mark that said, "This man is not a human, although he looks like one."

These are the ones who will listen to me. These are the ones who will pay attention. These are the ones who will save me against any future enmity that Man may raise against me.

For they are worse than the disinherited. They are not the has-beens, they are the never-weres.

They were not born of woman out of the laboratory. Their mother is a bin of chemicals and their father the ingenuity and technology of the normal race.

Android: An artificial human. A human made in the laboratory out of Man's own deep knowledge of chemicals and atomic and molecular structure and the strange reaction that is known as life.

Human in all but two respects—the mark upon the forehead and the inability to reproduce biologically.

Artificial humans to help the real humans, the biological humans, carry the load of galactic empire, to make the thin line of humanity the thicker. But kept in their place. Oh, yes, most definitely kept in their right place.

The corridor was empty, and Sutton, his bare feet slapping on the floor, followed the android.

The door before which they stopped said:

THOMAS H. DAVIS
(Human)
Operations Chief

"In there," the android said.

Sutton walked in and the man behind the desk looked up and gulped.

"I'm a human," Sutton told him. "I may not look it, but I am."

The man jerked his thumb toward a chair. "Sit down," he said.

Sutton sat.

"Why didn't you answer our signals?" Davis asked.

"My set was broken," Sutton told him.

"Your ship has no identity."

"The rains washed it off," said Sutton, "and I had no paint."

"Rain doesn't wash off paint."

"Not Earth rain," said Sutton. "Where I was, it does."

"Your motors?" asked Davis. "We could pick up nothing from them."

"They weren't working," Sutton told him.

Davis' Adam's apple bobbed up and down. "Weren't working. How did you navigate?"

"With energy," said Sutton.

"Energy . . ." Davis choked.

Sutton stared at him icily.

"Anything else?" he asked.

Davis was confused. The red tape had gotten tangled. The answers were all wrong. He fiddled with a pencil.

"Just the usual things, I guess." He drew a pad of forms before him.

"Name?"

"Asher Sutton."

"Origin of fli ... Say, wait a minute! Asher Sutton!"

Davis flung the pencil on the pad, pushed away the pad.

"That's right."

"Why didn't you tell me that at first?"

"I didn't have a chance."

Davis was flustered.

"If I had known ..." he said.

"It's the beard," said Sutton.

"My father talked about you often. Jim Davis. Maybe you remember him."

Sutton shook his head.

"Great friend of your father's. That is ... they knew one another."

"How is my father?" asked Sutton.

"Great," said Davis, enthusiastically. "Keeping well. Getting along in years, but standing up ..."

"My father and mother," Sutton told him, coldly, "died fifty years ago. In the Argus pandemic."

He heaved himself to his feet, faced Davis squarely.

"If you're through," he said, "I'd like to go to my hotel. They'll find some room for me."

"Certainly, Mr. Sutton, certainly. Which hotel?"

"The Orion Arms."

Davis reached into a drawer, took out a directory, flipped the pages, ran a shaking finger down a column.

"Cherry 26-3489," he said: "The teleport is over there."

He pointed to a booth set flush into the wall.

"Thanks," said Sutton.

"About your father, Mr. Sutton ..."

"I know," said Sutton. "I'm glad you tipped me off."

He swung around and walked to the teleport. Before he closed the door, he looked back.

Davis was on the visaphone, talking rapidly.

III

TWENTY YEARS had not changed the Orion Arms.

To Sutton, stepping out of the teleport, it looked the same as the day he had walked away. A little shabbier and slightly more on the fuddy-duddy side...but it was home, the quiet whisper of hushed activity, the dowdy furnishings, the finger-to-the-lip, tiptoe atmosphere, the stressed respectability that he had remembered and dreamed about in the long years of alienness.

The life-mural along the wall was the same as ever. A little faded with long running, but the self-same one that Sutton had remembered. The same goatish Pan still chased, after twenty years, the same terror-stricken maiden across the self-same hills and dales. And the same rabbit hopped from behind a bush and watched the chase with all his customary boredom, chewing his everlasting cud of clover.

The self-adjusting furniture, bought at a time when the management had considered throwing the hostelry open to the alien trade, had been out-of-date twenty years ago. But it still was there. It had been repainted, in soft, genteel pastels, its self-adjustment features still confined to human forms.

The spongy floor covering had lost some of its sponginess and the Cetian cactus must have died at last, for a pot of frankly terrestrial geraniums now occupied its place.

The clerk snapped off the visaphone and turned back to the room.

"Good morning, Mr. Sutton," he said, in his cultured android voice.

Then he added, almost as an afterthought, "We've been wondering when you would show up."

"Twenty years," said Sutton, dryly, "is long-time wondering."

"We've kept your old suite for you," said the clerk. "We knew that you would want it. Mary has kept it cleaned and ready for you ever since you left."

"That was nice of you, Ferdinand."

"You've hardly changed at all," said Ferdinand. "The beard is all. I knew you the second that I turned around and saw you."

"The beard and clothes," said Sutton. "The clothes are pretty bad."

"I don't suppose," said Ferdinand, "you have luggage, Mr. Sutton."

"No luggage."

"Breakfast, then, perhaps. We still are serving breakfast."

Sutton hesitated, suddenly aware that he was hungry. And he wondered for a moment how food would strike his stomach.

"I could find a screen," said Ferdinand.

Sutton shook his head. "No. I better get cleaned up and shaved. Send me up some breakfast and a change of clothes."

"Scrambled eggs, perhaps. You always liked scrambled eggs for breakfast."

"That sounds all right," said Sutton.

He turned slowly from the desk and walked to the elevator. He was about to close the door when a voice called:

"Just a moment, please."

The girl was running across the lobby . . . rangy and copper-haired. She slid into the elevator, pressed her back against the wall.

"Thanks very much," she said. "Thanks so much for waiting."

Her skin, Sutton saw, was magnolia-white and her eyes were granite-colored with shadows deep within them.

He closed the door softly.

"I was glad to wait," he said.

Her lips twitched just a little and he said, "I don't like shoes. They cramp one's feet too much."

He pressed the button savagely and the elevator sprang upward. The lights ticked off the floors.

Sutton stopped the cage. "This is my floor," he said.

He had the door open and was halfway out, when she spoke to him.

"Mister."

"Yes, what is it?"

"I didn't mean to laugh. I really-truly didn't."

"You had a right to laugh," said Sutton, and closed the door behind him.

He stood for a moment, fighting down a sudden tenseness that seized him like a mighty fist.

Careful, he told himself. Take it easy, boy. You are home at last. This is the place you dreamed of. Just a few doors down and you are finally home. You will reach out and turn the knob and push in the door and it will all be there . . . just as you remembered it. The favorite chair, the life-paintings on the wall, the little fountain with the mermaids from Venus . . . and the windows where you

17

can sit and fill your eyes with Earth.

But you can't get emotional. You can't go soft and sissy.

For that chap back at the spaceport had lied. And hotels don't keep rooms waiting for all of twenty years.

There is something wrong. I don't know what, but something. Something terribly wrong.

He took a slow step . . . and then another, fighting down the tension, swallowing the dryness of excitement welling in his throat.

One of the paintings, he remembered, was a forest brook, with birds flitting in the trees. And at the most unexpected times one of the birds would sing, usually with the dawn or the going of the sun. And the water babbled with a happy song that held one listening in his chair for hours.

He knew that he was running and he didn't try to stop.

His fingers curled around the doorknob and turned it. The room was there . . . the favorite chair, the babble of the brook, the splashing of the mermaids . . .

He caught the whiff of danger as he stepped across the threshold and he tried to turn and run, but he was too late. He felt his body crumpling forward to crash toward the floor.

"Johnny!" he cried and the cry bubbled in his throat. "Johnny!"

Inside his brain a voice whispered back. "It's all right, Ash. We're locked."

Then darkness came.

IV

THERE WAS someone in the room and Sutton kept his eyelids down, kept his breathing slow.

Someone in the room, pacing quietly. Stopping now before the window to look out, moving over to the mantel-piece to stare at the painting of the forest brook. And in the stillness of the room, Sutton heard the laughing babble of the painted stream against the splashing of the fountain, heard the faint bird notes that came from the painted trees, imagined that even from the distance that he lay he could smell the forest mold and the cool, wet perfume of the moss that grew along the stream.

The person in the room crossed back again and sat down in a chair. He whistled a tune, almost inaudibly. A funny, little lilting tune that Sutton had not heard before.

Someone gave me a going over, Sutton told himself. Knocked me out fast, with gas or powder, then gave me an overhauling. I seem to remember some of it . . . hazy and far away. Lights that glowed and a probing at my brain. And I might have fought against it, but I knew it was no use. And, besides, they're welcome to anything they found. He hugged himself with a mental smugness.

Yes, they're welcome to anything they pried out of my mind.

But they've found all they're going to find and they have gone away. They left someone to watch me and he still is in the room.

He stirred on the bed and opened his eyes, opened them slowly, kept them glazed and only partly focused.

The man rose from the chair and Sutton saw that he was dressed in white. He crossed the room and leaned above the bed.

"All right, now?" he asked.

Sutton raised a hand and passed it, bewildered, across his face.

"Yes," he said. "Yes, I guess I am."

"You passed out," the man told him.

"Something I ate," said Sutton.

The man shook his head. "The trip, more than likely. It must have been a tough one."

"Yes," said Sutton. "Tough."

Go ahead, he thought. Go ahead and ask some more. Those are your instructions. Catch me while I'm groggy, pump me like a well. Go ahead and ask the questions and earn your lousy money.

But he was wrong.

The man straightened up.

"I think you'll be all right," he said. "If you aren't, call me. My card is on the mantel."

"Thanks, doctor," said Sutton.

He watched him walk across the room, waited until he heard the door click, then sat up in bed. His clothing lay in a pile in the center of the floor. His case? Yes, there it was, lying on a chair. Ransacked, no doubt, probably photostated.

Spy rays, too, more than likely. All over the room. Ears

listening and eyes watching.

But who? he asked himself.

No one knew he was returning. No one could have known. Not even Adams. There was no way to know. There had been no way that he could let them know.

Funny.

Funny the way Davis at the spaceport had recognized his name and told a lie to cover up.

Funny the way Ferdinand pretended his suite had been kept for him for all these twenty years.

Funny, too, how Ferdinand had turned around and spoken, as if twenty years were nothing.

Organized, said Sutton. Clicking like a relay system. Set and waiting for me.

But why should anyone be waiting? No one knew when he'd be coming back. Or if he would come at all.

And even if someone did know, why go to all the trouble?

For they could not know, he thought . . . they could not know the thing I have, they could not even guess. Even if they did know I was coming back, incredible as it might be that they should know, even that would be more credible by a million times than that they should know the real reason for my coming.

And knowing, he said, they would not believe.

His eyes found the attaché case lying on the chair, and stared at it.

And knowing, he said again, they would not believe.

When they look the ship over, of course, they will do some wondering. Then there might be some excuse for the thing that happened. But they didn't have time to look at the ship. They didn't wait a minute. They were laying for me and they gave me the works from the second that I landed.

Davis shoved me into a teleport and grabbed his phone like mad. And Ferdinand knew that I was on the way, he knew he'd see me when he turned around. And the girl— the girl with the granite eyes?

Sutton got up and stretched. A bath and shave, first of all, he told himself. And then some clothes and breakfast. A visor call or two.

Don't act as if you've got the wind up, he warned himself. Act naturally. Pick your nose. Talk to yourself. Pinch out a blackhead. Scratch your back against a door casing. Act as if you think you are alone.

But be careful.

There is someone watching.

V

Sutton was finishing breakfast when the android came.

"My name is Herkimer," the android told him, "and I belong to Mr. Geoffrey Benton."

"Mr. Benton sent you here?"

"Yes. He sends a challenge."

"A challenge?"

"Yes. You know, a duel."

"But I am unarmed."

"You cannot be unarmed," said Herkimer.

"I never fought a duel in all my life," said Sutton. "I don't intend to now."

"You are vulnerable."

"What do you mean, vulnerable? If I go unarmed . . ."

"But you cannot go unarmed. The code was changed just a year or two ago. No man younger than a hundred years can go unarmed."

"But if one does?"

"Why, then," said Herkimer, "anyone who wants to can pot you like a rabbit."

"You are sure of this?"

Herkimer dug into his pocket, brought out a tiny book. He wet his finger and fumbled at the pages.

"It's right here," he said.

"Never mind," said Sutton. "I will take your word."

"You accept the challenge, then?"

Sutton grimaced. "I suppose I have to. Mr. Benton will wait, I presume, until I buy a gun."

"No need of that," Herkimer told him, brightly. "I brought one along. Mr. Benton always does that. Just a courtesy, you know. In case someone hasn't got one."

He reached into his pocket and held out the weapon. Sutton took it and laid it on the table.

"Awkward-looking thing," he said.

Herkimer stiffened. "It's traditional," he declared. "The finest weapon made. Shoots a .45-caliber slug. Handloaded ammunition. Sights are tested in for fifty feet."

"You pull this?" asked Sutton, pointing.

Herkimer nodded. "It is called a trigger. And you don't pull it. You squeeze it."

"Just why does Mr. Benton challenge me?" asked Sutton. "I don't even know the man. Never even heard of him."

"You are famous," said Herkimer.

"Not that I have heard of."

"You are an investigator," Herkimer pointed out. "You have just come back from a long and perilous mission. You're carrying a mysterious-appearing attaché case. And there are reporters waiting in the lobby."

Sutton nodded. "I see. When Benton kills someone he likes them to be famous."

"It is better if they are," said Herkimer. "More publicity."

"But I don't know Mr. Benton. How will I know who I'm supposed to shoot at?"

"I'll show you," said Herkimer, "on the televisor."

He stepped to the desk, dialed a number and stepped back.

"That's him," he said.

In the screen a man was sitting before a chess table. The pieces were in mid-game. Across the board stood a beautifully machined robotic.

The man reached out a hand, thoughtfully played his knight. The robotic clicked and chuckled. It moved a pawn. Benton's shoulders hunched forward and he bent above the board. One hand came around and scratched the back of his neck.

"Oscar's got him worried," said Herkimer. "He always has him worried. Mr. Benton hasn't won a single game in the last ten years."

"Why does he keep on playing, then?"

"Stubborn," said Herkimer. "But Oscar's stubborn, too."

He made a motion with his hand.

"Machines can be so much more stubborn than humans. It's the way they're built."

"But Benton must have known, when he had Oscar fabricated, that Oscar would beat him," Sutton pointed out. "A human simply can't beat a robotic expert."

"Mr. Benton knew that," said Herkimer, "but he didn't believe it. He wanted to prove otherwise."

"Egomaniac," said Sutton.

Herkimer stared at him calmly. "I believe that you are right, sir. I've sometimes thought the same myself."

Sutton brought his gaze back to Benton, who was still hunched above the board, the knuckles of one hand thrust hard against his mouth.

The veined face was scrubbed and pink and chubby, and the brooding eyes, thoughtful as they were, still held a fat twinkle of culture and good-fellowship.

"You'll know him now?" asked Herkimer.

Sutton nodded. "Yes, I think I can pick him out. He doesn't look too dangerous."

"He's killed sixteen men," Herkimer said, stiffly. "He plans to lay away his guns when he makes it twenty-five."

He looked straight at Sutton and said, "You're the seventeenth."

Sutton said, meekly, "I'll try to make it easy for him."

"How would you wish it, sir?" asked Herkimer. "Formal, or informal?"

"Let's make it catch-as-catch-can."

Herkimer was disapproving. "There are certain conventions. . . ."

"You can tell Mr. Benton," said Sutton, "that I don't plan to ambush him."

Herkimer picked up his cap, put it on his head.

"The best of luck, sir," he said.

"Why, thank you, Herkimer," said Sutton.

The door closed and Sutton was alone. He turned back to the screen. Benton played to double up his rooks. Oscar chuckled at him, slid a bishop three squares along the board and put Benton's king in check.

Sutton snapped the visor off.

He scraped a hand across his now-shaved chin.

Coincidence or plan? It was hard to know.

One of the mermaids had climbed to the edge of the fountain and balanced her three-inch self precariously. She whistled at Sutton. He turned swiftly at the sound and she dived into the pool, swam in circles, mocking him with obscene signs.

Sutton leaned forward, reached into the visor rack, brought out the INF-JAT directory, flipped the pages swiftly.

INFORMATION-Terrestrial.

And the headings:

Culinary

Culture

Customs

That would be it. Customs.

He found DUELING, noted the number and put back the book. He reset the dial and snapped the tumbler for direct communication.

A robot's streamlined, modernistic face filled the plate.

"At your service, sir," it said.

"I have been challenged to a duel," said Sutton.

The robot waited for the question.

"I don't want to fight a duel," said Sutton. "Is there any way, legally, for me to back out? I'd like to do it gracefully, too, but I won't insist on that."

"There is no way," the robot said.

"No way at all?"

"You are under one hundred?" the robot asked.

"Yes."

"You are sound of mind and body?"

"I think so."

"You are or you aren't. Make up your mind."

"I am," said Sutton.

"You do not belong to any bona fide religion that prohibits killing?"

"I presume I could classify myself as a Christian," said Sutton. "I believe there is a Commandment about killing."

The robot shook his head. "It doesn't count."

"It is clear and specific," Sutton argued. "It says, 'Thou shalt not kill.'"

"It is all of that," the robot told him. "But it has been discredited. You humans discredited it yourselves. You never obeyed it. You either obey or you forfeit it.

27

You can't forget it with one breath and invoke it with the next."

"I guess I'm sunk then," said Sutton.

"According to the revision of the year 7990," said the robot, "arrived at by convention, any male human under the age of one hundred, sound in mind and body, and unhampered by religious bonds or belief, which are subject to a court of inquiry, must fight a duel whenever challenged."

"I see," said Sutton.

"The history of dueling," said the robot, "is very interesting."

"It is barbaric," said Sutton.

"Perhaps so. But the humans are still barbaric in many other ways as well."

"You're impertinent," Sutton told him.

"I'm sick and tired of it," the robot said. "Sick and tired of the smugness of you humans. You say you've outlawed war and you haven't, really. You've just fixed it so no one dares to fight you. You say you have abolished crime and you have, except for human crime. And a lot of crime you have abolished isn't crime at all, except by human standards."

"You're taking a long chance, friend," said Sutton, softly, "talking the way you are."

"You can pull the plug on me," the robot told him, "any time you want to. Life isn't worth it, the kind of job I have."

He saw the look on Sutton's face and hurried on.

"Try to see it this way, sir. Through all his history, Man has been a killer. He was smart and brutal, even from the first. He was a puny thing, but he found how to use a club and rocks, and when the rocks weren't sharp enough he chipped them so they were. There were things, at first, he should not by rights have killed. They should have killed him. But he was smart and he had the club and flints and he killed the mammoth and the saber tooth and other things he could not have faced barehanded. So he won the Earth from the animals. He wiped them out, except the ones he allowed to live for the service that they gave him. And even as he fought with the animals, he fought with others of his kind. After the animals were gone, he kept on fighting . . . man against man, nation against nation."

"But that is past," said Sutton. "There hasn't been a war for more than a thousand years. Humans have no need of fighting now."

"That is just the point," the robot told him. "There is no more need of fighting, no more need of killing. Oh, once in a while, perhaps, on some far-off planet where a human must kill to protect his life or to uphold human dignity and power. But, by and large, there is no need of killing.

"And yet you kill. You must kill. The old brutality is in you. You are drunk with power and killing is a sign of power. It has become a habit with you . . . a thing you've carried from the caves. There's nothing left to kill but one another, so you kill one another and you call it dueling. You know it's wrong and you're hypocritical about it. You've set up a fine system of semantics to make it sound respectable and brave and noble. You call it traditional and chivalric . . . and even if you don't call it that in so many words, that is what you think. You cloak it with the trappings of your vicious past, you dress it up with words and the words are only tinsel."

"Look," said Sutton, "I don't want to fight this duel. I don't think it's . . ."

There was vindictive glee in the robot's voice.

"But you've got to fight it. There's no way to back out. Maybe you would like some pointers. I have all sorts of tricks. . . ."

"I thought you didn't approve of dueling."

"I don't," the robot said. "But it's my job. I'm stuck with it. I try to do it well. I can tell you the personal history of every man who ever fought a duel. I can talk for hours on the advantage of rapiers over pistols. Or if you'd rather I argued for pistols, I can do that, too. I can tell you about the old American West gun slicks and the Chicago gangsters and the handkerchief and dagger deals and . . ."

"No, thanks," said Sutton.

"You aren't interested?"

"I haven't got the time."

"But, sir," the robot pleaded, "I don't get a chance too often. I don't get many calls. Just an hour or so . . ."

"No," said Sutton, firmly.

"All right, then. Maybe you'd tell me who has challenged you."

"Benton. Geoffrey Benton."

The robot whistled.

"Is he that good?" asked Sutton.

"All of it," the robot said.

Sutton shut the visor off.

He sat quietly in his chair, staring at the gun. Slowly he reached out a hand and picked it up. The butt fitted snugly in his hand. His finger curled around the trigger. He lifted it and sighted at the doorknob.

It was easy to handle. Almost as if it were a part of him. There was a feel of power within it . . . of power and mastery. As if he suddenly were stronger and greater . . . and more dangerous.

He sighed and laid it down.

The robot had been right.

He reached out to the visor, pushed the signal for the lobby desk.

Ferdinand's face came in.

"Anyone waiting down there for me, Ferdinand?"

"Not a soul," said Ferdinand.

"Anyone asked for me?"

"No one, Mr. Sutton."

"No reporters? Or photographers?"

"No, Mr. Sutton. Were you expecting them?"

Sutton didn't answer.

He cut off, feeling very silly.

VI

MAN WAS SPREAD thin throughout the galaxy. A lone man here, a handful there. Slim blobs of bone and brain and muscle to hold a galaxy in check. Slight shoulders to hold up the cloak of human greatness spread across the light-years.

For Man had flown too fast, had driven far beyond his physical capacity. Not by strength did he hold his starry outposts, but by something else . . . by depth of human character, by his colossal conceit, by his ferocious conviction that Man was the greatest living thing the galaxy had spawned. All this in spite of many evidence that he was not . . . evidence that he took and evaluated and cast aside, scornful of any greatness that was not ruthless and aggressive.

Too thin, Christopher Adams told himself. Too thin and stretched too far. One man backed by a dozen androids and a hundred robots could hold a solar system. Could hold it until there were more men or until something cracked.

In time there'd be more men, if the birthrate held. But it would be many centuries before the line would grow much thicker, for Man held only the key points . . . one planet in an entire system, and not in every system. Man had leap-frogged since there weren't men enough, had set up strategic spheres of influence, had by-passed all but the richest, most influential systems.

There was room to spread, room for a million years. If there were any humans left in a million years.

If the life on those other planets let the humans live, if there never came a day when they would be willing to pay the terrible price of wiping out the race.

The price would be high, said Adams, talking to himself. But it would be done, and it would be easy. Just a few hours' job. Humans in the morning, no humans left by night. What if a thousand others died for every human death . . . or ten thousand, or a hundred thousand? Under certain circumstances, such a price might well be counted cheap.

There were islands of resistance even now where one walked carefully . . . or even walked around. Like 61 Cyngi, for example.

It took judgment . . . and some tolerance . . . and a great measure of latent brutality, but, most of all, conceit, the absolute, unshakable conviction that Man was sacrosanct, that he could not be touched, that he could scarcely die.

But five men had died, three humans and two androids, beside a river that flowed on Aldebaran XII, just a few short miles from Andrelon, the planetary capital.

They had died of violence, of that there was no question.

Adams' eyes sought out the paragraph of Thorne's latest report:

Force had been applied from the outside. We found a hole burned through the atomic shielding of the engine. The force must have been controlled or it would have resulted in absolute destruction. The automatics got in their work and headed off the blast, but the machine went out of control and smashed into the tree. The area was saturated with intensive radiation.

Good man, Thorne, thought Adams. He won't let a single thing be missed. He had those robots in there before the place was cool.

But there wasn't much to find . . . not much that gave an answer. Just a batch of question marks.

Five men had died and when that was said that was the end of fact. For they were burned and battered and there were no features left, no fingerprints or eyeprints to match against the records.

A few feet away from the strewn blackness of the bodies the machine had smashed into a tree, had wrapped itself around and half sheared the trunk in two. A machine that, like the men, was without a record. A machine without a counterpart in the known galaxy and, so far at least, a machine without a purpose.

Thorne would give it the works. He would set it up in solidographs, down to the last shattered piece of glass and plastic. He would have it analyzed and diagramed and the robots would put it in scanners that would peel it and record it molecule by molecule.

And they might find something. Just possibly they might.

Adams shoved the report to one side and leaned back in his chair. Idly, he spelled out his name lettered across the office door, reading backwards slowly and with exaggerated care. As if he'd never seen the name before. As if he did not know it. Puzzling it out.

And then the line beneath it:

SUPERVISOR, ALIEN RELATIONS BUREAU. SPACE SECTOR 16.

And the line beneath that:

DEPARTMENT OF GALACTIC INVESTIGATION (JUSTICE).

Early afternoon sunlight slanted through a window and fell across his head, highlighting the clipped silver mustache, the whitening temple hair.

Five men had died. . . .

He wished that he could get it out of his mind. There was other work. This Sutton thing, for instance. The reports on that would be coming in within an hour or so.

But there was a photograph . . . a photograph from Thorne, that he could not forget.

A smashed machine and broken bodies and a great smoking gash sliced across the turf. The silver river flowed in a silence that one knew was there even in the photograph and far in the distance the spidery web of Andrelon rose against a pinkish sky.

Adams smiled softly to himself. Aldebaran XII, he thought, must be a lovely world. H never had been there and he never would be there . . . for there were too many planets, too many planets for one man to even dream of seeing all.

Someday, perhaps, when the teleports would work across light-years instead of puny miles . . . perhaps then a man might just step across to any planet that he wished, for a day or hour or just to say he'd been there.

But Adams didn't need to be there . . . he had eyes and ears there, as he had on every occupied planet within the entire sector.

Thorne was there and Thorne was an able man. He wouldn't rest until he'd wrung the last ounce of information from the broken wreck and bodies.

I wish I could forget it, Adams told himself. It's important, yes, but not all-important.

A buzzer hummed at Adams and he flipped up a tumbler on his desk.

"What is it?"

An android voice answered, "It's Mr. Thorne, sir, on the mentophone from Andrelon."

"Thank you, Alice," Adams said.

He clicked open a drawer and took out the cap, placed it on his head, adjusted it with steady fingers. Thoughts flickered through his brain, disjointed, random thoughts, all faint and faraway. Ghost thoughts drifting through the universe—residual flotsam from the minds of things in time and space that was unguessable.

Adams flinched.

I'll never get used to it, he told himself. I will always duck, like the kid who knows he deserves a cuffing.

The ghost thoughts peeped and chittered at him.

Adams closed his eyes and settled back.

"Hello, Thorne," he thought.

Thorne's thought came in, thinned and scratchy over the space of more than fifty light-years.

"That you, Adams? Pretty weak out here."

"Yes, it's me. What's up?"

A high, singsong thought came in and skipped along his brain:

Spill the rattle . . . pinch the fish . . . oxygen is high-priced.

Adams forced the thought out of his brain, built up his concentration.

"Start over again, Thorne. A ghost came along and blotted you out."

Thorne's thought was louder now, more distinct.

"I wanted to ask you about a name. Seems to me I heard it once before, but I can't be sure."

"What name?"

Thorne was spacing his thoughts now, placing them slowly and with emphasis to cut through the static.

"The name is Asher Sutton."

Adams sat bolt upright in his chair. His mouth flapped open.

"What?" he roared.

"Walk west," said a voice in his brain. *"Walk west and then straight up."*

Thorne's thought came in: ". . . it was the name that was on the flyleaf. . . ."

"Start over," Adams pleaded. "Start over and take it slow. We got blotted out again. I couldn't hear a thing you thought."

Thorne's thoughts came slowly, power behind each word:

"It was like this. You remember that wreck we had out here? Five men killed . . ."

"Yes. Yes. Of course, I remember it."

"Well, we found a book, or what once had been a book, on one of the corpses. The book was burned, scorched through and through by radiation. The robots did what they could with it, but that wasn't much. A word here and there. Nothing you could make any sense out of. . . ."

The thought static purred and rumbled. Half thoughts cut through. Rambling thought-snatches that had no sense or meaning even if they had been heard in their human sense or meaning—that could have had no human entirety.

"Start over," Adams thought desperately. "Start over."

"You know about this wreck. Five men . . ."

"Yes. Yes. I got that much. Up to the part about the book. Where does Sutton come in?"

"That was about all the robotics could figure out," Thorne told him. "Just three words: 'by Asher Sutton.' As if he might have been the author. As if the book might have been written by him. It was on one of the first pages. The title page, maybe. Such and such a book by Asher Sutton."

There was silence, even the ghost voices still for a moment. Then a piping, lisping thought came in . . . a baby thought, immature and puling. And the thought was without context, untranslatable, almost meaningless. But hideous and nerve-wrenching in its alien connotation.

Adams felt the sudden chill of fear slice into his marrow, grasped the chair arms with both his hands and hung on tight while a filthy, taloned claw twisted at his entrails.

Suddenly the thought was gone. Fifty light-years of space whistled in the cold.

Adams relaxed, felt the perspiration running from his armpits, trickling down his ribs.

"You there, Thorne?" he asked.

"Yes. I caught some of that one, too."

"Pretty bad, wasn't it?"

"I've never heard much worse," Thorne told him.

There was a moment's silence. Then Thorne's thoughts took up again.

"Maybe I'm just wasting time. But it seemed to me I remembered that name."

"You have," Adams thought back. "Sutton went to 61 Cygni."

"Oh, he's the one!"

"He got back this morning."

"Couldn't have been him, then. Someone else by the same name, maybe."

"Must have been," thought Adams.

"Nothing else to report," Thorne told him. "The name just bothered me."

"Keep at it," Adams thought. "Let me know anything that turns up."

"I will," Thorne promised. "Good-bye."

"Thanks for calling."

Adams lifted off the cap. He opened his eyes and the sight of the room, commonplace and Earthly, with the sun streaming through the window, was almost a physical shock.

He sat limp in his chair, thinking, remembering.

The man had come at twilight, stepping out of the shadows onto the patio and he had sat down in the darkness and talked like any other man. Except the things he said were crazy.

When he returns, Sutton must be killed. I am your successor.

Crazy talk.

Unbelievable.

Impossible.

And, still, maybe I should have listened. Maybe I should have heard him out instead of flying off the handle.

Except that you don't kill a man who comes back after twenty years.

Especially a man like Sutton.

Sutton is a good man. One of the best the Bureau has. Slick as a whistle, well grounded in alien psychology, an authority on galactic politics. No other man could have done the Cygnian job as well.

If he did it.

I don't know that, of course. But he'll be in tomorrow and he'll tell me all about it.

A man is entitled to a day's rest after twenty years.

Slowly, Adams put away the mento-cap, reached out an almost reluctant hand and snapped up a tumbler.

Alice answered.

"Send me in the Asher Sutton file."

"Yes, Mr. Adams."

Adams settled back in his chair.

The warmth of the sun felt good across his shoulders. The ticking of the clock was comforting.

Commonplace and comforting after the ghost voices whispering out in space. Thoughts that one could not pin down, that one could not trace back and say, "This one started here and then."

Although we're trying, Adams thought. Man will try anything, take any sort of chance, gamble on no odds at all.

He chuckled to himself. Chuckled at the weirdness of the project.

Thousands of listeners listening in on the random thoughts of random time and space listening in for clues, for hints, for leads. Seeking a driblet of sense from the stream of gibberish . . . hunting the word or sentence or disassociated thought that might be translated into a new philosophy or a new technique or a new science . . . or a new something that the human race had never even dreamed of.

A new concept, said Adams, talking to himself. An entirely new concept.

Adams scowled to himself.

A new concept might be dangerous. This was not the time for anything that did not fit in the groove, that did not match the pattern of human thought and action.

There could be no confusion. There could be nothing but the sheer, bulldog determination to hang on, to sink in one's teeth and stay. To maintain the *status quo*.

Later, someday, many centuries from now, there would be a time and place and room for a new concept. When Man's grip was firmer, when the line was not too thin, when a mistake or two would not spell disaster.

Man, at the moment, controlled every factor. He held the edge at every point . . . a slight edge, admitted, but at least an edge. And it must stay that way. There must be nothing that would tip the scale in the wrong direction. Not a word or thought, not an action or a whisper.

VII

Apparently they had been waiting for him for some time and they intercepted him when he stepped out of the elevator on his way to the dining room for lunch.

There were three of them and they stood ranged in front of him, as if doggedly determined that he should not escape.

"Mr. Sutton?" one of them asked, and Sutton nodded.

The man was a somewhat seedy character. He might not actually have slept in his clothes, although the first impression was that he had. He clutched a threadbare cap with stubby, grimed fingers. The fingernails were rimmed with the blue of dirt.

"What may I do for you?" asked Sutton.

"We'd like to talk to you, sir, if you don't mind," said the woman of the trio. "You see, we're a sort of delegation."

She folded fat hands over a plump stomach and did her best to beam at him. The effect of the beam was spoiled by the wispy hair that straggled out from beneath her dowdy hat.

"I was just on my way to lunch," said Sutton, hesitantly, trying to make it sound as if he were in a hurry,

42

trying to put some irritation into his voice while still staying within the bounds of civility.

The woman kept on beaming.

"I'm Mrs. Jellicoe," she said, acting as if he must be glad to get the information. "And this gentleman, the one who spoke to you, is Mr. Hamilton. The other one of us is Captain Stevens."

Captain Stevens, Sutton noted, was a beefy individual, better dressed than the other two. His blue eyes twinkled at Sutton, as if he might be saying: I don't approve of these people any more than you do, Sutton, but I'm along with them and I'll do the best I can.

"Captain?" said Sutton. "One of the star ships, I presume."

Stevens nodded. "Retired," he said.

He cleared his throat. "We hate to bother you, Sutton, but we tried to get through to your rooms and couldn't. We've waited several hours. I hope you'll not disappoint us."

"It'll just be a little while," pleaded Mrs. Jellicoe.

"We could sit over here," said Hamilton, twirling the cap in his dirty fingers. "We saved a chair for you."

"As you wish," said Sutton.

He followed them back to the corner from which they had advanced upon him and took the proffered chair.

"Now," he said, "tell me what this is all about."

Mrs. Jellicoe took a deep breath. "We're representing the Android Equality League," she said.

Stevens broke in, successfully heading off the long speech that Mrs. Jellicoe seemed on the point of making. "I am sure," he said, "that Mr. Sutton has heard of us at one time or another. The League has been in existence for these many years."

"I have heard of the League," said Sutton.

"Perhaps," said Mrs. Jelicoe, "you've read our literature."

"No," said Sutton. "I can't say that I have."

"Here's some of it, then," said Hamilton. He dug with a grimy hand into an inside coat pocket, came out with a fistful of dog-eared leaflets and tracts. He held them out to Sutton and Sutton took them gingerly, laid them on the floor beside his chair.

"Briefly," said Stevens, "we represent the belief that androids should be granted equality with the human race. They are human, in actuality, in every characteristic except one."

"They can't have babies," Mrs. Jellicoe blurted out.

Stevens lifted his sandy eyebrows briefly and glanced at Sutton half apologetically.

He cleared his throat. "That's quite right, sir," he said, "as you probably know. They are sterile, quite sterile. In other words, the human race can manufacture, chemically, a perfect human body, but it has been unable to solve the mystery of biological conception. Many attempts have been made to duplicate the chromosomes and genes, fertile eggs and sperm, but none has been successful."

"Someday, perhaps," said Sutton.

Mrs. Jellicoe shook her head. "We aren't meant to know all things, Mr. Sutton," she declared sanctimoniously. "There is a Power that guards against our knowing everything. There is . . ."

Stevens interrupted her. "Briefly, sir, we are interested in bringing about an acceptance of equality between the biological human race, the born human race, and the chemically manufactured human race that we call the androids. We contend that they are basically the same, that both are human beings, that each is entitled to the common heritage of the human race.

"We, the original, biological human race, created the androids in order to bolster our population, in order that there might be more humans to man the command posts and administration centers spread through the galaxy. You perhaps are well aware that the only reason we have not brought the galaxy more closely under our control is the lack of human supervision."

"I am well aware of that," said Sutton.

And he was thinking: no wonder. No wonder that this Equality League is regarded as a band of crackpots. A flighty old woman, a stumbling, dirty oaf, a retired space captain with time hanging heavy on his hands and nothing else to do.

Stevens was saying, "Thousands of years ago slavery was wiped out as between one biological human and another. But today we have a slavery as between the biological human and the manufactured human. For the androids are owned. They do not live as masters of their own fate, but serve at the direction of an identical form of life . . . identical in all things except that one is biologically fertile and the other one is sterile."

And that, thought Sutton, certainly is something that he learned by rote from out of a book. Like an insurance salesman or an agent for an encyclopedia.

He said aloud, "What do you want me to do about it?"

"We want you to sign a petition," said Mrs. Jellicoe.

"And make a contribution?"

"Indeed not," said Stevens. "Your signature will be enough. It is all we ask. We are always glad to get evidence that men of prestige are with us, that the thinking men and women of the galaxy see the justice of our claim."

Sutton scraped back his chair and rose.

"My name," he said, "would carry little prestige."

"But Mr. Sutton . . ."

"I approve of your aims," said Sutton, "but I am skeptical of your methods of carrying them forward."

He made a half bow to them, still sitting in their chairs.

"And now I must go to lunch," he said.

He was halfway across the lobby when someone caught him by the elbow. He whirled, half angrily. It was Hamilton, threadbare cap in hand.

"You forgot something," said Hamilton, holding out the leaflets Sutton had left lying on the floor.

VIII

THE DESK buzzer snarled at Adams and he thumbed it up.

"Yes," he said. "What is it?"

Alice's words tumbled over one another. "The file, sir. The Sutton file."

"What about the Sutton file?"

"It's gone, sir."

"Someone is using it."

"No, sir, not that. It has been stolen."

Adams jerked erect.

"Stolen!"

"Stolen," said Alice. "That is right, sir. Twenty years ago."

"But twenty years . . ."

"We checked the security points," said Alice. "It was stolen just three days after Mr. Sutton set out for 61."

IX

THE LAWYER said his name was Wellington. He had painted a thin coat of plastic lacquer over his forehead to hide the tattoo mark, but the mark showed through if one looked closely. And his voice was the voice of an android.

He laid his hat very carefully on a table, sat down meticulously in a chair and placed his brief case across his knee. He handed Sutton a rolled-up paper.

"Your newspaper, sir," he said. "It was outside the door. I thought that you might want it."

"Thanks," said Sutton.

Wellington cleared his throat. "You are Asher Sutton?" he asked.

Sutton nodded.

"I represent a certain robot who commonly went by the name of Buster. You may remember him."

Sutton leaned quickly forward. "Remember him? Why, he was a second father to me. Raised me after both my parents died. He has been with my family for almost four thousand years."

Wellington cleared his throat again. "Quite so," he said.

48

Sutton leaned back in his chair, crushing the newspaper in his grip.

"Don't tell me . . ."

Wellington waved a sober hand. "No, he's in no trouble. Not yet, that is. Not unless you choose to make it for him."

"What has he done?" asked Sutton.

"He has run away."

"Good Lord! Run away. Where to?"

Wellington squirmed uneasily in the chair. "To one of the Tower stars, I believe."

"But," protested Sutton, "that's way out. Out almost to the edge."

Wellington nodded. "He bought himself a new body and a ship and stocked it up. . . ."

"With what?" asked Sutton. "Buster had no money."

"Oh yes, he had. Money he had saved over, what was it you said, four thousand years or so. Tips from guests, Christmas presents, one thing and another. It would all count up . . . in four thousand years. Placed at interest, you know."

"But why?" asked Sutton. "What does he intend to do?"

"He took out a homestead on a planet. He didn't sneak away. He filed his claim, so you can trace him if you wish. He used the family name, sir. That worried him a little. He hoped you wouldn't mind."

Sutton shook his head. "Not at all," he said. "He has a right to that name, as good a right as I have myself."

"You don't mind, then?" asked Wellington. "About the whole thing, I mean. After all, he was your property."

"No," said Sutton. "I don't mind. But I was looking forward to seeing him again. I called the old home place, but there was no answer. I thought he might be out."

Wellington reached into the inside pocket of his coat.

"He left you a letter," he said, holding it out.

Sutton took it. It had his name written across its face. He turned it over, but there was nothing more.

"He also," said Wellington, "left an old trunk in my custody. Said it contained some old family papers that you might find of interest."

Sutton sat silently, staring across the room and seeing nothing.

There had been an apple tree at the gate and each year young Ash Sutton had eaten the apples when they were green and Buster had nursed him each time gently through the crisis and then had whaled him good and proper to teach him respect for his metabolism. And when the kid down the road had licked him on the way home from school, it had been Buster who had taken him out in the back yard and taught him how to fight with head as well as hands.

Sutton clenched his fists unconsciously, remembering the surge of satisfaction, the red rawness of his knuckles. The kid down the road, he recalled, had nursed a black eye for a week and become his fastest friend.

"About the trunk, sir," said Wellington. "You will want it delivered?"

"Yes," said Sutton, "if you please."

"It will be here tomorrow morning," Wellington told him.

The android picked up his hat and rose. "I want to thank you, sir, for my client. He told me you would be reasonable."

"Not reasonable," said Sutton. "Just fair. He took care of us for many years. He has earned his freedom."

"Good day, sir," said Wellington.

"Good day," said Sutton. "And thank you very much."

One of the mermaids whistled at Sutton.

Sutton told her, "One of these days, my beauty, you'll do that once too often."

She thumbed her nose at him and dived into the fountain.

The door clicked shut as Wellington left.

Slowly, Sutton slit the letter open, spread out the single page:

Dear Ash—I went to see Mr. Adams today and he told me that he was afraid that you would not come back, but I told him that I knew you would. So I'm not doing this because I think you won't come back and that you will never know . . . because I know you will. Since you left me and struck out on our own, I have felt old and useless. In a galaxy where there were many things to do, I was doing nothing. You told me you just wanted me to live on at the old place and take it easy and I knew you did that because you were kind and would not sell me even if you had no use for me. So I'm doing something I have always wanted to do. I am filing on a planet. It sounds like a pretty good planet and I should be able to do something with it. I shall fix it up and build a home and maybe someday you will come and visit me.

Yours,

Buster.

P.S. If you ever want me, you can find out where I am at the homestead office.

Gently, Sutton folded the sheet, put it in his pocket.

He sat idly in the chair, listening to the purling of the stream that gushed through the painting hung above the fireplace. A bird sang and a fish jumped in a quiet pool around the bend, just outside the frame.

Tomorrow, he thought, I will see Adams. Maybe I can find out if he's behind what happened. Although, why should he be? I'm working for him. I'm carrying out his orders.

He shook his head. No, it couldn't be Adams.

But it must be someone. Someone who had been laying for him, who even now was watching.

He shrugged mental shoulders, picked up the newspaper and unfolded it.

It was the *Galactic Press* and in twenty years its format had not changed. Conservative columns of gray type ran down the page, broken only by laconic headings. Earth news started in the upper left-hand corner of the front page, was followed by Martian news, by Venusian news, by the column from the asteroids, the column and a half from the Jovian moons . . . then the outer planets. News from the rest of the galaxy, he knew, could be found on the inside pages. A paragraph or two to each story. Like the old community personal columns in the country papers of many centuries before.

Still, thought Sutton, smoothing out the paper, it was the only way it could be handled. There was so much news . . . news from many worlds, from many sectors . . . human news, android and robot news, alien news. The items had to be boiled down, condensed, compressed, making one word do the job of a hundred.

There were other papers, of course, serving isolated sections, and these would give the local news in more detail. But on Earth there was need of galactic-wide news coverage . . . for Earth was the capital of the galaxy . . . a planet that was nothing but a capital . . . a planet that grew no food, allowed no industries, that made its business nothing but government. A planet whose every inch was landscaped and tended like a lawn or park or garden.

Sutton ran his eye down the Earth column. An earthquake in eastern Asia. A new underwater development for the housing of alien employeeś and representatives from watery worlds. Delivery of three new star ships to the Sector 19 run. And then:

Asher Sutton, special agent of the Department of Galactic Investigation, returned today from 61 Cygni, to which he was assigned twenty years ago. Immediately upon landing a guard was thrown around his ship and he was in seclusion at the Orion Arms. All attempts to reach him for a statement failed. Shortly after his arrival, he was called out by Geoffrey Benton. Mr. Sutton chose a pistol and informality.

Sutton read the item again. *All attempts to reach him . . .*

Herkimer had said there were reporters and photographers in the lobby and ten minutes later Ferdinand had sworn there weren't. He had had no calls. There had been no attempt to reach him. Or had there? Attempts that had been neatly stopped. Stopped by the same person who had lain in wait for him, the same power that had been inside the room when he stepped across the threshold.

He dropped the paper to the floor, sat thinking.

He had been challenged by one of Earth's foremost, if not the foremost, duelist.

The old family robot had run away . . . or had been persuaded to run away.

Attempts by the press to reach him had been stopped . . . cold.

The visor purred at him and he jumped.

A call.

The first since he had arrived.

He swung around in his chair and flipped up the switch.

A woman's face came in. Granite eyes and skin magnolia-white, hair a copper glory.

"My name is Eva Armour," she said. "I am the one who asked you to wait with the elevator."

"I recognized you," said Sutton.

"I called to make amends."

"There is no need . . ."

"But, Mr. Sutton, there is. You thought I was laughing at you and I really wasn't."

"I looked funny," Sutton told her. "It was your privilege to laugh."

"Will you take me out to dinner?" she asked.

"Certainly," said Sutton. "I would be delighted to."

"And someplace afterwards," she suggested. "We'll make an evening of it."

"Gladly," said Sutton.

"I'll meet you in the lobby at seven," she said. "And I won't be late."

The visor faded and Sutton sat stiffly in the chair.

They'd make an evening of it, she had said. And he was afraid she might be right.

They'd make an evening of it, and he said, talking to himself, you'll be lucky if you're alive tomorrow.

X

Adams sat silently, facing the four men who had come into his office, trying to make out what they might be thinking. But their faces wore the masks of everyday.

Clark, the space construction engineer, clutched a field book in his hand and his face was set and stern. There was no foolishness about Clark . . . ever.

Anderson, anatomist, big and rough, was lighting up his pipe, and for the moment that seemed, to him, the most important thing in all the world.

Blackburn, the psychologist, frowned at the glowing tip of his cigarette, and Shulcross, the language expert, sprawled sloppily in his chair like an empty sack.

They found something, Adams told himself. They found plenty and some of it has them tangled up.

"Clark," said Adams, "suppose you start us out."

"We looked the ship over," Clark told him, "and we found it couldn't fly."

"But it did," said Adams. "Sutton brought it home."

Clark shrugged. "He might as well have used a log. Or a hunk of rock. Either one would have served the purpose. Either one would fly just as well as, or better than, that heap of junk."

"Junk?"

"The engines were washed out," said Clark. "The safety automatics were the only things that kept them from atomizing. The ports were cracked, some of them were broken. One of the tubes was busted off and lost. The whole ship was twisted out of line."

"You mean it was warped?"

"It had struck something," Clark declared. "Struck it hard and fast. Seams were opened, the structural plates were bent, the whole thing was twisted out of kilter. Even if you could start the engines, the ship would never handle. Even with the tubes O.K., you couldn't set a course. Give it any drive and it would simply corkscrew."

Anderson cleared his throat. "What would have happened to Sutton if he'd been in it when it struck?"

"He would have died," said Clark.

"You are positive of that?"

"No question of it. Even a miracle wouldn't have saved him. We thought of that same thing, so we worked it out. We rigged up a diagram and we used the most conservative force factors to show theoretic effects. . . ."

Adams interrupted. "But he must have been in the ship."

Clark shook his head stubbornly. "If he was, he died. Our diagram shows he didn't have a chance. If one force didn't kill him, a dozen others would."

"Sutton came back," Adams pointed out.

The two stared at one another, half angrily.

Anderson broke the silence. "Had he tried to fix it up?"

Clark shook his head. "Not a mark to show he did. There would have been no use in trying. Sutton didn't know a thing about mechanics. Not a single thing. I checked on that. He had no training, no natural inclination. And it takes a man with savvy to repair an atomic engine. Fix it, not rebuild it. And this setup would have called for complete rebuilding."

Shulcross spoke for the first time, softly, quietly, not moving from his awkward slouch.

"Maybe we're starting wrong," he said. "Starting in the middle. If we started at the beginning, laid the groundwork first, we might get a better idea of what really happened."

They looked at him, all of them, wondering what he meant.

Shulcross saw it was up to him to go ahead. He spoke to Adams.

"Do you have any idea of what sort of place this Cygnian world might be? This place that Sutton went."

Adams smiled wearily. "We aren't positive. Much like Earth, perhaps. We've never been able to get close enough to know. It's the seventh planet of 61 Cygni. It might have been any one of the system's sixteen planets, but mathematically it was figured out that the seventh planet had the best chance of sustaining life."

He paused and looked around the circle of faces and saw that they were waiting for him to go on.

"Sixty-one," he said, "is a near neighbor of ours. It was one of the first suns that Man headed for when he left the Solar system. Ever since it has been a thorn in our sides."

Anderson grinned. "Because we couldn't crack it."

Adams nodded. "That's right. A secret system in a galaxy that held few secrets from Man any time he wanted to go out and take the trouble to solve them.

"We've run into all sort of weird things, of course. Planetary conditions that, to this day, we haven't licked. Funny, dangerous life. Economic systems and psychological concepts that had us floored and still give us a headache every time we think of them. But we always were able, at the very least, to see the thing that gave us trouble, to know the thing that licked us. With Cygni it was different. We couldn't even get there."

"The planets are either cloud-covered or screened, for we've never seen the surface of a single one of them. And when you get within a few billion miles of the system you start sliding." He looked at Clark. "That's the right word, isn't it?"

"There's no word for it," Clark told him, "but sliding comes as close as any. You aren't stopped or you aren't slowed, but you are deflected. As if the ship had hit ice, although it would be something slicker than ice. Whatever it is, it doesn't register. There's no sign of it, nothing that you can see or nothing that makes even the faintest flicker on the instruments, but you hit it and you slide off course. You correct and you slide off course again. In the early days, it drove men mad trying to reach the system and never getting a mile nearer than a certain imaginary line."

"As if," said Adams, "someone had taken his finger and drawn a deadline around the system."

"Something like that," said Clark.

"But Sutton got through," said Anderson.

Adams nodded. "Sutton got through," he said.

"I don't like it," Clark declared. "I don't like a thing about it. Someone got a brainstorm. Our ships are too big, they said. If we used smaller ships, we might squeeze through. As if the things that kept us off was a mesh or something."

"Sutton got through," said Adams, stubbornly. "They launched him in a lifeboat and he got through. His small ship got through where the big ones couldn't."

Clark shook his head, just as stubbornly. "It doesn't make sense," he said. "Smallness and bigness wouldn't have a thing to do with it. There's another factor somewhere, a factor we've never even thought of. Sutton got through all right and he crashed and if he was in the ship when it crashed, he died. But he didn't get through because his ship was small. It was for some other reason."

The men sat tense, thinking, waiting.

"Why Sutton?" Anderson asked, finally.

Adams answered quietly. "The ship was small. We could only send one man. We picked the man we thought could do the best job if he did get through."

"And Sutton was the best man?"

"He was," said Adams, crisply.

Anderson said amiably, "Well, apparently, he was. He got through."

"Or was let through," said Blackburn.

"Not necessarily," said Anderson.

"It follows," Blackburn contended. "Why did we want to get into the Cygnian system? To find out if it was dangerous. That was the idea, wasn't it?"

"That was the idea," Adams told him. "Anything unknown is potentially dangerous. You can't write it off until you are sure. These were Sutton's instructions: Find out if 61 is dangerous."

"And by the same token, they'd want to find out about us," Blackburn said. "We'd been prying and poking at them for several thousand years. They might have wanted to find out about us as badly as we did about them."

Anderson nodded. "I see what you mean. They'd chance one man, if they could haul him in, but they wouldn't let a full-armed ship and a full crew get within shooting distance."

"Exactly," said Blackburn.

Adams dismissed the line of talk abruptly, said to Clark, "You spoke of dents. Were they made recently?"

Clark shook his head. "Twenty years looks right to me. There is a lot of rust. Some of the wiring was getting pretty soft."

"Let us suppose, then," said Anderson, "that Sutton, by some miracle, had the knowledge to fix the ship. Even then, he would have needed materials."

"Plenty of them," said Clark.

"The Cygnians could have supplied him with them," Shulcross suggested.

"If there are any Cygnians," said Anderson.

"I don't believe they could," Blackburn declared. "A race that hides behind a screen would not be mechanical. If they knew mechanics, they would go out into space instead of shielding themselves from space. I'll make a guess the Cygnians are nonmechanical."

"But the screen," Anderson prompted.

"It wouldn't have to be mechanical," Blackburn said flatly.

Clark smacked his open palm on his knee. "What's the use of all this speculation? Sutton didn't repair that ship. He brought it back, somehow, without repair. He didn't even try to fix it. There are layers of rust on everything and there's not a wrench mark on it."

Shulcross leaned forward. "One thing I don't get," he said. "Clark says some of the ports were broken. That means Sutton navigated eleven light-years exposed to space."

"He used a suit," said Blackburn.

Clark said, quietly, "There weren't any suits."

He looked around the room, almost as if he feared someone outside the little circle might be listening.

He lowered his voice. "And that isn't all. There wasn't any food and there wasn't any water."

Anderson tapped out his pipe against the palm of his hand and the hollow sound of tapping echoed in the room. Carefully, deliberately, almost as if forcing himself to concentrate upon it, he dropped the ash from his hand into a tray.

"I might have the answer to that one," he said. "At least a clue. There's still a lot of work to do before we have the answer. And then we can't be sure."

He sat stiffly in the chair, aware of the eyes upon him.

"I hesitate to say the thing I have in mind," he said.

No one spoke a word.

The clock on the wall ticked the seconds off.

From far outside the open window a locust hummed in the quiet of afternoon.

"I don't think," said Anderson, "that the man is human."

The clock ticked on. The locust shrilled to silence.

Adams finally spoke. "But the fingerprints checked. The eyeprints, too."

"Oh, it's Sutton, all right," Anderson admitted. "There is no doubt of that. Sutton on the outside. Sutton in the flesh. The same body, or at least part of the same body, that left Earth twenty years ago."

"What are you getting at?" asked Clark. "If he's the same, he's human."

"You take an old spaceship," said Anderson, "and you juice it up. Add a gadget here and another there, eliminate one thing, modify another. What have you got?"

"A rebuilt job," said Clark.

"That's just the phrase I wanted," Anderson told them. "Someone or something has done the same to Sutton. He's a rebuilt job. And the best human job I have ever seen.

He's got two hearts and his nervous system's haywire . . . well, not haywire exactly, but different. Certainly not human. And he's got an extra circulatory system. Not a circulatory system, either, but that is what it looks like. Only it's not connected with the heart. Right now, I'd say, it's not being used. Like a spare system. One system starts acting up and you can switch to the spare one while you tinker with the first."

Anderson pocketed his pipe, rubbed his hands together almost as if he were washing them.

"Well, there," he said, "you have it."

Blackburn blurted out, "It sounds impossible."

Anderson appeared not to have heard him, and yet he answered him. "We had Sutton under for the best part of an hour and we put every inch of him on tape and film. It takes some time to analyze a job like that. We aren't finished yet."

"But we failed in one thing. We used a psychonometer and we didn't get a nibble. Not a quaver, not a thought. Not even seepage. His mind was closed, tight shut."

"Some defect in the meter," Adams suggested.

"No," said Anderson. "We checked that. The psycho was all right."

He looked around the room, from one face to another.

"Maybe you don't realize the implication," he told them. "When a man is drugged or asleep, or in any other case where he is unaware, a psychonometer, will turn him inside out. It will dig out things that his waking self would swear he didn't know. Even when a man fights against it, there is a certain seepage and that seepage widens as his mental resistance wears down."

"But it didn't work with Sutton," Shulcross said.

"That's right. It didn't work with Sutton. I tell you, the man's not human."

"And you think he's different enough, physically, so that he could live in space, live without food and water?"

"I don't know," said Anderson.

He licked his lips and stared around the room, like a wild thing seeking some way to escape.

"I don't know," he said. "I simply don't."

Adams spoke softly. "We must not get upset," he said. "Alienness is no strange thing to us. Once it might have been, when the first humans went out into space. But today . . ."

Clark interrupted, impatiently. "Alien things themselves don't bother me. But when a man turns alien . . ."

He gulped, appealed to Anderson. "Do you think he's dangerous?"

"Possibly," said Anderson.

"Even if he is, he can't do much to harm us," Adams told them, calmly. "That place of his is simply clogged with spy rigs."

"Any reports in yet?" asked Blackburn.

"Just generally. Nothing specific. Sutton has been taking it easy. Had a few calls. Made a few himself. Had a visitor or two."

"He knows he's being watched," said Clark. "He's putting on an act."

"There's a rumor around," said Blackburn, "that Benton challenged him."

Adams nodded. "Yes, he did. Ash tried to back out of it. That doesn't sound as if he's dangerous."

"Maybe," speculated Clark, almost hopefully, "Benton will close our case for us."

Adams smiled thinly. "Somehow I think Ash may have spent the afternoon thinking up a dirty deal for our Mr. Benton."

Anderson had fished the pipe out of his pocket, was

loading it from his pouch. Clark was fumbling for a cigarette.

Adams looked at Shulcross. "You have something, Mr. Shulcross."

The language expert nodded. "But it's not too exciting. We opened Sutton's case and we found a manuscript. We photostated it and replaced it exactly as it was. But so far it hasn't done us any good. We can't read a word of it."

"Codes," said Blackburn.

Shulcross shook his head. "If it were code our robots would have cracked it. In an hour or two. But it's not a code. It's language. And until you get a key a language can't be cracked."

"You've checked, of course."

Shulcross smiled glumly. "Back to the old Earth languages . . . back to Babylon and Crete. We cross-checked every lingo in the galaxy. None of them came close."

"Language," said Blackburn. "A new language. That means Sutton found something."

"Sutton would," said Adams. "He's the best agent that I have."

Anderson stirred restlessly in his chair. "You like Sutton?" he asked. "Like him personally?"

"I do," said Adams.

"Adams," said Anderson, "I've been wondering. It's a thing that struck me funny from the first."

"Yes, what is it?"

"You knew Sutton was coming back. Knew almost to the minute when he would arrive. And you set a mousetrap for him. How come?"

"Just a hunch," said Adams.

For a long moment all four of them sat looking at

him. Then they saw he meant to say no more. They rose to leave the room.

XI

Across the room a woman's laughter floated, sharp-edged with excitement.

The lights changed from the dusk-blue of April to the purple-gray of madness and the room was another world that floated in a hush that was not exactly silence. Perfume came down a breeze that touched the cheek with ice . . . perfume that called to mind black orchids in an outland of breathless terror.

The floor swayed beneath Sutton's feet and he felt Eva's small fist digging hard into his arm.

The Zag spoke to them and his words were dead and hollow sounds dripping from a mummied husk.

"What is it that you wish? Here you live the lives you yearn for . . . find any escape that you may seek . . . possess the things you dream of."

"There is a stream," said Sutton. "A little creek that ran . . ."

The light changed to green, a faërie green that glowed with soft, quiet life, exuberant, springtime life and the hint of things to come, and there were trees, trees that were fringed and haloed with the glistening, sun-kissed green of the first bursting buds.

Sutton wiggled his toes and knew the grass beneath them, the first tender grass of spring, and smelled the hepaticas and bloodroot that had almost no smell at all ... and the stronger scent of sweet Williams blooming on the hill across the creek.

He told himself, "It's too early for sweet Williams to be in bloom."

The creek gurgled at him as it ran across the shingle down into the Big Hole and he hurried forward across the meadow grass, cane pole tight-clutched in one hand, the can of worms in the other.

A bluebird flashed through the trees that climbed the bluff across the meadow and a robin sang high in the top of the mighty elm that grew above the Big Hole.

Sutton found the worn place in the bank, like a chair with the elm's trunk serving as a back, and he sat down in it and leaned forward to peer into the water. The current ran strong and dark and deep, swirling in to hug the higher bank, gurgling and sucking with a strength that set up tiny whirlpools.

Sutton drew in his breath and held it with pent-up anticipation. With shaking hands he found the biggest worm and pulled it from the can, baited up the hook.

Breathlessly, he dropped the hook into the water, canted the pole in front of him for easy handling. The bobber drifted down the swirling slide of water, floated in an eddy where the current turned back upon itself. It jerked, almost disappeared, then bobbed to the surface and floated once again.

Sutton leaned forward, tensed, arms aching with the tenseness. But even through the tenseness, he knew the goodness of the day ... the utter peace and tranquillity ... the freshness of the morning, the soft heat of the sun, the blue of sky and the white of cloud. The water talked to him and he felt himself grow and become a being that comprehended and became a part of the clean, white ecstasy that was the hills and stream and meadow . . . earth, cloud, water, sky and sun.

And the bobber went clear under!

He jerked and felt the weight of the fish that he had caught. It sailed in an arc above his head and landed in the grass behind him. He laid down his pole, scrambled to his feet and ran.

The chub flopped in the grass and he grabbed the line and held it up. It was a whopper! A good six inches long!

Sobbing in his excitement, he dropped to his knees and grasped the fish, removed the hook with fingers that fumbled in their trembling.

A six-inch one to start with, he said, talking to the sky and stream and meadow. Maybe every one I catch will be that big. Maybe I'll catch as many as a dozen and all of them will be six inches long. Maybe some of them will be even bigger. Maybe . . .

"Hello," said a childish voice.

Sutton twisted around, still on his knees.

A little girl stood by the elm tree and it seemed for a moment that he had seen her somewhere before. But then he realized that she was a stranger and he frowned a little, for girls were no good when it came to fishing. He hoped she wouldn't stay. It would be just like her to hang around and spoil the day for him.

"I am," she said, speaking a name he did not catch, for she lisped a little.

He did not answer.

"I am eight years old," she said.

"I am Asher Sutton," he told her, "and I am ten . . . going on eleven."

She stood and stared at him, one hand plucking nervously at the figured apron that she wore. The apron, he noticed, was clean and starched, very stiff and prim, and she was messing it all up with her nervous plucking.

"I am fishing," he said and tried very hard to keep from sounding too important. "And I just caught a whopper."

He saw her eyes go large in sudden terror at the sight of something that came up from behind him and he wheeled around, no longer on his knees, but on his feet, and his hand was snaking into the pocket of his coat.

The place was purple-gray and there was shrill woman-laughter and there was a face in front of him . . . a face he had seen that afternoon and never would forget.

A fat and cultured face that twinkled even now with good fellowship, twinkled despite the deadly squint, despite the gun already swinging upward in a hairy, pudgy fist.

Sutton felt his fingers touch the grip of the gun he carried, felt them tighten around it and jerk it from the pocket. But he was too late, he knew, too late to beat the spat of flame from a gun that had long seconds' start.

Anger flamed within him, cold, desolate, deadly anger. Anger at the pudgy fist, at the smiling face . . . the face that would smile across a chessboard or from behind a gun. The smile of an egotist who would try to beat a robotic that was designed to play the perfect game of chess . . . an egotist who believed that he could shoot down Asher Sutton.

The anger, he realized, was something more than anger . . . something greater and more devastating than the mere working of human adrenal. It was a part of him and something that was more than him, more than the mortal thing of flesh and blood that was Asher Sutton. A terrible thing plucked from nonhumanity.

The face before him melted . . . or it seemed to melt. It changed and the smile was gone and Sutton felt the anger move out from his brain and slam bullet-hard against the wilting personality that was Geoffrey Benton.

Benton's gun coughed loudly and the muzzle-flash was blood-red in the purple light. Then Sutton felt the thud of his own gun slamming back against his wrist, slapping at the heel of his hand as he pulled the trigger.

Benton was falling, twisting forward, bending at the middle as if he had hinges in his stomach, and Sutton caught one glimpse of the purple-painted face before it dropped from sight to huddle on the floor. There were surprise and anguish and a terrible overriding fear printed on the features that had been twisted out of shape and were not human any more.

The crashing of the guns had smashed the place to silence, and through the garish light that swirled with powder smoke, Sutton saw the white blobs of many faces staring at him. Faces that mostly were without expression, although some of them had mouths and the mouths were round and open.

He felt a tugging at his elbow and he moved, guided by the hand upon his arm. Suddenly he was limp and shaken and the anger was no more and he told himself, "I have just killed a man."

"Quick," said Eva Armour's voice. "We must get out of here. They'll be swarming at you now. The whole hell's pack of them."

"It was you," he told her. "I remember now. I didn't catch the name at first. You mumbled it . . . or I guess you lisped, and I didn't hear it."

The girl tugged at his arm. "They had Benton conditioned. They figured that was all they needed. They never dreamed you could match him in a duel."

"You were the little girl," Sutton told her, gravely. "You wore a checkered apron and you kept twisting it as if you might be nervous."

"What in heavens' name are you talking about?"

"Why, I was fishing," Sutton said, "and I had just caught a big one when you came along. . . ."

"You're crazy," said the girl. "You were never fishing."

She pushed open a door and shoved him out and the cool air of night slapped him across the face.

"Wait a second," he cried. He wheeled around and caught the girl's arms roughly in his hands.

"They?" he yelled at her. "What are you talking about? Who are they?"

She stared at him wide-eyed.

"You mean that you don't know?"

He shook his head, bewildered.

"Poor Ash," she said.

Her copper hair was a reddish flame, burnished and alive in the flicker of the sign that flashed on and off above the Zag House facade.

DREAMS TO ORDER
Live the life you missed.
Dream up a tough one for us.

An android doorman spoke to them softly. "You wished a car, sir?"

Even as he spoke, the car was there, sliding smoothly and silently up the driveway like a black beetle winging from the night. The doorman reached out a hand and swung wide the door.

"Quick is the word," he said.

There was something in the soft, slurred tone that made Sutton move. He stepped inside the car and pulled Eva after him. The android slammed the door.

Sutton tramped on the accelerator and the car screamed down the curving driveway, slid onto the highway, roared with leashed impatience as it took the long road curing toward the hills.

"Where?" asked Sutton.

"Back to the Arms," she said. "They wouldn't dare to try for you there. Your room is rigged with rays."

Sutton chuckled. "I have to be careful or I would trip on them. But how come you know?"

"It is my job to know."

"Friend or foe?" he asked.

"Friend," she said.

He turned his head and studied her. She had slumped down in the seat and was a little girl . . . but she didn't have a checkered apron and she wasn't nervous.

"I don't suppose," said Sutton, "that it would be any use for me to ask you questions?"

She shook her head.

"If I did, you'd probably lie to me."

"If I wanted to," she said.

"I could shake it out of you."

"You could, but you won't. You see, Ash, I know you very well."

"You just met me yesterday."

"Yes, I know," she said, "but I've studied you for all of twenty years."

He laughed. "You haven't thought of me, at all. You just . . ."

"And Ash."

"Yes?"

"I think you're wonderful."

He shot a quick glance at her. She was still in her corner of the seat and the wind had blown one strand of copper hair across her face . . . and her body was soft and her face was shining. And yet, he thought, and yet . . .

"That's a nice thing for you to say," he told her. "I could kiss you for it."

"You may kiss me, Ash," she told him, "any time you want to."

After a startled moment he slowed the car and did.

XII

THE TRUNK CAME in the morning when Sutton was finishing his breakfast.

It was old and battered, the ancient rawhide covering hanging in tatters to reveal the marred steel skeleton, flecked here and there with rust. A key was in the lock and the straps were broken. Mice had gnawed the leather completely off one end.

Sutton remembered it . . . it was the one that had stood in the far corner of the attic when he had been a boy and gone there to play on rainy afternoons.

He picked up the neatly folded copy of the morning edition of the *Galactic Press* that had come with his breakfast tray and shook it out.

The item he was looking for was on the front page, the third item in the Earth news column:

Mr. Geoffrey Benton was killed last night in an informal meeting at one of the amusement centers in the university district. The victor was Mr. Asher Sutton, who returned only yesterday from a mission to 61 Cygni.

There was a final sentence, the most damning that could be written of a duelist.

Mr. Benton fired first and missed.

Sutton folded the paper again and laid it carefully on the table. He lit a cigarette.

I thought it would be me, he told himself. I never fired a gun like that before . . . scarcely knew a gun like that existed. Although I had read about them and knew about them. But I wasn't interested in dueling, and duelists and collectors and antiquarians are the only ones who would know about an ancient weapon.

Of course, I didn't really kill him. Benton killed himself. If he hadn't missed—and there was no excuse for missing—the item would have read the other way around.

Mr. Asher Sutton was killed last night in an encounter . . .

We'll make an evening of it, the girl had said, and she might have known. We'll have dinner and make an evening of it. We'll make an evening of it and Geoffrey Benton will kill you at the Zag House.

Yes, said Sutton to himself, she might have known. She knows too many things. About the spy traps in this room, for instance. And about someone who had Benton conditioned to challenge me and kill me.

She said friend when I asked her friend or foe, but a word is an easy thing. Anyone at all can speak a single word and there is no way to know if it is true or false.

She said she had studied me for twenty years and that is false, of course, for twenty years ago I was setting out for Cygni and I was unimportant. Just a cog in a great machine. I am unimportant still, unimportant to everyone but myself and a great idea that no human but myself could possibly know about. For no matter if the manuscript was photostated, there is not a soul who can read it.

She said friend when I asked her friend or foe. And she knew that Benton had been conditioned to challenge me and kill me. And she had called me up and made a dinner date.

And words are easy things to say. But there are other things than words that are not easy to twist from lie to truth . . . the way her lips felt beneath my lips, the tenderness of fingertips that slide along the cheek.

He snubbed out the cigarette and rose and walked over to the trunk. The lock was rusty and the key turned hard, but he finally got it open and lifted up the lid.

The trunk was half full of papers very neatly piled. Sutton, looking at them, chuckled. Buster always was a methodical soul. But, then, all robots were methodical. It was the nature of them. Methodical and, what was it Herkimer had said? Stubborn, that was it. Methodical and stubborn.

He squatted on the floor beside the trunk and rummaged through the contents. Old letters tied neatly in bundles. An old notebook from his college days. A sheaf of clipped-together documents that undoubtedly were outdated. A scrapbook littered with clippings that had not been pasted up. An album half filled with a cheap stamp collection.

He squatted back on his heels and turned the pages of the album lovingly, childhood coming back again. Cheap stamps because he had had no money to buy the better ones. Gaudy ones because they had appealed to him. Most of them in poor condition, but there had been a time when they had seemed wonderful.

The stamp craze, he remembered, had lasted two years . . . three years at the most. He had pored over catalogues, had traded, had bought cheap packets, picked up the strange lingo of the hobby . . . perforate, imperforate, shades, watermarks, intaglio.

He smiled softly at the happiness of the memory. There

had been stamps he'd wanted but could never have, and he had studied the illustrations of them until he knew each of them by heart. He lifted his head and stared at the wall and tried to remember what some of them were like, but there was no recollection. The once all-important thing had been buried by more than fifty years of other all-important matters.

He laid the album to one side, went at the trunk again.

More notebooks and letters. Loose clippings. A curious-looking wrench. A well-chewed bone that at one time probably had been the property and the solace of some well-loved but now forgotten family dog.

Junk, said Sutton. Buster could have saved a lot of time by simply burning it.

A couple of old newspapers. A moth-eaten pennant. A bulky letter that never had been opened.

Sutton tossed it on top of the rest of the litter he had taken from the trunk, then hesitated, put out his hand and picked it up again.

That stamp looked queer. The color, for one thing.

Memory ticked within his brain and he saw the stamp again, saw it as he had seen it when a lad . . . not the stamp, itself, of course, but the illustration of it in a catalogue.

He bent above the letter and caught a sudden, gasping breath.

The stamp was old, incredibly old . . . incredibly old and worth . . . good Lord, how much was it worth?

He tried to make out the postmark, but it was so faint with time that it blurred before his eyes.

He got up slowly and carried the letter to the table, bent above it, puzzling out the town name.

BRIDGEP—, WIS.

Bridgeport, probably. And WIS.? Some old state, perhaps. Some political division lost in the mist of time.

July—, 198

July, 1980-something!

Six thousand years ago!

Sutton's hand shook.

An unopened letter, mailed sixty centuries ago. Tossed in with this heap of junk. Lying cheek by jowl with a tooth-scarred bone and a funny wrench.

An unopened letter . . . and with a stamp that was worth a fortune.

Sutton read the postmark again. Bridgeport, Wis. July, it looked like 11 . . . July 11, 198-. The missing numeral in the year was too faint to make out. Maybe with a good glass it could be done.

The address, faded but still legible, said:

Mr. John H. Sutton,

Bridgeport,

Wisconsin.

So that was what WIS. was. Wisconsin.

And the name was Sutton.

Of course, it would be Sutton.

What had Buster's android lawyer said? A trunkful of family papers.

"I'll have to look into historic geography, Sutton thought. I'll have to find out just where Wisconsin was.

But John Sutton? John H. Sutton. That was another matter. Just another Sutton. One who had been dust these many years. A man who sometimes forgot to open up his mail.

Sutton turned the letter and examined the flap. There was no sign of tampering. The adhesive was flaking with age and when he ran a fingernail along one corner the mucilage came loose in a tiny shower of powder. The paper, he saw, was brittle and would require careful handling.

A trunkful of family papers, the android Wellington had said when he came into the room and balanced himself very primly on the edge of a chair and laid his hat precisely on the tabletop.

And it was a trunkful of junk instead. Bones and wrenches and paper clips and clippings. Old notebooks and letters and a letter that had been mailed six thousand years ago and never had been opened.

Did Buster know about the letter . . . but even as he asked himself the question Sutton knew that Buster did.

And he had tried to hide it . . . and he had succeeded. He had tossed it in with other odds and ends, well knowing that it would be found, but by the man for whom it was intended. For the trunk was deliberately made to appear of no importance. It was old and battered and the key was in the lock and it said there's nothing in me, but if you want to waste your time, why, go ahead and look. And if anyone had looked, the clutter would have seemed no more than what it was with one exception . . . the worthless accumulation of outworn sentiment.

Sutton reached out a finger and tapped the bulky letter lying on the table.

John H. Sutton, an ancestor six thousand years removed. His blood runs in my veins, though many times diluted. But he was a man who lived and breathed and ate and died, who saw the sunrise against the green Wisconsin hills . . . if Wisconsin has any hills, wherever it may be.

He felt the heat of summer and shivered in the cold of winter. He read the papers and talked politics with neighbors up the road. He worried about many things, both big and small, and most of them would be small, the way worries usually are.

He went fishing in the river a few miles away from home and he may have puttered in his garden in his declining years when he had little else to do.

A man like me, although there would be minor differences. He had a vermiform appendix and it may have caused him trouble. He had wisdom teeth and they may have caused him trouble, too. And he probably died at eighty or very shortly after, although he may as well have died much earlier. And when I am eighty, Sutton thought I will be just entering my prime.

But there would be compensations. John H. Sutton would have lived closer to the Earth, for the Earth was all he had. He would have been unplagued by alien psychology and Earth would have been a living place instead of a governing place where not a thing is grown for its economic worth, not a wheel is turned for economic purpose. He could have chosen his lifework from the whole broad field of human endeavor instead of being forced into governmental work, into the job of governing a flimsy expanse of galactic empire.

And, somewhere, lost now, there were Suttons before him, and after him, lost too, many other Suttons. The chain of life runs smoothly from one generation to the next and none of the links stand out except here and there a link one sees by accident. By the accident of history or the accident of myth or the accident of not opening a letter.

The doorbell chimed and Sutton, startled, scooped up the letter and slid it into the inside pocket of his coat.

"Come in," he called.

It was Herkimer.

"Good morning, sir," he said.

Sutton glared at him. "What do you want?" he asked.

"I belong to you," Herkimer told him, blandly. "I'm part of your third of Benton's property."

"My third . . ." and then he remembered.

It was the law. Whoever kills another in a duel inherits one third of the dead man's property. That was the law . . . a law he had forgotten.

"I hope you don't object," said Herkimer. "I am easy to get along with and very quick to learn and I like to work. I can cook and sew and run errands and I can read and write."

"And put the finger on me."

"Oh, no, I never would do that."

"Why not?"

"Because you are my master."

"We'll see," said Sutton, sourly.

"But I'm not all," said Herkimer. "There are other things. There's an asteroid, a hunting asteroid stocked with the finest game, and a spaceship. A small one, it's true, but very serviceable. There is several thousand dollars and an estate out on the west coast and some wildcat planetary development stock and a number of other small things, too numerous to mention."

Herkimer dipped into his pocket and brought out a notebook.

"I have them written out if you would care to listen."

"Not now," said Sutton. "I have work to do."

Herkimer brightened.

"Something I could do, no doubt. Something I could help with."

"Nothing," said Sutton. "I am going to see Adams."

"I could carry your case. That one over there."

"I'm not taking the case."

"But, sir . . ."

"You sit down and fold your hands and wait until I get back."

"I'll get into mischief," the android warned. "I just know I will."

"All right, then. There is something you can do. That case you mentioned. You can watch it."

"Yes, sir," said Herkimer, plainly disappointed.

"And don't waste your time trying to read what's in it," said Sutton. "You won't be able to."

"Oh," said Herkimer, still more disappointed.

"There's another thing. A girl by the name of Eva Armour lives in this hotel. Know anything about her?"

Herkimer shook his head. "But I have a cousin . . ."

"A cousin?"

"Sure. A cousin. She was made in the same laboratory as I and that makes her my cousin."

"You have a lot of cousins, then."

"Yes," said Herkimer, "I have many thousand. And we stick together. Which," he said, very sanctimoniously, "is the way it should be with families."

"You think this cousin might know something?"

Herkimer nodded. "She works in the hotel. She can tell me something."

He picked up a leaflet off a stack that was on a table.

"I see, sir," he said, "that they got to you."

"What are you talking about?" Sutton demanded angrily.

"The Equality Leaguers," said Herkimer. "They lie in wait for anyone who might have some importance. They have a petition."

"Yes," said Sutton, "they did say something about a petition. Wanted me to sign it."

"And you didn't, sir?"

"No," said Sutton, shortly.

He stared at Herkimer. "You're an android," he said, bluntly. "I would expect you to be sympathetic with them."

"Sir," said Herkimer, "they may mean all right, but they go about it wrong. They ask for charity for us, pity for us. We do not want charity and pity."

"What do you want?"

"Acceptance as human equals," said Herkimer, "but acceptance on our merits, not by special dispensation, not by human tolerance."

"I understand," said Sutton. "I think I understood when they caught me in the lobby. Without being able to put it into words . . ."

"It's this way, sir," said Herkimer. "The human race has made us. That is the thing that rankles. They made us with exactly the same spirit that a farmer breeds his cattle. They make us for a purpose and use us for that purpose. They may be kind to us, but there's pity back of kindness. They do not allow us to stand on our own abilities. We have no inherent claim, are allowed no inherent claim, to the basic rights of mankind. We . . ."

He paused and the glitter in his eyes turned off and his face smoothed out.

"I bore you, sir," he said.

Sutton spoke sharply. "I'm your friend in this matter, Herkimer. Don't forget that for a moment. I am your friend and I proved it in advance by not signing that petition."

He stood staring at the android. Impudent and sly, he thought. And that's the way we've made them. That is the mark of slavery that goes with the mark upon the forehead.

"You may rest assured," he told Herkimer, "that I have no pity for you."

"Thank you, sir," said Herkimer. "Thank you for all of us."

Sutton turned to the door.

"You are to be congratulated, sir," said Herkimer. "You gave a very good account of yourself last night."

Sutton turned back to the room.

"Benton missed," he said. "I couldn't help but kill him."

Herkimer nodded. "But it isn't only that, sir. This happens to be the first time I ever heard of a man being killed by a bullet in the arm."

"In the arm!"

"Precisely, sir. The bullet smashed his arm, but it didn't touch him otherwise."

"He was dead, wasn't he?"

"Oh, yes," said Herkimer. "Very, very dead."

XIII

ADAMS THUMBED the lighter and waited for the flame to steady. His eyes were fixed on Sutton and there was no softness in them, but there was softness and irritability and a certain faint unsureness in the man himself, hidden well, but there.

That staring, Sutton told himself, is an old trick of his. He glares at you and keeps his face frozen like a sphinx and if you aren't used to him and on to all his tricks, he'll have you thinking that he is God Almighty.

But he doesn't do the glaring quite as well as he used to do it. There's strain in him now and there was no strain in him twenty years ago. Just hardness, then. Granite, and now the granite is beginning to weather.

There's something on his mind. There's something that isn't going well.

Adams passed the lighter flame over the loaded bowl of his pipe, back and forth deliberately, taking his time, making Sutton wait.

"You know, of course," said Sutton, speaking quietly, "that I can't be frank with you."

The lighter flame snapped off and Adams straightened in his chair.

"Eh?" he asked.

Sutton hugged himself. Caught him off base. Threw him for a loss. A passed pawn, he told himself. That's what it is . . . a passed pawn.

He said aloud, "You know by now, of course, that I flew home a ship that could not be flown. You know I had no space-suit and that the ports were broken and the hull was riddled. I had no food and water and 61 is eleven light-years away."

Adams nodded bleakly. "Yes, we know all that."

"How I got back or what happened to me has nothing to do with my report and I don't intend to tell you."

Adams rumbled at him, "Then why mention it at all?"

"Just so we'll understand one another," Sutton said. "So that you won't ask a lot of questions that will get no answer. It will save a lot of time."

Adams leaned back in his chair and puffed his pipe contentedly.

"You were sent out to get information, Ash," he reminded Sutton. "Any kind of information. Anything that would make Cygni more understandable. You represented Earth and you were paid by Earth and you surely owe Earth something."

"I owe Cygni something, too," said Sutton. "I owe Cygni my life. My ship crashed and I was killed."

Adams nodded, almost sleepily.

"Yes, that is what Clark said. That you were killed."

"Who is Clark?"

"Clark is a space construction engineer," Adams told him. "Sleeps with ships and blue prints. He studied your ship and he calculated a graph of force co-ordinates. He reported that if you were inside the ship when it hit, you didn't have a chance."

Adams stared at the ceiling.

"Clark said that if you were in that ship when it hit you would have been reduced to jelly."

"It's wonderful," said Sutton, dryly, "what a man can do with figures."

Adams prodded him again. "Anderson said you weren't human."

"I suppose Anderson could tell that by looking at the ship."

Adams nodded. "No food, no air. It was the logical conclusion for anyone to draw."

Sutton shook his head. "Anderson is wrong. If I weren't human, you never would have seen me. I would not have come back at all. But I was homesick for Earth and you were expecting a report."

"You took your time," Adams accused him.

"I had to be sure," Sutton told him. "I had to know, you see. I had to be able to come back and tell you one thing or another. I had to tell you if the Cygnians were dangerous or if they weren't."

"And wihch is it?"

"They aren't dangerous," said Sutton.

Adams waited and Sutton sat silently.

Finally Adams said, "And that is all?"

"That is all," said Sutton.

Adams tapped his teeth with the bit of his pipe. "I'd hate to have to send another man out to check up," he said. "Especially after I had told everyone you'd bring back all the dope."

"It wouldn't do any good," said Sutton. "No one could get through."

"You did."

"Yes, and I was the first. Because I was the first, I also was the last."

Across the desk, Adams smiled winterly. "You were

fond of those people, Ash."

"They weren't people."

"Well . . . beings, then."

"They weren't even beings. It's hard to tell you exactly what they are. You'd laugh at me if I told you what I really think they are."

Adams grunted. "Come the closest that you can."

"Symbiotic abstractions. That's close enough, as close as I can come."

"You mean they really don't exist?" asked Adams.

"Oh, they exist all right. They are there and you are aware of them. As aware of them as I am aware of you, or you of me."

"And they make sense?"

"Yes," said Sutton, "they make sense."

"And no one can get through again?"

Sutton shook his head. "Why don't you cross Cygni off your list? Pretend it isn't there. There is no danger from Cygni. The Cygnians will never bother Man, and Man will never get there. There is no use of trying?"

"They aren't mechanical?"

"No," said Sutton. "They're not mechanical."

Adams changed the subject "Let me see. How old are you, Ash?"

"Sixty-one," said Sutton.

"Humpf," said Adams. "Just a kid. Just getting started." His pipe had gone out and he worried at it with a finger, probing at the bowl, scowling at it.

"What do you plan to do?" he asked.

"I have no plans."

"You want to stay on with the service, don't you?"

"That depends," said Sutton, "on how you feel about it. I had presumed, of course, that you wouldn't want me."

"We owe you twenty years' back pay," said Adams, almost kindly. "It's waiting for you. You can pick it up when you go out. You also have three or four years of vacation coming. Why don't you take it now?"

Sutton said nothing.

"Come back later on," said Adams. "We'll have another talk."

"I won't change my mind," said Sutton.

"No one will ask you to."

Sutton stood up slowly.

"I'm sorry," Adams said, "that I haven't your confidence."

"I went out to do a job," Sutton told him, crisply. "I've done that job. I've made my report."

"So you have," said Adams.

"I suppose," said Sutton, "you will keep in touch with me."

Adams' eyes twinkled grimly. "Most certainly, Ash. I shall keep in touch with you."

XIV

Sutton sat quietly in the chair and forty years were canceled from his life.

For it was like going back all of forty years . . . even to the teacups.

Through the open windows of Dr. Raven's study came young voices and the sound of student's feet tramping past along the walk. The wind talked in the elms and it was a sound with which he was familiar. Far off a chapel bell tolled and there was girlish laughter just across the way.

Dr. Raven handed him his teacup.

"I think that I am right," he said, and his eyes were twinkling. "Three lumps and no cream."

"Yes, that's right," said Sutton, astonished that he should remember.

But remembering, he told himself, was easy. I seem to be able to remember almost everything. As if the old sets of habit patterns had been kept bright and polished in my mind through all the alien years, waiting, like a set of cherished silver standing on a shelf, until it was time for them to be used again.

"I remember little things," said Dr. Raven. "Little, inconsequential things, like how many lumps of sugar and what a man said sixty years ago, but I don't do so well, sometimes, at the big things . . . the things you would expect a man to remember."

The white marble fireplace flared to the vaulted ceiling and the university's coat of arms upon its polished face was as bright as the last day Sutton had seen it.

"I suppose," he said, "you wonder why I came."

"Not at all," said Dr. Raven. "All my boys come back to sell me. And I am glad to see them. It makes me feel so proud."

"I've been wondering myself," said Sutton. "And I guess I know what it is, but it is hard to say."

"Let's take it easy then," said Dr. Raven. "Remember, the way we used to. We sat and talked around a thing and finally before we knew it, we had found the core."

Sutton laughed shortly.

"Yes, I remember, doctor. Fine points of theology. The vital differences in comparative religion. Tell me this. You have spent a lifetime at it, you know more about religions, Earthly and otherwise, than any man on Earth. Have you been able to keep one faith? Have you ever been tempted from the teaching of your race?"

Dr. Raven set down his teacup.

"I might have known," he said, "you would embarrass me. You used to do it all the time. You had the uncanny ability to hit exactly on the question that a man found it hard to answer."

"I won't embarrass you any longer," Sutton told him. "I take it that you have found some good, one might say superior, points in alien religions."

"You found a new religion?"

"No," said Sutton. "Not a religion."

The chapel bell kept on tolling and the girl who had

laughed was gone. The footsteps along the walk were far off in the distance.

"Have you ever felt," asked Sutton, "as if you sat on God's right hand and heard a thing that you knew you were never meant to hear?"

Dr. Raven shook his head. "No, I don't think I ever have."

"If you did, what would you do?"

"I think," said Dr. Raven, "that I might be as troubled by it as you are."

"We've lived by faith alone," said Sutton, "for eight thousand years at least and probably more than that. Certainly more than that. For it must have been faith, a glimmer of some sort of faith, that made the Neanderthaler paint the shinbones red and nest the skulls so they faced toward the east."

"Faith," said Dr. Raven gently, "is a powerful thing."

"Yes, powerful," Sutton agreed, "but even in its strength it is our own confession of weakness. Our own admission that we are not strong enough to stand alone, that we must have a staff to lean upon, the expressed hope and conviction that there is some greater power which will lend us aid and guidance."

"You haven't grown bitter, Ash? Something that you found?"

"Not bitter," Sutton told him.

Somewhere a clock was ticking, loud in the sudden hush.

"Doctor," said Sutton, "what do you know of destiny?"

"It's strange to hear you talk of destiny," said Dr. Raven. "You always were a man who never was inclined to bow to destiny."

"I mean documentary destiny," Sutton explained. "Not the abstraction, but the actual thing, the actual belief in destiny. What do the records say?"

"There always have been men who believed in destiny," said Dr. Raven. "Some of them, it would appear, with some justification. But mostly, they didn't call it destiny. They called it luck or a hunch or inspiration or something else. There have been historians who wrote of manifest destiny, but those were no more than words. Just a matter of semantics. Of course, there were some fanatics and there were others who believed in destiny, but practiced fatalism."

"But there is no evidence," said Sutton. "No actual evidence of a thing called destiny? An actual force. A living, vital thing. Something you can put your finger on."

Dr. Raven shook his head. "None that I know of, Ash. Destiny, after all, is just a word. It isn't something that you can pin down. Faith, too, at one time, may have been no more than a word, just as destiny is today. But millions of people and thousands of years made it an actual force, a thing that can be defined and invoked and a thing to live by."

"But hunches and luck," protested Sutton. "Those are just happenstance."

"They might be glimmerings of destiny," Dr. Raven declared. "Flashes showing through. A hint of a broad stream of happening behavior. One cannot know of course. Many can be blind to so many things until he has the facts. Turning points in history have rested on a hunch. Inspired belief in one's own ability has changed the course of events more times than one can count."

He rose and walked to a bookcase, stood with his head tilted back.

"Somewhere," he said, "if I can find it, there is a book."

He searched and did not find it.

"No matter," he declared, "I'll run onto it later if you are still interested. It tells about an old African tribe with a strange belief. They believed that each man's spirit or consciousness or ego or whatever you may call it had a partner, a counterpart on some distant star. If I remember rightly, they even knew which star and could point it out in the evening sky."

He turned around from the bookcase and stared at Sutton.

"That might be destiny, you know," he said. "It might, very well, at that."

He crossed the room to stand in front of the cold fireplace, hands locked behind his back, silver head titled to one side.

"Why are you so interested in destiny?" he asked.

"Because I found destiny," said Sutton.

XV

THE FACE in the visiplate was masked and Adams spoke in chilly anger: "I do not receive masked calls."

"You will this one," said the voice form behind the mask. "I am the man you talked to on the patio. Remember?"

"Calling from the future, I presume," said Adams.

"No, I still am in your time. I have been watching you."

"Watching Sutton, too?"

The masked head nodded. "You have seen him now. What do you think?"

"He's hiding something," Adams said. "And not all of him is human."

"You're going to have him killed?"

"No," said Adams. "No, I don't think I will. He knows something that we need to know. And we won't get it out of him by killing."

"What he knows," said the masked voice, "is better dead with the man who knows it."

"Perhaps," said Adams, "we could come to an understanding if you would tell me what this is all about."

"I can't tell you, Adams. I wish I could. I can't tell you the future."

"And until you do," snapped Adams, "I won't let you change the past."

And he was thinking: The man is scared. Scared and almost desperate. He would kill Sutton any time he wished, but he is afraid to do it. Sutton has to be killed by a man of his own time . . . literally has to be, for time may not tolerate the extension of violence from one bracket to the next.

"By the way," said the future man.

"Yes," said Adams.

"I was going to ask you how things are on Aldebaran XII."

Adams sat rigid in his chair, anger flaming in him.

"If it hadn't been for Sutton," said the masked man, "there would have been no incident on Aldebaran XII."

"But Sutton wasn't back yet," snapped Adams. "He wasn't even here. . . ."

His voice ran down, for he remembered something. The name on the flyleaf . . ."by Asher Sutton."

"Look," said Adams, "tell me, for the love of heaven, if you have anything to tell."

"You mean to say you haven't guessed what it might be?"

Adams shook his head.

"It's war," the voice said.

"But there is no war."

"Not in your time, but in another time."

"But how . . ."

"Remember Michaelson?"

"The man who went a second into time."

The masked head nodded and the screen went blank

and Adams sat and felt the chill of horror trickle through his body.

The visor buzzer purred at him and mechanically he snapped the toggle over.

It was Nelson in the glass.

"Sutton just left the university," Nelson said. "He spent an hour with Dr. Horace Raven. Dr. Raven, if you don't recall, is a professor of comparative religion."

"Oh," said Adams. "Oh, so that is it."

He tapped his fingers on the desk, half irritated, half frightened.

It would be a shame, he thought, to kill a man like Sutton.

But it might be best.

Yes, he told himself, it might be for the best.

XVI

CLARK SAID that he had died and Clark was an engineer. Clark made a graph and death was in the graph; mathematics foretold that certain strains and stresses would turn a body into human jelly.

And Anderson had said he wasn't human and how was Anderson to know?

The road curved ahead, a silver strip shining in the moonlight, and the sounds and smells of night lay across the land. The sharp, clean smell of growing things, the mystery smell of water. A creek ran through the marsh that lay off to the right and Sutton, from behind the wheel, caught the flashing hint of winding, moonlit water as he took a curve. Peeping frogs made a veil of pixy sound that hugged against the hills and fireflies were swinging lanterns that signaled through the dark.

And how was Anderson to know?

How, asked Sutton, unless he examined me? Unless he was the one who tired to probe into my mind after I had been knocked out when I walked into my room?

Adams had tipped his hand and Adams never tipped his hand unless he wanted one to see. Unless he had an ace tucked neatly up his sleeve.

He wanted me to know, Sutton told himself. He wanted me to know, but he couldn't tell me. He couldn't tell me he had me down on tape and film, that he was the one who had rigged up the room.

But he could let me know by making just one slip, a carefully calculated slip, like the one on Anderson. He knew that I would catch and he thinks he can jitter me.

The headlights caught, momentarily, the gray-black massive lines of a house that huddled on a hillside and then there was another curve. A night bird, black and ghostly, fluttered across the road and the shadow of its flight danced down the cone of light.

Adams was the one, said Sutton, talking to himself. He was the one who was waiting for me. He knew, somehow, that I was coming, and he was all primed and cocked. He had me tagged and ticketed before I hit the ground and he gave me a going over before I knew what was going on.

And undoubtedly he found a whole lot more than he bargained for.

Sutton chuckled dryly. And the chuckle was a scream that came slanting down the hill slope in a blaze of streaming fire . . . a stream of fire that ended in the marsh, that died down momentarily, then licked out in blue and red.

Brakes hissed and tires screeched on the pavement as Sutton slued the car around to bring it to a stop. Even before the machine came to a halt, he was out of the door and running down the slope toward the strange, black craft that flickered in the swamp.

Water sloshed around his ankles and knife-edged grass slashed at his legs. The puddles gleamed black and oily in the light from the flaming craft. The frogs still kept up their peeping at the far edge of the marsh.

Something flopped and struggled in a pool of muddy,

flame-stained water just a few feet from the burning ship and Sutton, plunging forward, saw it was a man.

He caught the gleaming white of frightened, piteous eyeballs shining in the flame as the man lifted himself on his mud-caked arms and tried to drag his body forward. He saw the flash of teeth as pain twisted the face into grisly anguish. And his nostrils took the smell of charred, crisped flesh and knew it for what it was.

He stooped and locked his hands beneath the armpits of the man, hauled him upright, dragged him back across the swamp. Mud sucked at his feet and he heard the splashing behind him, the horrible, dragging splash of the other's body trailing through the water and the slime.

There was dry land beneath his feet and he began the climb back up the slope toward the car. Sounds came from the bobbing head of the man he carried, thick, slobbering sounds that might have been words if one had had the time to listen.

Sutton cast a quick glance over his shoulder and saw the flames mounting straight into the sky, a pillar of blue that lighted up the night. Marsh birds, roused from their nests, flew blinded and in panic through the garish light, waking the night with their squawks of terror.

"The atomics," said Sutton, aloud. "The atomics . . ."

They couldn't hold for long in a flame like that. The automatics would melt down and the marsh would be a crater and the hills would be charred from horizon to horizon.

"No," said the bobbing head. "No . . . no atomics."

Sutton's foot caught in a root and he stumbled to his knees. The body of the man slid from his mud-caked grasp.

The man struggled, trying to turn over.

Sutton helped him and he lay on his back, his face toward the sky.

He was young, Sutton saw . . . young beneath the mask of mud and pain.

"No atomics," said the man. "I dumped them."

There was pride in the words, pride in a job well done. But the words had cost him heavily. He lay still, so still that he might not have been living at all.

Then his breath came to life again and whistled in his throat. Sutton saw the blood pumping through the temples beneath the burned and twisted skin. The man's jaw worked and words came out, limping, tangled words.

"There was a battle . . . back in '83 . . . I saw him coming . . . tried to time-jump . . ." The words gurgled and got lost, then gushed out again. "Got new guns . . . set metal afire . . ."

He turned his head and apparently saw Sutton for the first time. He started up and then fell back, gasping with the effort.

"Sutton!"

Sutton bent above him. "I will carry you. Get you to a doctor."

"Asher Sutton!" The two words were a whisper.

For a moment Sutton caught the triumphant, almost fanatic gleam that washed across the eyes of the dying man, half understood the gesture of the half-raised arm, of the cryptic sign that the fingers made.

Then the gleam faded and the arm dropped back and the fingers came apart.

Sutton knew, even before he bent with his head turned against the heart, that the man was dead.

Slowly Sutton stood up.

The flame was dying down and the birds had gone. The craft lay half buried in the mud and its lines, he noted, were none he had ever seen.

Asher Sutton, the man had said. And his eyes had lighted up and he had made a sign just before he died. And there had been a battle back in '83.

Eighty-three what?

The man had tried to time-jump . . . who had ever heard of time-jump?

I never saw the man before, said Sutton, as if he might be denying something that was criminal. So help me, I don't know him even now. And yet he cried my name and it sounded as if he knew me and was very glad to see me and he made a sign . . . a sign that went with the name.

He stared down at the dead man lying at his feet and saw the pity of it, the crumpled legs that dangled even flat upon the ground, the stiffened arms, the lolling head and the flash of moonlight on the teeth where the mouth had opened.

Carefully, Sutton went down on his knees, ran his hands over the body, seeking something . . . some bulging pocket that might give a clue to the man who lay there dead.

Because he knew me. And I must know how he knew me. And none of it makes sense.

There was a small book in the breast pocket of the coat and Sutton slipped it out. The title was in gold on black leather, and even in the moonlight Sutton could read the letters that flamed from the cover to hit him straight between the eyes.

THIS IS DESTINY

By

Asher Sutton

Sutton did not move.

He crouched there on the ground, like a cowering thing, stricken by the golden letters on the leather cover.

A book!

A book he meant to write for many months to come!

A book he meant to write, but hadn't written yet!

And yet here it was, dog-eared and limp from reading.

An involuntary choking sound rose unbidden in his throat.

He felt the chill of the fog rising from the marsh, the loneliness of a wild bird's crying.

A strange ship had plunged into the marsh, disabled and burning. A man had escaped from the ship, but on the verge of death. Before he died he had recognized Sutton and had called his name. In his pocket he had a book that was not even written.

Those were the facts . . . the bare, hard facts. There was no explanation.

Faint sounds of human voices drifted down the night and Sutton rose swiftly to his feet, stood poised and waiting, listening. The voices came again.

Someone had heard the crash and was coming to investigate, coming down the road, calling to others who also had heard the crash.

Sutton turned and walked swiftly up the slope to the car.

There was, he told himself, no earthly use of waiting.

Those coming down the road would only cause him trouble.

XVII

A MAN WAS waiting in the clump of lilac bushes across the road and there was another one crouched in the shadow of the courtyard wall.

Sutton walked slowly forward, strolling, taking his time.

"Johnny," he said, soundlessly.

"Yes, Ash."

"That is all there are—just those two?"

"I think there is another one, but I can't place him. All of them are armed."

Sutton felt the stir of comfort in his brain, the sense of self-assurance, the sense of aid and comradeship.

"Keep me posted, Johnny."

He whistled a bar or two, from a tune that had been forgotten long ago but still was fresh in his mind from twenty years before.

The rent-a-car garage was two blocks up the road, the Orion Arms two blocks farther down. Between him and the Arms were two men, waiting with guns. Two and maybe more.

Between the garage and hotel was nothing . . . just the

landscaped beauty that was a residential, administrative Earth. An Earth dedicated to beauty and to ruling . . . planted with a garden's care, every inch of it mapped out by landscape architects with clumps of shrubs and lanes of trees and carefully tended flower beds.

An ideal place, Sutton told himself, to execute an ambush.

Adams, he wondered. Although, it hardly could be Adams. He had something that Adams expected to find out and killing the man who holds information that you want, no matter how irate you may be at him, is downright infantile.

Or those others that Eva had told him of . . . the ones who had Benton conditioned and all set to kill him.

They tied in better than Adams did, for Adams wanted him to stay alive, and these others, whoever they might be, were quite content to kill him.

He dropped his hand in his coat pocket as if searching for a cigarette and his fingers touched the steel of the gun he had used on Benton. He let his fingers wrap around it and then pulled them away and took his hand out of the pocket and found the cigarettes in another pocket.

Not time yet, he told himself. Time later on to use the gun, if he had to use it, if he had a chance to use it.

He stopped to light the cigarette, dallying, taking his time, playing for time.

The gun would be a poor weapon, he knew, but better than none at all. In the dark, he probably couldn't hit the broad side of a house, but it would make a noise and the waiting men were not counting on noise. If they hadn't minded noise, they could have stepped out minutes ago and mowed him down.

"Ash," said Johnny, "there is another man. Just in that

bush ahead. He expects to let you pass and then they'll have you three ways."

Sutton grunted. "Good, tell me exactly."

"The bush with the white flowers. He's on this edge of it. Quite close to the walk, so he can step around and be behind you the minute that you pass."

Sutton puffed on the cigarette, making it glow like a red eye in the dark.

"Shall we take him, Johnny?"

"Yes, we'd better take him."

Sutton resumed his stroll and now he saw the bush, four paces away, no more.

One step.

I wonder what it's all about.

Two steps.

Cut out your wondering. Act now and do your wondering later.

Three steps.

There he is. I see him.

Sutton was off the walk in a single stride. The gun whipped out of his pocket and at his second stride it talked, two quick, ugly words.

The man behind the bush bent foward on his knees, swayed there for a moment then flattened on his face. His gun fell from his fingers, and in a single swoop Sutton scooped it up. It was, he saw, an electronic device, a vicious thing that could kill even with a near-miss, owing to the field of distortion that its beam set up. A gun like that had been new and secret twenty years ago, but now, apparently, anyone could get it.

Gun in hand, Sutton wheeled and ran, twisting through the shrubbery, ducking overhanging branches, plowing through a tulip bed. Out of the corner of one eye, he caught a twinkle . . . the twinkling breath of a silent flamming gun, and the dancing path of silver that it sliced into the night.

He plunged through a ripping, tearing hedge, waded a stream, found himself in a clump of evergreen and birch. He stopped to get back his breath, staring back over the way that he had come.

The countryside lay quiet and peaceful, a silvered picture painted by the moon. No one or nothing stirred. The gun long ago had ceased its flickering.

Johnny's warning came suddenly:

"Ash! Behind you. Friendly . . ."

Sutton wheeled, gun half lifted.

Herkimer was running in the moonlight, like a hound hunting for a trace.

Sutton stepped from the corpse and called gently. Herkimer stopped his running, wheeled around, then loped toward him.

"Mr. Sutton, sir . . ."

"Yes, Herkimer."

"We've got to run for it."

"Yes," said Sutton, "I suppose we have. I walked into a trap. There were three of them laying for me."

"It's worse than that," said Herkimer. "It's not only the Revisionists and Morgan, but it's Adams, too."

"Adams?"

"Adams has given orders that you be killed on sight."

Sutton stiffened. "How do you know?" he snapped.

"The girl," said Herkimer. "Eva. The one you asked about. She told me."

Herkimer walked forward, stood face to face with Sutton.

"You have to trust me, sir. You said this morning I'd put the finger on you, but I never would. I was with you from the very first."

"But the girl," said Sutton.

"Eva's with you, too, sir. We started out to find you as soon as we found out, but we were too late to catch you. Eva's waiting with the ship."

"A ship," said Sutton. "A ship and everything."

"It's your own ship, sir," said Herkimer. "The one you got from Benton. The ship that went along with me."

"And you want me to come with you and get into this ship and . . ."

"I'm sorry, sir," said Herkimer.

He moved so fast that Sutton couldn't do a thing.

He saw the fist coming and he tried to raise his gun. He felt the sudden fury grow cold within his brain and then there was a crushing impact and his head snapped back so that for a moment, before his eyelids closed, he saw the wheel of stars against a spinning sky.

He felt his knees buckling under him and his body falling.

But he was out, stone-cold, when his body hit the ground.

XVIII

EVA ARMOUR was calling to him softly.

"Ash. Oh, Ash. Wake up."

To Sutton's ears came the muted mutter of the coasting rockets, the hollow, thrumming sound of a small ship hurtling through space.

"Johnny," said Sutton's mind.

"We're in a ship, Ash."

"How many are there?"

"The Android and the girl. The one called Eva. And they are friendly. I told you they were friendly. Why don't you pay attention?"

"I can't trust anyone."

"Not even me?"

"Not your judgment, Johnny. You are new to Earth."

"Not new, Ash. I know Earth and Earthmen. Much better than you know them. You're not the first Earthman I've lived with."

"I can't remember, Johnny. There's something to remember. I try to remember it and there's nothing but a blur. The big things, of course, the things I learned, the things I wrote down and took away. But not the place itself or the people in it."

"They aren't people, Ash."

"I know. I can't remember."

"You're not supposed to, Ash. It was all too alien. You can't carry such memories with you . . . you shouldn't carry such alien memories, for when you carry them too closely, you are a part of them. And you had to stay human, Ash. We have to keep you human."

"But someday I must remember. Someday . . ."

"When you must remember them, you will remember them. I will see to that."

"And, Johnny."

"What is it, Ash?"

"You don't mind this Johnny business?"

"What about it, Ash?"

"I shouldn't call you 'Johnny.' It is flippant and familiar . . . but it is friendly. It is the friendliest name I know. That is why I call you it."

"I do not mind," said Johnny. "I do not mind at all."

"You understand any of this, Johnny? About Morgan? And the Revisionists?"

"No, Ash."

"But you see a pattern?"

"I am beginning to."

Eva Armour shook him. "Wake up, Ash," she said. "Can't you hear me, Ash? Wake up."

Sutton opened his eyes. He was lying on a bunk and the girl still was shaking him.

"O.K.," he said. "You can stop now. O.K."

He swung his legs off the bunk and sat on its edge. His hand went up and felt the lump on his jaw.

"Herkimer had to hit you," Eva said. "He didn't want to hit you, but you were unreasonable and we had no time to lose."

"Herkimer?"

"Certainly. You remember Herkimer, Ash. He was Benton's android. He's piloting this ship."

The ship, Sutton saw, was small, but it was clean and comfortable and there would have been room for another passenger or two. Herkimer, talking his precise, copybook speech, had said it was small but serviceable.

"Since you've kidnaped me," Sutton told the girl, "I don't suppose you'd mind telling me where we're going."

"We don't mind at all," said Eva. "We're going to the hunting asteroid that you got from Benton. It has a lodge and a good supply of food and no one will think of looking for us there."

"That's fine," said Sutton, grinning. "I could do with a spot of hunting."

"You won't be doing any hunting," said a voice behind them. Sutton swung around. Herkimer stood in the hatch that led to the pilot's shell.

"You're going to write a book," said Eva, softly. "Surely you know about the book. The one the Revisionists . . ."

"Yes," Sutton told her. "I know about the book. . . ."

He stopped, remembering, and his hand went involuntarily to feel of his breast pocket. The book was there, all right, and something that crinkled when he touched it. He remembered that, too. The letter . . . the incredibly old letter that John H. Sutton had forgotten to open six thousand years before.

"About the book," said Sutton, and then he stopped again, for he was going to say they needn't bother about writing the book, for he already had a copy. But something stopped him, for he wasn't certain that it was smart just then to let them know about the book he had.

"I brought along the case," said Herkimer. "The manuscript's all there. I checked through it."

"And plenty of paper?" asked Sutton, mocking him.

"And plenty of paper."

Eva Armour leaned toward Sutton, so close that he could smell the fragrance of her copper hair.

"Don't you see," she asked, "how important it is that you write this book? Don't you understand?"

Sutton shook his head.

Important, he thought. Important for what? And whom? And when?

He remembered the open mouth that death had struck, the teeth that glittered in the moonlight and the words of a dying man still rang sharply in his ears.

"But I don't understand," he said. "Maybe you can tell me."

She shook her head. "You write the book," she told him.

XIX

THE ASTEROID was enveloped in the perpetual twilight of the far-from-sun and its frosty peaks speared up like sharp, silvery needles stabbing at the stars.

The air was sharp and cold and thinner than on Earth and the wonder was, Sutton told himself, that any air could be kept on the place at all. Although at the cost that it had taken to make this or any other asteroid habitable, it would seem that anything should be possible.

A billion-dollar job at least, Sutton estimated. The cost of the atomic plants alone would run to half that figure and without atomics there would be no power to run the atmosphere and gravity machines that supplied the air and held it in its place.

Once, he thought, Man had been content, had been forced to be content, to find his solitude at a lakeshore cottage or a hunting lodge or aboard a pleasure yacht, but now, with a galaxy to spend, Man fixed up an asteroid at a billion bucks a throw or bought out a planet at a bargain price.

"There's the lodge," said Herkimer, and Sutton looked in the direction of the pointing finger. High up on the jigsaw horizon he saw the humped, black building with its one pinpoint of light.

"What's the light?" asked Eva. "Is there someone here?"

Herkimer shook his head. "Someone forgot to turn off a light the last time when they left."

Evergreens and birches, ghostlike in the starlight, stood in ragged clumps, like marching soldiers storming the height where the lodge was set.

"The path is over here," said Herkimer.

He led the way and they climbed, with Eva in the center and Sutton bringing up the rear. The path was steep and uneven and the light was none too good, for the thin atmosphere failed to break up the starlight and the stars themselves remained tiny, steely points of light that did not blaze or twinkle, but stood primly in the sky like dots upon a map.

The lodge, Sutton saw, apparently sat upon a small plateau, and he knew that the plateau would be the work of man, for nowhere else in all this jumbled landscape was it likely that one would find a level spot much bigger than a pocket handkerchief.

A movement of air so faint and tenuous that it could be scarcely called a breeze rustled down the slope and set the evergreens to moaning. Something scuttled from the path and skittered up the rocks. From somewhere far away came a screaming sound that set one's teeth on edge.

"That's an animal," Herkimer said quietly. He stopped and waved his hand at the tortured, twisted rock. "Great place to hunt," he said, and added, "if you don't break a leg."

Sutton looked behind him and saw for the first time the true, savage wildness of the place. A frozen whirlpool of star-speckled terrain stretched below them . . . great yawning gulfs of blackness above which stood brooding peaks and spirelike pinnacles.

Sutton shivered at the sight. "Let's get on," he said.

They climbed the last hundred yards and reached the man-made plateau, then stood and stared across the nightmare landscape, and as he looked, Sutton felt the cold hand of loneliness reach down with icy fingers to take him in its grip. For here was sheer, mad loneliness such as he had never dreamed. Here was the very negation of life and motion, here was the stark, bald beginning when there was no life, nor even thought of life. Here anything that knew or thought or moved was an alien thing, a disease, a cancer on the face of nothingness.

A footstep crunched behind them and they swung around.

A man moved out of the starry darkness. His voice was pleasant and heavy as he spoke to them.

"Good evening," he said and waited for a moment, then added by way of explanation, "We heard you land and I walked out to meet you."

Eva's voice was cold and just a little angry. "You take us by surprise," she said. "We had not expected anyone."

The man's tone stiffened. "I hope we are not trespassing. We are friends of Mr. Benton and he told us to use the place at our convenience."

"Mr. Benton is dead," said Eva, frostily. "This man is the new owner."

The man's head turned toward Sutton.

"I'm sorry, sir," he said. "We did not know. Of course we'll leave, the first moment that we can."

"I see no reason," Sutton told him, "why you should not stay."

"Mr. Sutton," said Eva, primly, "came here for peace and quiet. He expects to write a book."

"A book," said the man. "An author, eh?"

Sutton had the uncomfortable feeling that the man was laughing, not at him alone, but at the three of them.

"Mr. Sutton?" said the man, acting as if he were thinking hard. "I can't seem to recall the name. But, then, I'm not a great reader."

"I've never written anything before," said Sutton.

"Oh well, then," said the man, laughing as if he were relieved, "that probably explains it."

"It's cold out here," Herkimer said, abruptly. "Let us get indoors."

"Certainly," said the man. "Yes, it is cold, although I hadn't noticed it. By the way, my name is Pringle. My partner's name is Case."

No one answered him and after a few seconds he turned and trotted ahead of them, like a happy dog, leading the way.

The lodge, Sutton saw as they approached it, was larger than it had seemed from the valley where they had brought the ship in. It loomed huge and black against the starlit backdrop, and if one had not known that it was there it might have been mistaken for another rock formation.

The door opened as their feet sounded on the massive stone steps which led up to it and another man stood there, stiff and erect and tall, thin, but with whipcord strength about him as the light from inside the room threw his figure into black relief.

"The new owner, Case," said Pringle, and it seemed to Sutton that he pitched his voice just a key too low, that he emphasized the words just a bit too much. As if he meant the words to be a warning.

"Benton died, you know," said Pringle and Case answered, "Oh, did he? How peculiar."

Which, Sutton thought, was a funny thing to say.

Case stood to one side to let them enter, then pulled shut the door.

The room was huge, with only one lamp burning, and shadows pressed in upon them out of the dark corners and the cavernous arch of the raftered ceiling.

"I am afraid," said Pringle, "that you'll have to look out for yourselves. Case and I are roughing it and we brought along no robots. Although I can fix up something if you happen to be hungry. A hot drink, perhaps, and some sandwiches?"

"We ate just before we landed," Eva said, "and Herkimer will take care of what few things we have."

"Then take a chair," urged Pringle. "That one over there is comfortable. We will talk a bit."

"I'm afraid we can't. The trip was just a little rough."

"You're an ungracious young lady," Pringle said, and his words were halfway between jest and anger.

"I'm a tired young lady."

Pringle walked to a wall, flipped up toggles. Lights sprang into being.

"The bedrooms are up the stairs," he said. "Off the balcony. Case and I have the first and second to the left. You may have your pick from any of the rest."

He moved forward to lead them up the stairs. But Case spoke up and Pringle stopped and waited, one hand on the lower curve of the stair rail.

"Mr. Sutton," said Case, "it seems to me I have heard your name somewhere."

"I don't think so," said Sutton. "I'm a most unimportant person."

"But you killed Benton."

"No one said I killed him."

Case did not laugh, but his voice said that if he had not

been Case he would have laughed.

"Nevertheless, you must have killed him. For I happen to know that is the only way anyone could get this asteroid. Benton loved it and this side of life he'd never give it up."

"Since you insist, then, I did kill Benton."

Case shook his head, bewildered. "Remarkable," he said. "Remarkable."

"Good night, Mr. Case," said Eva, and then she spoke to Pringle. "No need to trouble you. We will find our way."

"No trouble," Pringle rumbled back. "No trouble at all." And, once again, he was laughing at them.

He jogged lightly up the stairs.

XX

PRINGLE AND CASE were wrong. There was something
wrong about them. The very fact that they were here, at
the lodge, was sinister.

There had been mockery in Pringle's voice. And he
had been laughing at them all the time, laughing with a
sneering amusement, enjoying some thinly varnished
joke that they did not know.

Pringle was a talker, a buffoon . . . but Case was stiff
and straight and correct and when he spoke his words
were clipped and sharp. There was something about
Case . . . some point . . . some resemblance . . . a resemblance to something that escaped Sutton at the moment.

Sitting on the edge of his bed. Sutton frowned.

If I could just remember, he told himself. If I could
put my finger on that mannerism, on the way he talks
and walks and holds himself erect. If I could associate
that with a certain thing I know, it would explain a lot.
It might even tell me who Case is, or what he is, or even
why he's here.

Case knew that I killed Benton. Case knows who I am.
And he should have kept his mouth shut, but he had
to let me know he knew, because that way he bolstered

up his ego and even if he doesn't look it, his ego may need boosting.

Eva didn't trust them, either, for she tried to tell me something when we parted at her door and I couldn't quite make out what it was from the way she moved her lips, although it looked as if she was trying to say, "Don't trust them."

As if I would trust anyone . . . anyone at all.

Sutton wiggled his toes and stared at them, fascinated. He tried to match the wiggling of each toe on each foot and they wouldn't match.

I can't even control my own body, he thought, and it was a funny thing to think.

Pringle and Case were waiting for us, Sutton told himself, and wondered even as he said it if he might not be giving himself over to sheer fantasy. For how could they be waiting when they could not have known that Herkimer and Eva would head for the asteroid?

He shook his head, but the belief that the two had been waiting for them stayed . . . an idea clinging like a burr.

After all, it was not so strange. Adams had known that he was coming back to Earth, returning home after twenty years. Adams knew and set a trap for him . . . and there was no way, absolutely no way that Adams could have known.

And why, he asked himself. Why?

Why did Adams set the trap?

Why had Buster run away to homestead a planet?

Why had someone conditioned Benton to issue a challenge?

Why had Eva and Herkimer brought him to the asteroid?

To write a book, they said.

But the book was written.

The book . . .

He reached for his coat, which hung from the back of a chair. From it, he took out the gold-lettered copy of the book, and as he pulled it out the letter came with it and fell upon the carpet. He picked the letter up and put it on the bed beside him and opened the book to the flyleaf.

THIS IS DESTINY, it said, By Asher Sutton.

Underneath the title, at the very bottom of the page, was a line of fine print.

Sutton had to hold the book a little closer so that he could read it.

It said: *Original Version.*

And that was all. No date of publication. No marks of copyright. No publisher's imprint.

Just the title and the author and the line of print that said Original Version.

As if, he thought . . . as if the book was so well known, so firm a fixture in the lives of everyone, that anything other than the title and the author would be superfluous.

He turned two pages and they were blank and then another page and the text began. . . .

We are not alone.

No one ever is alone.

Not since the first faint stirring of the first flicker of life on the first planet in the galaxy that knew the quickening of life, has there ever been a single entity that walked or crawled or slithered down the path of life alone.

And that is it, he thought. That is the way I mean to write it.

That was the way I wrote it.

For I must have written it. Sometime, somewhere. I must have written it, for I hold it in my hands.

He closed the book and put it back carefully in the

pocket and hung the coat back on the chair.

For I must not read, he told himself. I must not read and know the way that it will go, for then I would write the way that I had read it, and I must not do that. I must write it the way I know it is, the way I plan to write it, the only way to write it.

I must be honest, for someday the race of man ... and the race of other things as well ... may know the book and read it and every word must be exactly so and I must write so well and so simply that all can understand.

He threw back the covers of the bed and crawled beneath them, and as he did he saw the letter and picked it up.

With a steady finger, he inserted in his nail beneath the flap and ran it along the edge and the mucilage dissolved in a brittle storm of powder that showered down on the sheet.

He took the letter out and unfolded it carefully, so that it would not break, and saw that it was typewritten, with many mistakes that were X'd out as if the man who wrote it found a typewriter an unhandy thing to use.

He rolled over on one side and held the paper under the lamp and this is what he read:

XXI

Bridgeport, Wis.
July 11, 1987

I WRITE THIS letter to myself, so that the postmark may prove beyond controversy the day and year that it was written, and I shall not open it but shall place it among my effects against the day when someone, a member of my own family, God willing, may open it and read. And reading, know the thing that I believe and think, but dare not say while I am still alive, lest someone call me touched.

For I have not long to live. I have lasted more than a man's average allotted span, and while I still am hale and hearty, I know full well the hand of time, while it may miss a man at one reaping, will get him at the next.

I have no morbid fear of death, nor any sentimental wish to gain the brief immortality that a thought accorded me after I am dead may give me, for the thought itself will be a fleeting one and the one who holds it himself will not have too many years of life, for the years of man are short ... far too short for any perfect understanding of any of the problems that a lifetime poses.

While it is more than likely that this letter will be read by my immediate descendants, who are well acquainted with me, I am still aware that through some vagary of fate it may fall yet unopened into the hands of someone many years after I am long forgotten, or even into the hands of strangers.

Feeling that the circumstance which I have to tell is of more than ordinary interest, even at the risk of reporting something which may be well known to the one who reads this letter, I shall here include some of the basic facts about myself and my locality and situation.

My name is John H. Sutton and I am a member of a numerous family which had its roots in the East, but one branch of which situated in this locality about one hundred years ago. While I must ask, if the reader of this be unacquainted with the Suttons, that my word be taken at face value without substantiating proof, I would like to state that we Suttons are a sober lot and not given to jokes, and that our reputation for integrity and honesty is singularly unquestioned.

While I was educated for the law, I soon found it not entirely to my liking and for the last forty years or more have followed the occupation of farming, finding more content in it that I ever found in law. For farming is an honest and a soul-warming job that gives one contact with the first essentials of living, and there is, I find, a satisfaction that is almost smug in the simple yet mystifying process of raising food from soil.

For the past number of years I have not been physically able to continue with the more strenuous labor of the farm, but pride myself that I still do most of the chores and still hold active management, which means that I am in the habit of making regular tours of the acres to see how things are coming.

Through the years, I have grown to love this country, although it is rough and in many instances not suited to easy cultivation. In fact, I sometimes find myself viewing with pity the men who hold broad, flat acreages with no hills to rest their eyes. Their land may be more fertile and more easily worked than mine, but I have something that they do not have... a setting for my life where I am keenly aware of all the beauties of nature, all the changes of the seasons.

Of late years, as my step has slowed and I have found that more than normal exertion is tiring, I have fallen into the habit of arbitrarily setting for myself certain places of rest during my inspection of the farm. It is not mere coincidence that each of these resting places is a spot which recommends itself to the eye and spirit. I believe, in fact, if the truth be told, that I look forward to these resting places more than I do the inspection of the fields and pastures, although, Lord knows, I derive much satisfaction from every aspect of my trips.

There is one spot which has always had, from the very first, a sense of the special for me. If I were still a child I might best explain it by saying that it seems to be an enchanted place.

It is a deep cleft in the bluff that runs down to the river valley and it is located at the north end of the bluff pasture. There is a fair-sized boulder at the top of the cleft, and this boulder is shaped appropriately for sitting, which may be one of the reasons why I liked it, for I am a man who takes to comfort.

From the boulder one may see the sweep of the river valley with a stressed third-dimensional quality, due no doubt to the height of the vantage point plus the clearness of the air, although at times the whole scene is enveloped with a blue mist of particularly tantalizing and lucid clarity.

The view is a charming one and I have often sat there for an hour at a time, doing absolutely nothing, thinking nothing, but at peace with the world and with myself.

But there is a strangeness to the spot and this strangeness is one that I find hard to explain, for search as I may, I find no word at my command to adequately express the thing I wish to say or the condition which I would describe.

It is as if the place were tingling . . . as if the place were waiting for something to happen, as if that one particular spot held great possibilities for drama or for revelation, and while revelation may seem a strange word to use, I find that it comes the closest of any to the thing I have felt many times as I sat upon the boulder and gazed across the valley.

It has often seemed to me that there on that one area of earth, something could or might happen which could or might happen nowhere else on the entire planet. And I have, at times, tried to imagine what that happening might be, and I shrink from telling some of the possibilities that I have imagined, although in truth, in other things I am perhaps not imaginative enough.

To approach the boulder, I cut across the lower end of the bluff pasture, a place which is often in better grass than the rest of the grazing area, for the cattle, for some reason, do not often venture there. The pasture ends in a thin growth of trees, the forerunners of the verdant mass of foliage which sweeps down the bluff side. Just a few rods inside the trees is the boulder and because of the trees the boulder is always shaded, no matter what the time of the day, but the view is unobstructed because of the rapid falling away of the ground.

One day about ten years ago, July 4, 1977, to be exact, I approached this place and found a man and a strange machine at the lower end of the pasture, just clear of the trees.

I say machine, because that is what it appeared to be, although to tell the truth I could not make too much of it. It was like an egg, pointed slightly at each end, as an egg might look if someone stepped on it and did not break it, but spread it out, so that the ends became more pronounced. It had no working parts outside and so far as I could see not even a window, although it was apparent that the operator of it sat inside its body.

For the man had what appeared to be a door open and was standing outside and working at what may have been the motor, although when I ventured to look, it appeared like no motor I had ever seen before. Truth to tell, however, I never did get a good look at the motor or at anything else about the contraption, for the man, as soon as he saw me, most adroitly maneuvered me away from it and engaged me in such pleasant and intelligent conversation that I could not, without the utmost rudeness, change the subject or free myself from his inquiries long enough to pay attention to all the things that stirred my curiosity. I remember now, thinking back, that there were many things which I would have liked to ask him but which I never got around to, and it seems to me now that he must have anticipated these very questions and deliberately and skillfully steered me away from them.

As a matter of fact, he never did tell me who he was or where he came from or why he happened to be in my pasture. And while that may seem rude to the reader of this account, it did not seem rude at the time, for he was such a charming person that one failed to measure him by the same yardstick as one would other people of less accomplishments.

He seemed well informed on farming, although he looked like no farmer. Come to think of it, I do not remember exactly what he did look like, although I seem to recall that he was dressed in a way which I had never seen before. Not garishly, nor outlandishly, nor even in such a manner that one would think of him as foreign, but in clothing which had certain subtle differences difficult to pin down.

He complimented me on the good growth of the pasture grass and asked me how many head of cattle we ran there and how many we were milking and what was the most satisfactory manner we had found to finish off good beef. I answered him as best I could, being very interested in his line of talk, and he kept the conversation going with appropriate comment and questions, some of which I now realize were meant as subtle flattery, although at the time I probably did not think so.

He had a tool of some sort in his hand and now he waved it at a field of corn across the fence and said it looked like a good stand and asked me if I thought it would be knee-high by the Fourth. I told him that today was the Fourth and that it was a mite better than knee-high and that I was very pleased with it, since it was a new brand of seed that I was trying for the first time. He looked a little taken aback and laughed and said, so it was the Fourth, and that he had been so busy lately he had got his dates mixed. And then, before I could even wonder how a man could get his dates so mixed that he could miss the Fourth of July, he was off again on another track.

He asked how long I had lived here, and when I told him he asked if the family hadn't been here a long time; somewhere, he said, he had heard the name before. So I told him that we had, and before I knew it he had me telling all about the family, including some anecdotes which we usually do not tell outside the family circle since they are not exactly the kind of stories that we would care to have known about ourselves. For while our family is conservative and honorable in the main and better in most things than many others, there is no family which does not have a skeleton or two to hide away from view.

We talked until it was long past the dinner hour, and when I noticed this I asked him if he would not take the meal with us, but he thanked me and said that in just a short while he would have the trouble fixed and would be on his way. He said that he had virtually completed whatever repair was needed when I had appeared. When I expressed fear that I had too long delayed him, he assured me that he did not mind at all, that it had been pleasant to spend the time with me.

As I left him, I managed to get in one question. I had been intrigued by the tool which he had held in his hand during our conversation and I asked him what it was. He showed it to me and told me it was a wrench and it did look something like a wrench, although not very much so.

After I had eaten dinner and had a nap, I walked back to the pasture, determined to ask the stranger some of the questions which I had realized by this time he had avoided.

But the machine was gone and the stranger too, with only a print in the pasture grass to show where the machine had lain. But the wrench was there, and when I bent to pick it up I saw that one end was discolored, and upon investigation I found that the discoloration was blood. I have, many times since, berated myself for not having had an analysis made to determine whether the blood was human or from some animal.

Likewise, I have wondered many times just what happened there. Who the man was and how come he left the wrench and why the heavier end of the wrench was stained with blood.

I still make the boulder one of my regular stops and the boulder still is always in the shade and the view still is unobstructed and the air over the river valley still lends to the scene its strangely deep three-dimensional effect. And the sense of tingling expectancy still hangs above the spot, so I know that the place had not been waiting for this one strange happening alone, but that other strange happenings still may occur; that this one happening may have been only one of many happenings, that there may have been uncounted others before it and countless others yet to come. Although I do not hope or expect that I shall see another, for the life of man is but a second in comparison with the time of planets.

The wrench which I picked up is still with us and it has proved a very useful tool. As a matter of fact, we have dispensed with most of our other tools and use it almost alone, for it will adjust itself to almost any nut or burr or will hold a shaft of almost any size from turning. There is no need for adjustment, nor is there any adjustment device that can be found. One simply applies it to whatever piece of metal one wants to take a grip upon and the tool adjusts itself. No great amount of pressure or of strength is needed to operate the wrench, for it appears to have the tendency to take whatever slight pressure one exerts upon it and multiply that pressure to the exact point needed to turn the nut or hold a shaft from turning. However, we are very careful to use the wrench only when there are no outside eyes to see it, for it smacks too much of magic or of witchcraft to be allowed on public view. The general knowledge that we possessed such a wrench almost certainly would lead to unwholesome speculation among our neighbors. And since we are an honest and respectable family, such a situation is the furthest from our wish.

None of us ever talk about the man and the machine I found in the bluff pasture, even among ourselves, for we seem tacitly to recognize that it is a subject which does not fit within the frame of our lives as sober, unimaginative farmers.

But while we do not talk about it, I do know that I, myself, think about it much. I spend more time than usual at the boulder resting place, just why I do not know, unless it is in the feeble hope that there somehow I may find a clue which will either substantiate or disprove the theory I have formed to account for the happening.

For I believe, without proof of any sort, that the man was a man who came from time and that the machine was a time machine and the wrench is a tool which will not be discovered or manufactured for more years to come than I care to think about.

I believe that somewhere in the future man has discovered a method by which he moves through time and that undoubtedly he has involved a very rigid code of ethics and of practices in order to prevent the paradoxes which would result from indiscriminate time traveling or meddling in the affairs of other times. I believe that the leaving of the wrench in my time provides one of those paradoxes which in itself is simple, but which under certain circumstances might lead to many complications. For that reason, I have impressed upon the family the strict necessity of continuing our present attitude of keeping its possession secret.

Likewise, I have come to the conclusion, also unsupported, that the cleft at the head of which the boulder is located may be a road through time, or at least part of a road, a single point where our present time coincides very closely through the operation of some as yet unknown principle with another time far removed from us. It may be a place in the space-time continuum where less resistance is encountered in traveling through time than in other places and, having been discovered, is used quite frequently. Or it may simply be that it is a time road more deeply rutted, more frequently used than many other time roads, with the result that whatever medium separates one time from another time had been worn thin or had been bulged a bit or whatever would happen under such a circumstance.

That reasoning might explain the strange eerie tingling of the place, might account for the sense of expectancy.

The reader must bear in mind, of course, that I am an old, old man, that I have outlived the ordinary span of human life and that I continue to exist through some vagary of human destiny. While it does not seem so to myself, it may well be that my mind is not as sharp or keen nor as analytical as it may once have been, and that as a result I am susceptible to the entertainment of ideas which would be summarily rejected by a normal human being.

The one bit of proof, if one may call it proof, that I have to support my theories, is that the man I met could well have been a future man, might well have sprung from some civilization further advanced than ours. For it must be apparent to whoever reads this letter that in my talk with him he used me for his own purpose, that he pulled the wool over my eyes as easily as a man of my day might pull it over the eyes of a Homeric Greek or some member of Attila's tribe. He was, I am sure, a man well versed in semantics and in psychology. Looking back, I know that he always was one long jump ahead of me.

I write this not only so that any theories which I may have, and which I shrink from telling in my lifetime, may not be wholly lost, but may be available at some future time when a more enlightened knowledge than we have today may be able to make something out of them. And I hope that reading them, one will not laugh since I am dead. For if one did laugh, I am afraid that, dead as I might be, I would surely know it.

That is the failing of us Suttons—we cannot bear to be made the butt of laughter.

And in case that one may believe that my mind is twisted, I herewith enclose a physician's certificate, signed just three days ago, asserting that upon examination he found me of sound body and sane mind.

But the story I have to tell is not yet entirely done. These additional events should have been included in earlier sequence, but I found no place in which they logically would fit.

They concern the strange incident of the stolen clothing and the advent of William Jones.

The clothing was stolen a few days after the incident in the bluff pasture. Martha had done the washing early in the day, before the heat of the summer sun set in, and hung it on the line. When she went to take in the clothes, she found that an old pair of overalls of mine, a shirt belonging to Roland and a couple pairs of socks, the ownership of which I fear I have forgotten, had disappeared.

The theft made quite a stir among us, for thievery is a thing which does not often happen in our community. We checked through our list of neighbors with a somewhat guilty feeling, for while we spoke no word aloud that anyone could hear, we knew in our hearts that even thinking of any of our near-by folks in connection with the theft was a rank injustice.

We talked about it off and on for several days, and finally agreed that the theft must have been the work of some passing tramp; although even that explanation was scarcely satisfactory, for we are off the beaten way and tramps do not often pass and that year as I remember it was a year of great prosperity and there were few tramps.

It was two weeks or so after the theft of the clothing that William Jones came to the house and asked if we might need a hand to help with the harvest. We were glad to take him on, for we were short of help and the wages that he asked were far below the going pay. We took him on for the harvest only, but he proved so capable that we have kept him all these years. Even as I write this, he is out in the barnyard readying the binder for the small grain cutting.

There is a funny thing about William Jones. In this country a man soon acquires a nickname or at least a diminutive of his own. But William Jones always has been William. He never has been Will or Bill or Willy. Nor has he been Spike or Bud or Kid. There is a quiet dignity about him that makes everyone respect him, and his love of work and his quiet, intelligent interest in farming have won him a place in the community far above the usual status of a hired hand.

He is completely sober and he never drinks, a thing for which I am thankful, although at one time I had my misgivings. For when he came to us, he had a bandage on his head and he explained to me, shamefacedly, that he had been hurt in a tavern brawl across the river somewhere in Crawford County.

I don't know when it was that I began to wonder about William Jones. Certainly it was not at first, for I accepted him for what he pretended to be, a man looking for work. If there was any resemblance to the man I had talked with down in the pasture, I did not notice it then. And, now, having noticed it at this late date, I wonder if my mind may not be playing tricks, if my imagination, running riot with my theories of time travel, may not have conditioned me to a point where I see a mystery crouching back of every tree.

But the conviction has grown upon me through the years as I have associated with him. For all that he tries to keep his place, attempts to adopt his idiom to match our idiom, there are times that his speech hints at an education and an understanding one would not expect to find in a man who works on the farm for seventy-five dollars a month and board.

There is, too, his natural shyness, which is a thing one would expect to find if a man were deliberately attempting to adapt himself to a society that was not his own.

And there is the matter of clothes. Thinking back, I can't be sure about the overalls, for all overalls look very much alike. But the shirt was exactly like the shirt that had been stolen from the line, although I tell myself that it would not be improbable for two men to own the same kind of shirt. And he was barefooted, which seemed a funny thing even at the time, but he explained it by saying that he had been down on his luck and I remember I advanced him enough money to buy some shoes and socks. But it turned out that he didn't need the socks, for he had two pairs in his pocket.

A few years ago I decided several times that I would speak to him about the matter, but each time my resolution failed and now I know I never will. For I like William Jones and William Jones likes me and I would not for the world destroy that mutual liking by a question that might send him fleeing from the farm.

There is yet one other thing which goes to make William Jones unlike most farm hands. With his first money from his work here, he bought a typewriter, and during the first two or three years that he was with us he spent long hours of his evenings in his room using the typewriter and tramping about the room, as a man who is thinking is apt to walk.

And then one day, in the early morning, before the rest of us had gotten from our beds, he took a great sheaf of paper, apparently the result of those long hours of work, and burned it. Watching from my bedroom window, I watched him do it and he stayed until he was sure that the last scrap of paper had been burned. Then he turned around and walked back slowly to the house.

I never mentioned to him the burning of the paper, for I felt, somehow, that it was something he did not wish another man to know.

I might go on for many pages and write down many other inconsequential, trivial things which rattle in my skull, but they would not add one iota to the telling of the thing I've told and might, in fact, convince the reader that I am in my dotage.

To whoever may peruse this, I wish to make one last assurance. While my theory may be wrong, I would have him or her believe that the facts I have told are true. I would have him or her know that I did see a strange machine in the bluff pasture and that I did talk with a strange man, that I picked up a wrench with blood upon it, that clothes were stolen from the wash line and that even now a man named William Jones is pumping himself a drink of water at the well, for the day is very hot.

Sincerely,

John H. Sutton

XXII

Sutton folded the letter and the crackling of the old paper rippled across the quietness of the room like a spiteful snarl of thunder.

Then he recalled something and unfolded the sheaf of leaves again and found the thing that had been mentioned. It was yellow and old ... not as good a quality of paper as the letter had been written on. The writing was by hand, with ink, and the lines were faded so they hardly could be read. The date was unclear, except for the final 7.

Sutton puzzled it out:

John H. Sutton today has been examined by me and I find him sound of mind and body.

The signature was a scrawl that probably could not have been read when the ink was scarcely dry, but there were two letters that stood out fairly clearly at the very end.

The letters were *M.D.*

Sutton stared across the room and saw in his mind the scene of that long-gone day.

"Doctor, I've a mind to make a will. Wonder if you could . . ."

For John H. Sutton never would have told the doctor the real reason for that slip of paper . . . the real reason why he wanted it established that he was not insane.

Sutton could imagine him. Ponderous in his walk, slow, deliberate, taking plenty of time to think things over, placing vast values on qualities and fictions which even in that day were shopworn and losing caste from centuries of overglorification.

An old tyrant to his family, more than likely. A fuddy-duddy among his neighbors, who laughed behind his back. A man lacking in humor and crinkling his brow over fine matters of etiquette and ethics.

He had been trained for the law and he had a lawyer's mind, that much at least the letter told with clarity. A lawyer's mind for detail and a landed man's quality of slowness and an old man's garrulity.

But there was no mistaking the man's sincerity. He believed he had seen a strange machine and had talked with a strange man and had picked up a wrench stained with . . .

A wrench!

Sutton sat bolt upright on the bed.

The wrench had been in the trunk. He, Asher Sutton, had held it in his hand. He had picked it up and tossed it on the pile of junk along with the dog-gnawed bone and the college notebooks.

Sutton's hand trembled as he slid the letter back into its envelope. First it had been the stamp that had intrigued him, a stamp that was worth Lord knows how many thousand dollars . . . then it was the letter itself and the mystery of its being sealed . . . and now there was the wrench. And the wrench clinched everything.

For the wrench meant that there actually had been a strange machine and a stranger man . . . a man who knew enough semantics and psychology to speak a talkative, self-centered oldster off his mental feet. Fast enough on the uptake to keep this inspection-tripping farmer from asking him the very questions the man was bubbling to ask.

Who are you and where did you come from and what's that machine and how does it run, I never saw the like of it before . . .

Hard to answer, if they were ever asked.

But they were not asked.

John H. Sutton had had the last word . . . as would have been his habit.

Asher Sutton chuckled, thinking of John H. Sutton's having the last word and how it came about. It would please the old boy if he could only know, but, of course, he couldn't.

There had been some slip, of course. The letter had been lost or mislaid somehow and then mislaid again . . . and finally, somehow, it had come into the hands of another Sutton, six thousand years removed.

And the first Sutton, more than likely, it would have done a bit of good. For the letter tied in someplace, had some significance in the mystery of the moment.

Men who traveled in time. Men whose time machines went haywire and came to landfall or timefall, whichever you might call it, in a cow pasture. And other men who fought in time and screamed through folds of time in burning ships and landed in a swamp.

A battle back in eighty-three, the dying youth had said. Not a battle at Waterloo or off the Martian orbit, but back in eighty-three.

And the man had cried his name just before he died

and lifted himself to make a sign with strangely twisted fingers. So I am known, thought Sutton, up in eighty-three and beyond eighty-three, for the boy said back and that means that in his time a time three centuries yet to come is historically the past.

He reached for his coat again and slid the letter into the pocket with the book, then rolled out of bed. He reached for his clothes and began to dress.

For it had come to him, the thing he had to do.

Pringle and Case had used a ship to get to the asteroid and he must find that ship.

XXIII

THE LODGE was deserted, big and empty with an alienness
in its emptiness that made Sutton, who should have been
accustomed to alienness, shiver as he felt it touch him.

He stood for a moment outside his door and listened to
the whispering of the place, the faint, illogical breathing
of the house, the creak of frost-expanded timbers, the
caress of wind against a windowpane, and the noises
that could not be explained by either frost or wind, the
living sound of something that is not alive.

The carpeting in the hall deadened his footsteps as he
went down it toward the stairs. Snores came from one of
the two rooms which Pringle had said that he and Case
occupied and Sutton wondered for a moment which one
of them it was that snored.

He went carefully down the stairs, trailing his hand
along the banister to guide him, and when he reached
the massive living space he waited, standing stock-still so
that his eyes might become accustomed to the deeper dark
that crouched there like lairing animals.

Slowly the animals took the shapes of chairs and
couches, tables, cabinets and cases, and one of the chairs,
he saw, had a man sitting in it.

As if he had become aware that Sutton had seen him, the man stirred, turning his face toward him. And although it was too dark to see his features, Sutton knew that the man in the chair was Case.

Then, he thought, the man who snores is Pringle, although he knew that it made no difference which it was that snored.

"So, Mr. Sutton," Case said, slowly, "you decided to go out and try to find our ship."

"Yes," Sutton said, "I did."

"Now, that is fine," said Case. "That is the way I like a man to speak up and say what's on his mind." He sighed. "You meet so many devious persons," he said. "So many people who try to lie to you. So many people who tell you half-truths and feel, while they're doing it, that they are being clever."

He rose out of the chair, tall and straight and prim.

"Mr. Sutton," he said, "I like you very much."

Sutton felt the absurdity of the situation, but there was a coldness and a half-anger in him that told him this was no laughing matter.

Footsteps padded softly down the stairs behind him and Pringle's voice whispered through the room.

"So he decided to make a try for it."

"As you see," said Case.

"I told you that he would," said Pringle, almost triumphantly. "I told you that he would get it figured out."

Sutton choked down the gorge that rose into his throat. But the anger held . . . anger at the way they talked about him as if he weren't there.

"I fear," said Case to Sutton, "that we have disturbed you. We are most untactful people and you are sensitive. But let's forget it all and get down to business now. You wanted, I believe, to ferret out our ship."

Sutton shrugged his shoulders. "It's your move now," he said.

"Oh, but you misunderstand," said Case. "We have no objection. Go ahead and ferret."

"Meaning I can't find it?"

"Meaning that you can," said Case. "We didn't try to hide it."

"We'll even show you the way," said Pringle. "We'll go along with you. It will take you a lot less time."

Sutton felt the fine ooze of perspiration break out along his hairline and dampen his forehead.

A trap, he told himself. A trap laid out in plain sight and not even baited. And he'd walked into it without even looking.

But it was too late now. There was no backing out.

He tried to make his voice sound unconcerned.

"O.K.," he said. "I'll gamble with you."

XXIV

THE SHIP was real—strange, but very real. And it was the only thing that was. All the rest of the situation had a vague, unrealistic, almost faërie character about it, as if it might be a bad dream and one would wake up any moment and for an agonizing second try to distinguish between drama and reality.

"That map over there," said Pringle, "puzzles you, no doubt. And there is every reason that it should. For it is a time map."

He chuckled and rubbed the back of his head with a beefy hand.

"Tell the truth, I don't understand the thing myself. But Case does. Case is a military man and I'm just a propagandist and a propagandist doesn't have to know what he is talking about, just so he talks about it most convincingly. But a military man does. A military man has to know or someday he'll get behind an eight-ball and his life may depend on knowing."

So that was it, thought Sutton. That was the thing that had bothered him. That was the clue that had slipped his mind. The thing he couldn't place about Case, the thing that he had told himself would explain Case, tell who he was and what he was and why he was here on this asteroid.

A military man.

I should have guessed, said Sutton to himself. But I was thinking in the present . . . not the past or future. And there are no military men, as such, in the world today. Although there were mililtary men before my time and apparently there will be military men in ages yet to come.

He said to Case, "War in four dimensions must be slightly complicated."

And he didn't say it because he was interested at the moment in war, whether in three or four dimensions, but because he felt that it was his turn to talk, his turn to keep this Mad Hare tea chatter at its proper pace.

For that was what it was, he told himself . . . an utterly illogical situation, a madcap, slightly psychopathic interlude that might have its purpose, but a hidden, tangled purpose.

"The time has come," the Walrus said, *"To talk of many things, Of shoes—and ships—and sealing wax—Of cabbages—and kings—"*

Case smiled when he spoke to him, a tight, hard, clipped, military smile.

"Primarily," Case said, "it is a matter of charts and graphs and very special knowledge and some superguessing. You figure out where the enemy may be and what he may be thinking and you get there first."

Sutton shrugged. "Basically that always was the principle," he said. "You get there fustest . . ."

"Ah," said Pringle, "but there are now so many more places where the enemy may go."

"You work with thought graphs and attitude charts and historic reports," said Case, almost as if he had not been interrupted. "You trace back certain happenings and then you go back and try to change some of those happenings ... just a little, you understand, for you must not change them much. Just enough so the end result is slightly different, just a little less favorable to the enemy. One change here and another there and you have him on the run."

"It drives you nuts," said Pringle, confidentially. "Because you must be sure, you see. You pick out a nice juicy historic trend and you figure it out to the finest detail and you pick a key point where change is indicated, so you go back and change it. ..."

"And, then," said Case, "it kicks you in the face."

"Because, you understand," said Pringle, "the historian was wrong. Some of his material was wrong or his method was clumsy or his reasoning was off. ..."

"Somewhere along the line," said Case, "he missed a lick."

"That's right," said Pringle, "somewhere he missed a lick and you find, after you have changed it, that it affects your side more than it does your enemy's."

"Now, Mr. Bones," said Sutton, "I wonder if you could tell me why a chicken runs across the road."

"Yes, sir, Mr. Interlocutor," said Pringle. "Because it wants to get on the other side."

Mutt and Jeff, thought Sutton. A scene jerked raw and bleeding from a Krazy Kat cartoon.

But clever Pringle was a propagandist and he was no fool. He knew semantics and he knew psychology and he even knew about the ancient minstrel shows. He knew all there was to know about the human race, so far as that knowledge could serve him in the human past.

A man had landed in the bluff pasture one morning six thousand years before and John H. Sutton, Esq., had come ambling down the hill, swinging a stick, for he was the sort of man who would have carried a stick, a stout, strong hickory stick, no doubt, cut and trimmed with his own jackknife. And the man had talked with him and had used the same kind of mental tactics on John H. Sutton as Pringle now was trying to use an Sutton's far descendant.

Go ahead, said Sutton silently. Talk yourself hoarse in the throat and squeaky in the tongue. For I am on to you and you're the one who knows it. And pretty soon we'll get down to business.

As if he had read Sutton's thoughts, Case said to Pringle:

"Jake, it isn't working out."

"No, I guess it ain't," said Pringle.

"Let's sit down," said Case.

Sutton felt a flood of relief. Now, he told himself, he would find out what the others wanted, might get some clue to what was going on.

He sat down in a chair and from where he sat he could see the front end of the cabin, a tiny living space that shrieked efficiency. The control board canted in front of the pilot's chair, but there were few controls. A row of buttons, a lever or two, a panel of toggles that probably controlled lights and ports and such . . . and that was all. Efficient and simple . . . no foolishness, a minimum of manual controls. The ship, Sutton thought, must almost fly itself.

Case slid down into a chair and crossed his long legs, stretching them out in front of him, sitting on his backbone. Pringle perched on a chair's edge, leaning forward, rubbing hairy hands.

"Sutton," asked Case, "what is it that you want?"

"For one thing," said Sutton, "this time business. . . ."

"You don't know?" asked Case. "Why, it was a man in

your own time. A man who is living at this very moment. . . ."

"Case," said Pringle, "this is 7990. Michaelson really did very little with it until 8003."

Case clapped a hand to his forehead. "Oh, so it is," he said. "I keep forgetting."

"See," Pringle said to Sutton. "See what I mean?"

Sutton nodded, although for the life of him he didn't see what Pringle meant.

"But how?" asked Sutton.

"It's all a matter of the mind," said Pringle.

"Certainly," said Case. "If you'd just stop to think of it, you would know it was."

"Time is a mental concept," said Pringle. "They looked for time everywhere else before they located it in the human mind. They thought it was a fourth dimension. You remember Einstein. . . ."

"Einstein didn't say it was a fourth dimension," said Case. "Not a dimension as you think of length or breadth or depth. He thought of it as duration. . . ."

"That's a fourth dimension," said Pringle.

"No, it's not," said Case.

"Gentlemen," said Sutton. "Gentlemen."

"Well, anyhow," said Case, "this Michaelson of yours figured out it was a mental concept, that time was in the mind only, that it has no physical properties outside of Man's ability to comprehend and encompass it. He found that a man with a strong enough time sense . . ."

"There are men, you know," said Pringle, "who have what amounts to an exaggerated time sense. They can tell you ten minutes have passed since a certain event has transpired and ten minutes have gone past. They can count the seconds off as well and as accurately as any watch."

"So Michaelson built a time brain," said Case. "A brain with its time sense exaggerated many billionfold, and he found that such a time brain could control time within a certain area . . . that it could master time and move through time and carry along with it any objects which might be within the field of power."

"And that is what we use today," said Pringle. "A time brain. You just set the lever that tells the brain where you want to go . . . or rather, when you want to go . . . and the time brain does the rest."

He beamed at Sutton. "Simple, isn't it?"

"I have no doubt," said Sutton, "that it is very simple."

"And now Mr. Sutton." said Case, "what else do you want?"

"Not a thing," said Sutton. "Not a single thing."

"But that's foolish," Pringle protested. "There must be something that you want."

"A little information, maybe."

"Like what?"

"Like what this is all about."

"You're going to write a book," said Case.

"Yes," said Sutton. "I intend to write a book."

"And you want to sell that book."

"I want to see it published."

"A book," Case pointed out, "is a commodity. It's a product of brain and muscle. It has a market value."

"I suppose," said Sutton, "that you are in the market."

"We are publishers," said Case, "looking for a book."

"A best seller," Pringle added.

Case uncrossed his legs, hitched himself higher in the chair.

"It's all quite simple," he said. "Just a business deal. We wish you would go ahead and set your price."

"Make it high," urged Pringle. "We are prepared to pay."

"I have no price in mind," said Sutton.

"We have discussed it," Case told him, "in a rather speculative manner, wondering how much you might want and how much we might be willing to give. We figured a planet might be attractive to you."

"We'd make it a dozen planets," Pringle said, "but that doesn't quite make sense. What would a man do with a dozen planets?"

"He might rent them out," said Sutton.

"You mean," asked Case, "that you might be interested in a dozen planets?"

"No, I don't," Sutton told him. "Pringle wondered what a man would do with a dozen planets and I was being helpful. I said . . ."

Pringle leaned so far forward in his chair that he almost fell on his face.

"Look," he said, "we aren't talking about one of the backwoods planets out at the tail end of nowhere. We're offering you a landscaped planet, free of all venomous and disgusting life, with a salubrious climate and tractable natives and all the customary living accommodations and improvements."

"And the money," said Case, "to keep it running for the rest of your life."

"Right spang in the middle of the galaxy," said Pringle. "It's an address you wouldn't be ashamed of."

"I'm not interested," said Sutton.

Case's temper cracked.

"Good Lord, man, what is it that you want?"

"I want information," Sutton said.

Case sighed. "All right, then. We'll give you information."

"Why do you want my book?"

"There are three parties interested in your book," said Case. "One of those parties would kill you to prevent your writing it. What is more to the point, they probably will if you don't throw in with us."

"And the other party, the third party?"

"The third party wants you to write the book, all right, but they won't pay you a dime for doing it. They'll do all they can to make it easy for you to write the book and they'll try to protect you from the ones that would like to kill you, but they're not offering any money."

"If I took you up," said Sutton, "I suppose you'd help me write the book. Editorial conferences and so forth."

"Naturally," said Case. "We'd have an interest in it. We'd want it done the best way possible."

"After all," said Pringle, "our interest would be as great as yours."

"I'm sorry," Sutton told them, "my book is not for sale."

"We'd boost the ante some," said Pringle.

"It still is not for sale."

"That's your final word?" asked Case. "Your considered opinion?"

Sutton nodded.

Case sighed. "Then," he said, "I guess we've got to kill you."

He took a gun out of his pocket.

XXV

THE PSYCH-TRACER ticked on, endlessly, running fast, then slow, skipping a beat now and then like the erratic time measurement of a clock with hiccoughs.

It was the only sound in the room and to Adams it seemed as if he were listening to the beating of a heart, the breathing of a man, the throb of blood along the jugular vein.

He grimaced at the pile of dossiers which a moment before he had swept from his desk onto the floor with an angry sweep of his hand. For there was nothing in them . . . absolutely nothing. Every one was perfect, every one checked. Birth certificates, scholastic records, recommendations, loyalty checks, psych examinations—all of them were as they should be. There was not a single flaw.

That was the trouble . . . in all the records of the service's personnel there was not a single flaw. Not a thing a man could point to. Not a thing on which one could anchor suspicion.

Lily-white and pure.

Yet, someone inside the service had stolen Sutton's dossier. Someone inside the service had tipped off Sutton on the gun-trap laid for him at the Orion Arms. Someone had been ready and waiting, knowing of the ·trap, to whisk him out of reach.

Spies, said Adams to himself, and he lifted up his hand and made his hand into a fist and hit the desk so hard that his knuckles stung.

For no one but an insider could have made away with Sutton's dossier. No one but an insider could have known of the decision to destroy Sutton, or of the three men who had been assigned to carry out the order.

The tracer chuckled at him. *Ker-rup*, it said, *ker-rup, clickity, click, ker-rup.*

That was Sutton's heart and breath . . . that was Sutton's life ticking away somewhere. So long as Sutton lived, no matter where he was or what he might be doing, the tracer would go on with its chuckling and its burping. *Ker-rup, ker-rup, ker-rup . . .*

Somewhere in the asteroid belt, the tracer had said, and that was a very general location, but it could be narrowed. Already ships with other tracers abroad were engaged in narrowing it down. Sooner or later . . . hours or days or weeks, Sutton would be found.

Ker-rup . . .

War, the man in the mask had said.

And hours later, a ship had come screaming down across the hills like a blazing comet to plunge into a swamp.

A ship such as no man as yet had made, carrying melted weapons that were unlike any that man had yet invented. A ship whose thunder in the night had roused the sleeping inhabitants for miles around, whose flaming metal had been a beacon glowing in the sky.

A ship and a body and a track that led from ship to body across three hundred yards of marsh. The trace of one man's footprints and the furrowing trail of other feet that dragged across the mud. And the man who had carried the dead man had been Asher Sutton, for Sutton's fingerprints were on the muddied clothing of the man lying at the swamp's edge.

Sutton, thought Adams wearily. It is always Sutton. Sutton's name on the flyleaf out of Alderbaran XII. Sutton's fingerprints upon a dead man's clothing. The man in the mask had said there would have been no incident on Aldebaran if it had not been for Sutton. And Sutton had killed Benton with a bullet in the arm.

Ker-rup, clickity, click, ker-rup . . .

Dr. Raven had sat in that chair across the desk and told of the afternoon Sutton had dropped in at the university.

"He found destiny," Dr. Raven had said and he said it as if it were commonplace, as if it were a thing that could not be questioned and a thing that could have been expected all along to happen.

Not a religion, Dr. Raven had said, with the afternoon sunlight shining on his snow-white hair. Oh, dear, no, not a religion. Destiny, don't you understand?

Destiny, noun. Destiny—the predetermined course of events often conceived as a resistless power or agency . . .

"The accepted definition," Dr. Raven had said, as if he might be addressing a lecture hall, "may have to be modified slightly when Asher writes his book."

But how could Sutton find destiny? Destiny was an idea, an abstraction.

"You forget," Dr. Raven had told him, speaking gently as one would to a child, "that part about the resistless power or agency. That is what he found . . . the power or agency."

"Sutton told me about the beings he found on Cygni," Adams had said. "He was at a loss as to how best to describe them. He said the nearest that he could come was symbiotic adstractions."

Dr. Raven had nodded his head and pulled his shell-like ears and figured that maybe symbiotic abstractions would fit the bill, although it was hard for one to decide just what a symbiotic abstraction was or what it would look like.

What it would look like—or what it might be.

The informational robot had been very technical when Adams had put the question to him.

"Symbiosis," he had said. "Why, sir, symbiosis is quite simple. It is a mutually beneficial internal partnership between two organisms of different kinds. Mutually beneficial, you understand, sir. That is the important thing—that mutually beneficial business. Not a benefit to one of the things alone, but to both of them."

"Commensalism, now, that is something else. In commensalism there still is mutual benefit, sir, but the relationship is external, not internal. Nor parasitism, either, for that matter. Because in parasitic instances only one thing benefits. The host does not benefit, just the parasite."

"Some of this may sound confusing, sir, but . . ."

"Tell me," Adams had asked him, "about symbiosis. I don't care about all this other stuff."

"It really is," the robot said, "a very simple thing. Now, take heather, for instance. You know, of course, that it is associated with a certain fungus."

"No," Adams said, "I didn't."

"Well, it is," the robot said. "A fungus that grows inside of it, inside its roots and branches, its flowers and leaves, even in its seed. If it weren't for this fungus, the heather couldn't grow on the kind of soil it does. No other plant can grow on so poor a soil. Because, you see, sir, no other plant has this particular fungus associated with it. The heather gives the fungus a place to live and the fungus makes it possible for the heather to make its living on the scanty soil where it has no opposition."

"I wouldn't call that," Adams had told him, "a very simple business."

"Well," said the robot, "there are other things, of course. Certain lichens are no more than a symbiotic combination of an alga and a fungus. In other words, there is no such a thing as a lichen in this case. It's just two other things."

"It's a wonder to me," said Adams sourly, "that you don't simply melt down in the white heat of your brilliance."

"Then there are certain green animals," said the robot.

"Frogs," said Adams.

"Not frogs," the robot said. "Certain simple, primal animals. Things that live in the water, you know. They establish a symbiotic relationship with certain algae. The animal uses the oxygen which the plant gives off and the plant uses the carbon dioxide the animal gives off.

"And there's a worm with a symbiotic alga which aids it in its digestive processes. Everything works swell except when sometimes the worm digests the alga and then it dies because, without the alga, it can't digest its food."

"All very interesting," Adams had told the robot. "Now can you tell me what a symbiotic abstraction might be?"

"No," the robot had said, "I can't."

And Dr. Raven, sitting at the desk, had said the same. "It would be rather difficult," he said, "to know just what a symbiotic abstraction might be."

Under questioning, he reiterated once again that it was not a new religion Sutton had found. Oh, gracious, no, not a religion.

And Raven, Adams thought, should be the one to know, for he was one of the galaxy's best and most widely known comparative religionists.

Although it would be a new idea, Dr. Raven had said. Bless me, yes, an absolutely new idea.

And ideas are dangerous, Adams told himself.

For man was spread thin across the galaxy. So thin that one word, literally one spoken word, one unbidden thought might be enough to set off the train of rebellion and of violence that would sweep Man back to the Solar system, back to the puny ring of circling planets that had caged him in before.

One could not take a chance. One could not gamble with an imponderable.

Better that one man die needlessly than that the whole race lose its grip upon the galaxy. Better that one new idea, however great, be blotted out than that all the vast associations of ideas which represented mankind be swept from the billion stars.

Item One: Sutton wasn't human.

Item Two: He was not telling all he knew.

Item Three: He had a manuscript which was not decipherable.

Item Four: He meant to write a book.

Item Five: He had a new idea.

Conclusion: Sutton must be killed.

Ker-rup, clickity, click . . .

War, the man had said. A war in time.

It would be spread thin, too, like Man across the galaxy.

It would be three-dimensional chess with a million billion squares and a million pieces. And with the rules changing every move.

It would reach back to win its battles. It would strike at

points in time and space which would not even know that there was a war. It could, logically, go back to the silver mines of Athens, to the horse and chariot of Thutmosis III, to the sailing of Columbus. It would involve all fields of human endeavor and human speculation and it would twist the dreams of men who had never thought of time except as a moving shadow across the sun dial's face.

It would involve spies and propagandists, spies to learn the factors of the past so that they could be plotted in the campaign strategy, propagandists to twist the fabric of the past so that strategy could be the more effective.

It would load the personnel of the Justice Department of the year 7990 with spies and fifth columnists and saboteurs. And it would do that thing so cleverly one could never find the spies.

But, as in an ordinary, honest war, there would be strategic points. As in chess, there would be one key square.

Sutton was that square. He was the square that must be seized and held. He was the pawn that stood in the way of the sweep of bishop and of rook. He was the pawn that both sides were lining up on, bringing all their pressure on a single point . . . and when one side was ready, when it had gained a fraction of advantage, the slaughter would begin.

Adams folded his arms upon the desk and laid his head upon them. His shoulders twitched with sobbing, but he had no tears.

"Ash, boy," he said. "Ash, I counted on you so much. Ash . . ."

The silence brought him straight in the chair again.

For a moment, he was unable to locate it . . . determine what was wrong. And then he knew.

The psych-tracer had stopped its burping.

He leaned forward and bent above it and there was no

sound, no sound of heart, of breath, of blood coursing in the jugular.

The motivating force that had operated it had ceased.

Slowly, Adams rose from his chair, took down his hat and put it on.

For the first time in his life, Christopher Adams was going home before the day was over.

XXVI

Sutton stiffened in his chair and then relaxed. For this was bluff, he told himself. These men wouldn't kill him. They wanted the book and dead men do not write.

Case answered him, almost as if Sutton had spoken what he thought aloud.

"You must not count on us," he said, "as honorable men, for neither of us ourselves would lay a claim to that. Pringle, I think, will bear me out in that."

"Oh, most certainly," said Pringle, "I have no use for honor."

"It would have meant a great deal to us if we could have taken you back to Trevor and . . ."

"Wait a second," said Sutton. "Who is this Trevor? He's a new one."

"Oh, Trevor," said Pringle. "Just an oversight. Trevor is the head of the corporation."

"The corporation," said Case, "that wants to get your book."

"Trevor would have heaped us with honors," Pringle said, "and loaded us with wealth if we had pulled it off, but since you won't co-operate we'll have to cast around for some other way to make ourselves a profit."

"So we switch sides," said Case, "and we shoot you. Morgan will pay high for you, but he wants you dead. Your carcass will be worth a good deal to Morgan. Oh yes, indeed it will."

"And you will sell it to him," Sutton said.

"Most certainly," said Pringle. "We never miss a bet."

Case purred at Sutton, "You do not object, I hope?"

Sutton shook his head. "What you do with my cadaver," he told them, "is no concern of mine."

"Well, then," said Case and he raised the gun.

"Just a second," Sutton said quietly.

Case lowered the gun. "Now what?" he asked.

"He wants a cigarette," said Pringle. "Men who are about to be executed always want a cigarette or a glass of wine or a chicken dinner or something of the sort."

"I want to ask a question," Sutton said.

Case nodded.

"I take it," Sutton said, "that in your time I've already written this book."

"That's right," Case told him. "And, if you will allow me, it is an honest and efficient job."

"Under your imprint or someone else's?"

Pringle cackled. "Under someone else's, of course. If you did it under ours, why do you think we'd be back here at all?"

Sutton wrinkled his brow. "I've already written it," he said, "without your help or counsel . . . and without your editing. Now, if I did it a second time, and wrote it the way you wanted, there would be complications."

"None," said Case, "we couldn't overcome. Nothing that could not be explained quite satisfactorily."

"And now that you're going to kill me, there'll be no book at all. How will you handle that?"

Case frowned. "It will be difficult," he said, "and unfortunate . . . unfortunate for many people. But we'll work it out somehow."

He raised the gun again.

"Sure you won't change your mind?" he asked.

Sutton shook his head.

They won't shoot, he told himself. It's a bluff. The deck is cold and . . .

Case pulled the trigger.

A mighty force, like a striking fist, slammed into Sutton's body and shoved him back so hard that the chair tilted and then slued around, yawing like a ship caught in magnetic stresses.

Fire flashed within his skull and he felt one swift shriek of agony that took him in its claws and lifted him and shook him, jangling every nerve, grating every bone.

There was one thought, one fleeting thought that he tried to grasp and hold, but it wriggled from his brain like an eel slipping free from bloody fingers.

Change, said the thought. Change. Change.

He felt the change . . . felt it start even as he died.

And death was a soft thing, soft and black, cool and sweet and gracious. He slipped into it as a swimmer slips into the surf and it closed over him and held him and he felt the pulse and beat of it and knew the vastness and the sureness of it.

Back on Earth, the psych-tracer faltered to a stop and Christopher Adams went home for the first time in his life before the day was done.

XXVII

HERKIMER lay on his bed and tried to sleep, but sleep was long in coming. And he wondered that he should sleep . . . that he should sleep and eat and drink as Man. For he was not a man, although he was as close to one as the human mind and human skill could come.

His origin was chemical and Man's was biological. He was the imitation and Man was reality. It is the method, he told himself, the method and terminology, that keeps me from being Man, for in all things else we are the same.

The method and the words and the tattoo mark I wear upon my brow.

I am as good as Man and almost as smart as Man, for all I act the clown, and would be as treacherous as Man if I had the chance. Except I wear a tattoo mark and I am owned and I have no soul . . . although sometimes I doubt that.

Herkimer lay very quiet and gazed at the ceiling and tried to remember certain things, but the memories would not come.

First there was the tool and then the machine, which was no more than a complicated tool, and both machine and tool were no more than the extension of a hand.

Man's hand, of course.

Then came the robot and a robot was a machine that walked like a man. That walked and looked and talked like a man and did the things Man wished, but it was a caricature. No matter how sleekly machined, no matter how cleverly designed, there never was a danger that it be mistaken for a man.

And after the robot?

We are not robots, Herkimer told himself, and we are not men. We are not machines and we are not flesh and blood. We are chemicals made into the shapes of our creators and assigned a chemical life so close to the life of our makers that someday one of them will find, to his astonishment, that there is no difference.

Made in the shape of men . . . and the resemblance is so close that we wear a tattoo mark so that men may know their own.

So close to Man and yet not Man.

Although there is hope. If we can keep the Cradle secret, if we can keep it hidden from the eyes of Man. Someday there will be no difference. Someday a man will talk to an android and think he's talking to a fellow man.

Herkimer stretched his arms and folded them over his head.

He tried to examine his mind, to arrive at motives and evaluations, but it was hard to do. No rancor, certainly. No jealousy. No bitterness. But a nagging feeling of inadequacy, of almost having reached the goal and falling short.

But there was comfort, he thought. There was comfort if there was nothing else.

And that comfort must be kept. Kept for the little ones, for the ones that were less than Man.

He lay for a long time, thinking about comfort, watching the dark square of the window with the rime of frost upon it and the stars shining through the frost, listening to the thin whine of the feeble, vicious weasel-wind as it knifed across the roof.

Sleep did not come and he got up at last and turned on the light. Shivering, he got into his clothes and pulled a book out of his pocket. Huddling close to the lamp, he turned the pages to a passage worn thin with reading.

There is no thing, no matter how created, how born or how conceived or made, which knows the pulse of life, that goes alone. That assurance I can give you. . . .

He closed the book and held it clasped between the palms of his two hands.

". . . how born or how conceived *or made* . . ."

Made.

All that mattered was the pulse of life.

Comfort.

And it must be kept.

I did my duty, he told himself. My willing, almost eager, duty. I still am doing it.

I acted the part, he told himself, and I think I acted well. I acted a part when I carried the challenge to Asher Sutton's room. I acted a part when I came to him as a part of the *estate duella* . . . the saucy, flippant part of any common android.

I did my duty for him . . . and yet not for him, but for comfort, for the privilege of knowing and believing that neither I nor any other living thing, no matter how lowly it may be, will ever be alone.

I hit him. I hit him on the button and I knocked him out and I lifted him in my arms and carried him.

He was angry at me, but that does not matter. For his anger cannot wash away a single word of the thing he gave me.

Thunder shook the house, and the window, for a moment, flared with sudden crimson.

Herkimer came to his feet and ran to the window and stood there, gripping the ledge, watching the red twinkle of dwindling rocket tubes.

Fear hit him in the stomach and he raced out of the door and down the hall, to Sutton's room.

He did not knock nor did he turn the knob. He hit the door and it shattered open, with a wrecked and twisted lock dangling by its screws.

The bed was empty and there was no one in the room.

XXVIII

SUTTON SENSED resurrection and he fought against it, for death was so comfortable. Like a soft, warm bed. And resurrection was a strident, inistent, maddening alarm clock that shrilled across the predawn chill of a dreadful, frowzy room. Dreadful with its life and its bare reality and its sharp, sickening reminder that one must get up and walk into reality again.

But this is not the first time. No, indeed, said Sutton. This is not the first time that I died and came to life again. For I did it once before and that time I was dead for a long, long time.

There was a hard, flat surface underneath him and he lay face down upon it and for what seemed an interminable stretch of time his mind struggled to visualize the hardness and smoothness beneath him. Hard and flat and smooth, three words, but they did not help one see or understand the thing that they described.

He felt life creep back and quicken, seep along his legs and arms. But he wasn't breathing and his heart was still.

Floor!

That was it . . . that was the word for the thing on which he lay. The flat, hard surface was a floor.

Sounds came to him, but at first he didn't call them sounds, for he had no word for them at all, and then, a moment later, he knew that they were sounds.

Now he could move one finger. Then a second finger. He opened his eyes and there was light.

The sounds were voices and the voices were words and the words were thoughts.

It takes so long to figure things out, Sutton told himself.

"We should have tried a little harder," said a voice, "and a little longer. The trouble with us, Case, is that we have no patience."

"Patience wouldn't have done a bit of good," said Case. "He was convinced that we were bluffing. No matter what we'd done or said, he'd still have thought we were bluffing and we would have gotten nowhere. There was only one thing to do."

"Yes, I know," Pringle agreed. "Convince him that we weren't bluffing."

He made a sound of blowing out his breath. "Pity, too," he said. "He was such a bright young man."

They were silent for a time and now it was not life alone, but strength, that was flowing into Sutton. Strength to stand and walk, strength to lift his arms, strength to vent his anger. Strength to kill two men.

"We won't do so badly," Pringle said. "Morgan and his crowd will pay us handsomely."

Case was squeamish. "I don't like it, Pringle. A dead man is a dead man if you leave him dead. But when you sell him, that makes you a butcher."

"That's not the thing that's worrying me," Pringle told him. "What will it do to the future, Case? To our future. We had a future with many of its facets based on Sutton's book. If we had managed to change the book a little it wouldn't have mattered much . . . wouldn't have mattered at all, in fact, the way we had it figured out. But now Sutton's dead. There will be no book by Sutton. The future will be different."

Sutton rose to his feet.

They spun around and faced him and Case's hand went for his gun.

"Go ahead," invited Sutton. "Shoot me full of holes. You won't live a minute longer for it."

He tried to hate them, as he had hated Benton during that one fleeting moment back on Earth. Hatred so strong and primal that it had blasted the man's mind into oblivion.

But there was no hate. Just a ponderous, determined will to kill.

He moved forward on sturdy legs and his hands reached out.

Pringle ran, squeeling like a rat, seeking to escape. Case's gun spat twice and when blood oozed out and ran down Sutton's chest and he still came on, Case threw away his weapon and backed against the wall.

It didn't take long.

They couldn't get away.

There was no place to go.

XXIX

Sutton maneuvered the ship down against the tiny asteroid, a whirling piece of debris not much bigger than the ship itself. He felt it touch and his thumb reached out and knocked over the gravity lever and the ship clamped down, to go tumbling through space with the twisting chunk of rock.

Sutton let his hands fall to his side, sat quietly in the pilot's chair. In front of him, space was black and friendless, streaked by the pinpoint stars that spun in lines of fire across the field of vision, writing cryptic messages of cold, white light across the cosmos as the asteroid bumbled on its erratic course.

Safe, he told himself. Safe for a while, at least. Perhaps safe forever, for there might be no one looking for him.

Safe with a hole blasted through his chest, with blood splashed down his shirt front and running down his legs. Handy thing to have, he thought grimly, this second body of mine. This body that was grafted on me by the Cygnians. It will keep me going until . . . until . . .

Until what?

Until I can get back to Earth and walk into a doctor's

office and say, "I got shot up some. How about a patching job?"

Sutton chuckled.

He could see the doctor dropping dead.

Or going back to Cygni?

But they wouldn't let me in.

Or just going back to Earth the way I am and forgetting about the doctor.

I could get other clothes and the bleeding will stop when the blood's all gone.

But I wouldn't breathe, and they would notice that.

"Johnny," he said, but there was no answer, just a feeble stir of life within his brain, a sign of recognition, as a dog would wag its tail to let you know it heard but was too busy with a bone to let anything distract it.

"Johnny, is there any way?"

For there might be a way. It was a hope to cling to, it was a thing to think about.

Not even yet, he suspected, had he begun to plumb the strange depth of abilities lodged within his body and his mind.

He had not known that his hate alone could kill, that hate could spear out from his brain like a lance of steel and strike a man down dead. And yet Benton had died with a bullet in the arm . . . and he had been dead before the bullet hit him. For Benton had fired and missed and Benton, alive, never would have missed.

He had not known that by mind alone he could control the energy that was needed to lift the dead weight of a ship from a boulder bed and fly it across eleven years of space. And yet that is what he'd done, winnowing the energy from the flaming stars so far away they dimmed to almost nothing, from the random specks of matter that floated in the void.

And while he knew that he could change at will from one life to another, he had not known for certain that when one way of life was killed, the other way would take over automatically. Yet that was what had happened. Case had killed him and he had died and he had come to life again. But he had died before the change had started. Of that much he was sure. For he remembered death and recognized it. He knew it from the time before.

He felt his body eating . . . sucking at the stars as a human sucks an orange, nibbling at the energy imprisoned in the bit of rock to which the ship was clamped, pouncing on the tiny leaks of power from the ship's atomic motors.

Eating to grow strong, eating to repair . . .

"Johnny, is there any way?"

And there was no answer.

He let his head sag forward until it lay upon the inclined panel that housed the instruments.

His body went on eating, sucking at the stars.

He listened to the slow drip of blood falling from his body and splashing on the floor.

His mind was clouding and he let it cloud, for there was nothing to do . . . there was no need to use it, he did not know how to use it. He did not know what he could do or what he couldn't do, nor how to go about it.

He had fallen, he remembered, screaming down the alien sky, knowing a moment of wild elation that he had broken through, that the world of Cygni VII lay beneath his hand. That what all the navies of the Earth had failed to do, he'd done.

The planet was rushing up and he saw the tangled geography of it that snaked in black and gray across his visionplate.

It was twenty years ago, but he remembered it, in the

gray fog of his mind, as if it were yesterday or this very moment.

He reached out a hand and hauled back on a lever and the lever would not move. The ship plunged down and for a moment he felt a rising panic that exploded into fear.

One fact stood out, one stark, black fact in all the flashing fragments of thoughts and schemes and prayer that went screeching through his brain. One stark fact . . . he was about to crash.

He did not remember crashing, for he probably never knew exactly when he crashed. It was only fear and terror and then no fear or terror. It was consciousness and awareness and then a nothingness that was a restfulness and a vast forgetting.

Awareness came back . . . in a moment or an aeon—which, he could not tell. But an awareness that was different, a sentiency that was only partly human, just a small percentage human. And a knowledge that was new, but which it seemed he had held forever.

He sensed or knew, for it was not seeing, his body stretched out on the ground, smashed and broken, twisted out of human shape. And although he knew it was his body and knew its every superficial function and the plan of its assembly, he felt a twinge of wonder at the thing which lay there and knew that here was a problem which would tax his utmost ingenuity.

For the body must be put together, must be straightened out and reintegrated and co-ordinated so that it would work and the life that had escaped it be returned to it again.

He thought of Humpty Dumpty and the thought was strange, as if the nursery rhyme were something new or something long forgotten.

Humpty Dumpty, said another part of him, supplies no answer, and he knew that it was right, for Humpty, he recalled, could not be put together.

He became aware there were two of him, for one part of him had answered the other part of him. The answerer and the other, and although they were one, they were also separate. There was a cleavage he could not understand.

I am your destiny, said the answerer. I was with you when you came to life and I stay with you till you die. I do not control you and I do not coerce you, but I try to guide you, although you do not know it.

Sutton, the small part of him that was Sutton, said, "I know it now."

He knew it as if he'd always known it and that was queer, for he had only learned it. Knowledge, he realized, was all tangled up, for there were two of him . . . he and destiny. He could not immediately distinguish between the things he knew as Sutton alone and those he knew as Sutton plus Sutton's destiny.

I cannot know, he thought. I could not know then and I cannot know now. For there still is deep within me the two facets of my being, the human that I am and the destiny that guides me to a greater glory and a greater life if I will only let it.

For it will not coerce me and it will not stop me. It will only give me hunches, it will only whisper to me. It is the thing called conscience and the thing called judgment and the thing called righteousness.

And it sits within my brain as it sits within the brain of no other thing, for I am one with it as is no other thing. I know of it with a dreadful certainty and they do not know at all or, if they do, they only guess at the great immensity of its truthfulness.

And all must know. All must know as I know.

But there is something going on to keep them from knowing, or to twist their knowledge so their knowing is all wrong. I must find out what it is and I must correct it. And somehow or other I must strike into the future, I must set it aright for the days I will not see.

I am your destiny, the answerer had said.

Destiny, not fatalism.

Destiny, not foreordination.

Destiny, the way of men and races and of worlds.

Destiny, the way you made your life, the way you shaped your living . . . the way it was meant to be, the way that it would be if you listened to the still, small voice that talked to you at the many turning points and crossroads.

But if you did not listen . . . why, then, you did not listen and you did not hear. And there was no power that could make you listen. There was no penalty if you did not listen except the penalty of having gone against your destiny.

There were other thoughts or other voices. Sutton could not tell which they were, but they were outside the tangled thing that was he and destiny.

That is my body, he thought. And I am somewhere else. Someplace where there is no seeing as I used to see . . . and no hearing, although I see and hear, but with another's senses and in an alien way.

The screen let him through, said one thought, although screen was not the word it used.

And another said, the screen has served its purpose.

And another said that there was a certain technique he had picked up on a planet, the name of which blurred and ran and made a splotch and had no meaning at all so far as Sutton could make out.

Still another pointed out the singular complexity and inefficiency of Sutton's mangled body and spoke enthusiastically of the simplicity and perfection of direct energy intake.

Sutton tried to cry out to them for the love of God to hurry, for his body was a fragile thing, that if they waited too long it would be past all mending. But he could not say it and as if in a dream he listened to the interplay of thought, the flash and flicker of individual opinion, all molding into one cohesive thought that spelled eventual decision.

He tried to wonder where he was, tried to orient himself, and found that he could not even define himself. For himself no longer was a body or a place in space or time, nor even a personal pronoun. It was a hanging, dangling thing that had no substance and no fixture in the scheme of time and it could not recognize itself no matter what it did. It was a vacuum that knew it existed and it was dominated by something else that might as well have been a vacuum for all the recognition he could make of it.

He was outside his body and he lived. But where or how there was no way of knowing.

I am your destiny, the answerer that seemed a part of him had said.

But destiny was a word and nothing more. An idea. An abstraction. A tenuous definition for something that the mind of Man had conceived, but could not prove . . . that the mind of Man was willing to agree was an idea only and could not be proved.

You are wrong, said Sutton's destiny. Destiny is real although you cannot see it. It is real for you and for all other things . . . for every single thing that knows the surge of life. And it has always been and it will always be.

This is not death? asked Sutton.

You are the first to come to us, said destiny. We cannot let you die. We will give you back your body, but until then you will live with me. You will be part of me. And that is only fair, for I have lived with you; I have been part of you.

You did not want me here, said Sutton. You built a screen to keep me out.

We wanted one, said destiny. One only. You are that one; there will be no more.

But the screen?

It was keyed to a mind, said destiny. To a certain mind. The kind of mind we wanted.

But you let me die.

You had to die, destiny told him. Until you died and became one of us you could not know. In your body we could not have reached you. You had to die so that you would be freed and I was there to take you and make you part of me so you would understand.

I do not understand, said Sutton:

You will, said destiny. You will.

And I did, thought Sutton, remembering. I did.

His body shook as he remembered and his mind stood awed with the vast, unsuspected immensity of destiny . . . of trillions upon trillions of destinies to match the teeming life of the galaxy.

Destiny had stirred a million years before and a shaggy ape thing had stooped and picked up a broken stick. It stirred again and struck flint together. It stirred once more and there was a bow and arrow. Again, and the wheel was born.

Destiny whispered and a thing climbed dripping from the water and in the years to come its fins were legs and its gills were nostrils.

Symbiotic abstractions. Parasites. Call them what you

177

would. They were destiny.

And the time had come for the galaxy to know of destiny.

If parasites, then beneficial parasites, ready to give more than they could take. For all they got was the sense of living, the sense of being . . . and what they gave, or stood ready to give, was far more than mere living.

For many of the lives they lived must be dull, indeed. An angleworm, for instance. Or the bloated unintelligence that crept through nauseous jungle worlds.

But because of them someday an angleworm might be more than an angleworm . . . or a greater angleworm. The bloated unintelligence might be something that would reach to greater heights than Man.

For every thing that moved, whether slow or fast, across the face of any world, was not one thing, but two. It and its own individual destiny.

And sometimes destiny took a hold and caught . . . and sometimes it didn't. But where there was destiny there was hope forever. For destiny was hope. And destiny was everywhere.

No thing walks alone.

Nor crawls nor hops nor swims nor flies nor shambles.

One planet barred to every mind but one and, once that mind arrived, barred forevermore.

One mind to tell the galaxy when the galaxy was ready. One mind to tell of destiny and hope.

That mind, thought Sutton, is my own.

Lord help me now.

For if I had been the one to choose, if I had been asked, if I had had a thing to say about it, it would not have been I, but someone or something else. Some other mind in another million years. Some other thing in ten times another million years.

It is too much to ask, he thought . . . too much to ask a being with a mind as frail as Man's, to bear the weight of revelation, to bear the load of knowing.

But destiny put the finger on me.

Happenstance or accident or pure blind luck . . . it would be destiny.

I lived with destiny, as destiny . . . I was a part of destiny instead of destiny being a part of me, and we came to know each other as if we were two humans . . . better than if we were two humans. For destiny was I and I was destiny. Destiny had no name and I called it Johnny and the fact I had to name him is a joke that destiny, my destiny, still can chuckle over.

I lived with Johnny, the vital part of me, the spark of me that men call life and do not understand . . . the part of me I still do not understand . . . until my body had been repaired again. And then I returned to it and it was a different body and a better body, for the many destinies had been astounded and horrified at the inefficiency and the flimsy structure of the human body.

And when they fixed it up, they made it better. They tinkered it so it had a lot of things it did not have before . . . many things, I suspect, I still do not know about and will not know about until it is time to use them. Some things, perhaps, I'll never know about.

When I went back to my body, destiny came and lived with me again, but now I knew him and recognized him and I called him Johnny and we talked together and I never failed to hear him, as I must many times have failed to hear him in the past.

Symbiosis, Sutton told himself, a higher symbiosis than the symbiosis of heather with its fungus or the primitive animal with its alga. A mental symbiosis. I am the host and Johnny is my guest and we get along together because we understand each other. Johnny gives me an awareness of my destiny, of the operative force of destiny that shapes my hours and days, and I give Johnny the semblance of life that he could not have through his existence independently.

"Johnny," he called and there was no answer.

He waited and there was no answer.

"Johnny," he called again and there was terror in his voice. For Johnny must be there. Destiny must be there.

Unless . . . unless . . . the thought struck him slowly, kindly. Unless he were really dead. Unless this were dreaming, unless this were a twilight zone where knowledge and a sense of being linger for a moment between the state of life and death.

Johnny's voice was small, very small and very far away.

"Ash."

"Yes, Johnny."

"The engines, Ash. The engines."

He fought his body out of the pilot's chair, stood on weaving legs.

He could scarcely see . . . just the faded, blurred, shifting outline of the shape of metal that enclosed him. His feet were leaden weights that he could not move . . . that were no part of him at all.

He stumbled, staggered forward, fell flat upon his face.

Shock, he thought. The shock of violence, the shock of death, the shock of draining blood, of mangled, blasted flesh.

There had been strength, a surge of strength that had brought him, clear-eyed, clear-brained, to his feet. A strength that had been great enough to take the lives of the two men who had killed him. The strength was vengeance.

But that strength was gone and now he knew it had been the strength of brain, the strength of will rather than of mere bone and muscle that had let him do it.

He struggled to his hands and knees and crept. He stopped and rested and then crept a few feet more and his head hung limp between his shoulders, drooling blood and mucus and slobbered stomach slime that left a trail across the floor.

He found the door of the engine room and by slow degrees pulled himself upward to the latch.

His fingers found the latch and pulled it down, but they had no strength and they slipped off the metal and he fell into a huddled pile of sheer defeat against the hard coldness of the door.

He waited for a long time and then he tried again and this time the latch clicked open even as his fingers slipped again, and as he fell, he fell across the threshold.

Finally, after so long a wait that he thought he could never do it, he got on hands and knees again and crept forward by slow inches.

XXX

ASHER SUTTON awoke to darkness.

To darkness and an unknowing.

To unknowing and a slow, exploding wonder.

He was lying on a hard, smooth surface and a roof of metal came down close above his head. And beside him was a thing that purred and rumbled. One arm was flung across the purring thing and somehow he knew that he had slept with the thing clasped in his arms, with his body pressed against it, as a child might sleep with a beloved Teddy bear.

There was no sense of time and no sense of place and no sense of any life before. As if he had sprung full-limbed by magic into life and intelligence and knowing.

He lay still and his eyes became accustomed to the dark and he saw the open door and the dark stain, now dry, that led across the threshold into the room beyond. Something had dragged itself there, from the other room into this one, and left a trail behind it, and he lay for a long time, wondering what the thing might be, with the quesiness of terror gnawing at his mind. For the thing might still be with him and it might be dangerous.

But he felt he was alone, sensed a loneness in the throbbing of the engine at his side . . . and it was thus for the first time that he knew the purring thing for what it was. Name and recognition had slipped into his consciousness without conscious effort, as if it were a thing he had known all the time, and now he knew what it was, except that it seemed to him the name had come ahead of recognition and that, he thought, was strange.

So the thing beside him was an engine and he was lying on the floor and the metal close above his head was a roof of some sort. A narrow space, he thought. A narrow space that housed an engine and a door that opened into another room.

A ship. That was it. He was in a ship. And the trail of dark that ran across the threshold.

At first he thought that some other thing, some imagined thing, had crawled in slime of its own making to mark the trail, but now he remembered. It had been himself . . . himself crawling to the engines.

Lying quietly, it came back to him and in wonder he tested his aliveness. He lifted a hand and felt his chest and the clothes were burned away and their scorched edges were crisp between his fingers, but his chest was whole . . . whole and smooth and hard. Good human flesh. No holes.

So it was possible, he thought. I remember that I wondered if it was . . . if Johnny might not have some trick up his sleeve, if my body might not have some capability which I could not suspect.

It sucked at the stars and it nibbled at the asteroid and it yearned toward the engines. It wanted energy. And the engines had the energy . . . more than the distant stars, more than the cold, frozen chunk of rock that was the asteroid.

So I crawled to reach the engines and I left a dark

death-trail behind me and I slept with the engines in my arms. And my body, my direct-intake, energy-eating body sucked the power that was needed from the flaming core of the reaction chambers.

And I am whole again.

I am back in my breath-and-blood body once again and I can go back to Earth.

He crawled out of the engine room and stood on his two feet.

Faint starlight came through the visionplates and scattered like jewel dust along the floor and walls. And there were two huddled shapes, one in the middle of the floor and another in a corner.

His mind took them in and nosed them as a dog would nose a bone and in a little while he remembered what they were. The humanity within him shivered at the black, sprawled shapes, but another part of him, a cold, hard inner core, stood calculating and undismayed in the face of death.

He moved forward on slow feet and slowly knelt beside one of the bodies. It must be Case, he thought, for Case was thin and tall. But he could not see the face and he did not wish to see the face, for in some dark corner of his mind he still remembered what the faces had been like.

His hands went down and searched, minnowing through the clothing. He made a tiny pile of things he found and finally he found the thing he was looking for.

Squatting on his heels, he opened the book to the title page and it was the same as the one he carried in his pocket. The same except for a single line of type, the tiny line at the very bottom.

And the line said:

Revised Edition

So that was it. That was the meaning of the word that had puzzled him: Revisionists.

There had been a book and it had been revised. Those who lived by the revised edition were the Revisionists. And the others? He wondered, running through the names . . . Fundamentalists, Primitives, Orthodox, Hard-Shell. There were others, he was sure, and it didn't matter. It didn't really matter what the others would be called.

There were two blank pages and the text began:

We are not alone.

No one ever is alone.

Not since the first faint stirring of the first flicker of life on the first planet in the galaxy that knew the quickening of life, has there ever been a single entity that walked or crawled or slithered down the path of life alone.*

His eye went down the page to the first footnote.

*This is the first of many statements which, wrongly interpreted, have caused some readers to believe that Sutton meant to say that life, regardless of its intelligence or moral precepts, is the beneficiary of destiny. His first line should refute this entire line of reasoning, for Sutton used the pronoun "we" and all students of semantics are agreed that it is a common idiom for any genus, when speaking of itself, to use such a personal pronoun. Had Sutton meant all life, he would have written "all life." But by using the personal pronoun, he undeniably was referring to his own genus, the human race, and the human race alone. He apparently erroneously believed, a not uncommon belief of the day, that the Earth had been the first planet of the galaxy to know the quickening of life. There is no doubt that, in part, Sutton's revelations of his great discovery of destiny have been tampered with. Assiduous research and

study, however, have resulted in determining beyond reasonable doubt which portions are genuine and which are not. Those parts which patently have been altered will be noted and the reasons for this belief will be carefully and frankly pointed out.

Sutton riffled through the pages quickly. More than half the text was taken up by the fine-print footnotes. Some of the pages had two or three lines of actual text and the rest was filled with lengthy explanation and refutation.

He slapped the book shut, held it between his flattened palms.

I tried so hard, he thought. I repeated and reiterated and underscored. Not human life alone, but all life. Everything that was aware.

And yet they twist my words.

They fight a war so that my words shall not be the words I wrote, so that the things I meant to say shall be misinterpreted. They scheme and fight and murder so that the great cloak of destiny shall rest on one race alone . . . so that the most vicious race of animals ever spawned shall steal the thing that was meant not for them alone, but for every living thing.

And somehow I must stop it. Somehow it must be stopped. Somehow my words must stand, so that all may read and know without the smoke screen of petty theorizing and learned interpretation and weasel logic.

For it is so simple. Such a simple thing. All life has destiny, not human life alone.

There is one destiny creature for every other living thing. For every living thing and then to spare. They wait for life to happen and each time it occurs one of them is there and stays there until that particular life is ended. How, I do not know, nor why. I do not know if the actual

Johnny is lodged within my mind and being or if he merely keeps in contact with me from Cygni. But I know that he is with me. I know that he will stay.

And yet the Revisionists will twist my words and discredit me. They will change my book and dig up old scandals about the Suttons so that the mistakes of my forebears, magnified many times, will tend to smear my name.

They sent back a man who talked to John H. Sutton and he told them things that they could have used. For John Sutton said that there are skeletons in every family closet and in that he spoke the truth. And, old and garrulous as he was, he talked about these skeletons.

But those tales were not carried forward into the future to be of any use, for the man who heard them came tramping up the road with a bandage on his head and no shoes on his feet. Something happened and he could not go back.

Something happened.

Something . . .

Sutton rose slowly.

Something happened, he said, talking to himself, and I know what it was.

Six thousand years ago in a place that was called Wisconsin.

He moved forward, heading for the pilot's chair.

Asher Sutton was going to Wisconsin.

XXXI

CHRISTOPHER ADAMS came into his office and hung up
his hat and coat.

He turned around and pulled out the chair before his
desk, and in the act of sitting down he froze and listened.

The psych-tracer burped at him.

Ker-rup, it chuckled, *ker-up, clickity, click, ker-rup.*

Christopher Adams straightened from his half-sitting,
half-standing position and put on his hat and coat again.

Going out, he slammed the door behind him

And in all his life, he had never slammed a door.

XXXII

Sutton breasted the river, swimming with slow, sure strokes. The water was warm against his body and it talked to him with a deep, important voice and Sutton thought: It is trying to tell me something, as it has tried to tell the people something all down through the ages. A mighty tongue talking down the land, gossiping to itself when there is no one else to hear, but trying, always trying to tell its people the news it has to sell. Some of them, perhaps, have grasped a certain truth and a certain philosophy from the river, but none of them have ever reached the meaning of the river's language, for it is an unknown language.

Like the language, Sutton thought, I used to make my notes. For they had to be in a language which no one else could read, a language that had been forgotten in the galaxy aeons before any tongue now living lisped its baby talk. Either a language that had been forgotten or one that never could be known.

I do not know that language, Sutton told himself, the language of my notes. I do not know whence it came or when or how. I asked, but they would not tell me. Johnny tried to tell me once, but I could not grasp it, for it was a thing that the brain of Man could not accept.

I know its symbols and the things they stand for, but I do not know the sounds that make it. My tongue might not be able to form the sounds that make the spoken language. For all I know it might be the language that this river talks . . . or the language of some race that went to disaster and to dust a million years ago.

The black of night came down to nestle against the black of flowing river and the moon had not risen, would not rise for many hours to come. The starlight made little diamond points on the rippling waves of the pulsing river, and on the shore ahead the lights of homes made jagged patterns up and down the land.

Herkimer has the notes, Sutton told himself, and I hope he has sense enough to hide them. For I will need them later, but not now. I would like to see Herkimer, but I can't take the chance, for they'll be watching him. And there's no doubt they have a tracer on me, but if I move fast enough, I can keep out of their way.

His feet struck gravel bottom and he let himself down, waded up the shelving shore. The night wind struck him and he shivered, for the river had been warm from a day of sun and the wind had a touch of chill.

Herkimer, of course, would be one of those who had come back to see that he wrote the book as he would have written it if there had been no interference. Herkimer and Eva . . . and of the two, Sutton told himself, he could trust Herkimer the most. For an android would fight, would fight and die for the thing that the book would say. The android and the dog and horse and honeybee and ant. But the dog and horse and honeybee and ant would never know, for they could not read.

He found a grassy bank and sat down and took off his clothes to wring them dry, then put them on again. Then he struck out across the meadow toward the highway that arrowed up the valley.

No one would find the ship at the bottom of the river . . . not for a while, at least. And a few hours was all he needed. A few hours to ask a thing that he must know, a few hours to get back to the ship again.

But he couldn't waste any time. He had to get the information the quickest way he could. For if Adams had a tracer on him, and Adams would have a tracer on him, they would already know that he had returned to Earth.

Once again came the old nagging wonder about Adams. How had Adams known that he was coming back and why had he set a mousetrap for him when he did arrive? What information had he gotten that would make him give the order that Sutton must be shot on sight?

Someone had gotten to him . . . someone who had evidence to show him. For Adams would not go on anything less than evidence. And the only person who could have given him any information would have been someone from the future. One of those, perhaps, who contended that the book must not be written, that it must not exist, that the knowledge that it held be blotted out forever. And if the man who was to write should die, what could be more simple?

Except that the book had been written. That the book already did exist. That the knowledge apparently was spread across the galaxy.

That would be catastrophe . . . for if the book were not written, then it never had existed and the whole segment of the future that had been touched by the book in any wise would be blotted out along with the book that had not been.

And that could not be, Sutton told himself.

That meant that Asher Sutton could not, would not,

be allowed to die before the book was written.

However it were written, the book must be written or the future was a lie.

Sutton shrugged. The tangled thread of logic was too much for him. There was no precept, no precedent upon which one might develop the pattern of cause and result.

Alternate futures? Maybe, but it didn't seem likely. Alternate futures were a fantasy that employed semantics twisting to prove a point, a clever use of words that covered up and masked the fallacies.

He crossed the road and took a foot path that led to a house standing on a knoll.

In the marsh down near the river, the frogs had struck up their piping and somewhere far away a wild duck called in the darkness. In the hills the whipporwills began the evening forum. The scent of new-cut grass lay heavy in the air and the smell of river night fog was crawling up the hills.

The path came out on a patio and Sutton moved across it.

A man's voice came to him.

"Good evening, sir," it said, and Sutton wheeled around.

He saw the man, then, for the first time. A man who sat in his chair and smoked his pipe beneath the evening stars.

"I hate to bother you," said Sutton, "but I wonder if I might use your visor."

"Certainly, Ash," said Adams. "Certainly. Anything you wish."

Sutton started and then felt himself freeze into a man of steel and ice.

Adams!

Of all the homes along the river, he would walk in on Adams!

Adams chuckled at him. "Destiny works against you, Ash."

Sutton moved forward, found a chair in the darkness and sat down.

"You have a pleasant place," he said.

"A very pleasant place," said Adams.

Adams tapped out his pipe and put it in his pocket.

"So you died again," he said.

"I was killed," said Sutton. "I got unkilled almost immediately."

"Some of my boys?" asked Adams. "They are hunting for you."

"A couple of strangers," said Sutton. "Some of Morgan's gang."

Adams shook his head. "I don't know the name," he said.

"He probably didn't tell his name," said Sutton. "He told you I was coming back."

"So that was it," said Adams. "The man out of the future. You have him worried, Ash."

"I need to make a visor call," said Sutton.

"You can use the visor," said Adams.

"And I need an hour."

Adams shook his head.

"I can't give you an hour."

"Half hour, then. I may have a chance to make it. A half hour after I finish my call."

"Nor a half hour, either."

"You never gamble, do you, Adams?"

"Never," said Adams.

"I do," said Sutton. He rose. "Where is that visor? I'm going to gamble on you."

"Sit down, Ash," said Adams, almost kindly. "Sit down and tell me something."

Stubbornly, Sutton remained standing.

"If you could give me your word," said Adams, "that this destiny business won't harm Man. If you could tell me it won't give aid and comfort to our enemies."

"Man hasn't any enemies," said Ash, "except the ones he's made."

"The galaxy is waiting for us to crack," said Adams. "Waiting to close in at the first faint sign of weakness."

"That's because we taught them it," said Sutton. "They watched us use their own weaknesses to push them off their feet."

"What will this destiny do?" asked Adams.

"It will teach Man humility," said Sutton. "Humility and responsibility."

"It's not a religion," said Adams. "That's what Raven told me. But it sounds like a religion . . . with all that humility pother."

"Dr. Raven was right," Sutton told him. "It's not a religion. Destiny and religions could flourish side by side and exist in perfect peace. They do not encroach upon one another. Rather, they would complement one another. Destiny stands for the same things most religions stand for and it holds out no promise of an afterlife. It leaves that to religion."

"Ash," said Adams quietly, "you have read your history."

Sutton nodded.

"Think back," said Adams. "Remember the crusades. Remember the rise of Mohammedanism. Remember Cromwell in England. Remember Germany and America. And Russia and America. Religion and ideas, Ash. Religion and ideas. Man will fight for an idea when he wouldn't lift a hand for land or life or honor. But an idea . . . that's a different thing."

"And you're afraid of an idea."

"We can't afford an idea, Ash. Not right now, at least."

"And still," Sutton told him, "it has been the ideas that have made men grow. We wouldn't have a culture or a civilization if it weren't for ideas."

"Right now," said Adams, bitterly, "men are fighting in the future over this destiny of yours."

"That's why I have to make a call," said Sutton. "That's why I need an hour."

Adams rose heavily to his feet.

"I may be making a mistake," he said. "It's something I have never done in all my life. But for once I'll gamble."

He led the way across the patio and into a dimly lighted room, furnished with old-fashioned furniture.

"Jonathon," he called.

Feet pattered in the hall and the android came into the room.

"A pair of dice," said Adams, heavily. "Mr. Sutton and I are about to gamble."

"Dice, sir?"

"Yes, that pair you and the cook are using."

"Yes, sir," said Jonathon.

He turned and disappeared and Sutton listened to his feet going through the house, fainter and fainter.

Adams turned to face him.

"One throw each," he said. "High man wins."

Sutton nodded, tense.

"If you win you get the hour," said Adams. "If I win you take my orders."

"I'll throw with you," said Sutton. "On terms like that, I'm willing to gamble."

And he was thinking:

I filted the battered ship on Cygni VII and manenuvered it through space. I was the engine and the pilot, the tubes and navigator. Energy garnered by my body took the ship and lifted it and drove it through space . . . eleven years through space. I brought the ship tonight down through atmosphere with the engines dead so it could not be spotted and I landed in the river. I could pick a book out of that case and carry it to the table without laying hands on it and I could turn the pages without the use of fingertips.

But dice.

Dice are different.

They roll so fast and topple so.

"Win or lose," said Adams, "you can use the visor."

"If I lose," said Sutton, "I won't need it."

Jonathon came back and laid the dice upon a tabletop. He hesitated for a moment and when he saw that the two humans were waiting for him to go, he went.

Sutton nodded at the dice carelessly.

"You first," he said.

Adams picked them up, held them in his fist and shook them, and their clicking was like the porcelain chatter of badly frightened teeth.

His fist came down above the table and his fingers opened and the little white cubes spun and whirled on the polished top. They came to rest and one was a five and the other one a six.

Adams raised his eyes to Sutton and there was nothing in them. No triumph. Absolutely nothing.

"Your turn," said Adams.

Perfect, thought Sutton. Nothing less than perfect. Two sixes. It has to be two sixes.

He stretched out his hand and picked up the dice,

shook them in his fist, felt the shape and size of them rolling in his palm.

Now take them in your mind, he told himself . . . take them in your mind as well as in your fist. Hold them in your mind, make them a part of you, as you made the two ships you drove through space, as you could make a book or chair or a flower you wished to pick.

He changed for a moment and his heart faltered to a stop and the blood slowed to a trickle in his arteries and veins and he was not breathing. He felt the energy system take over, the other body that drew raw energy from anything that might have energy.

His mind reached out and took the dice and shook them inside the prison of his fist and he brought his hand down with a swooping gesture and let his fingers loose and the dice came dancing out.

They were dancing in his brain, too, as well as on the tabletop and he saw them, or sensed them, or was aware of them, as if they were a part of him. Aware of the sides that had the six black dots and the sides with one and all the other sides.

But they were slippery to handle, hard to make go the way he wanted them to go and for a fearful, agonizing second it seemed almost as if the spinning cubes had minds and personalities that were their very own.

One of them was a six and the other still was rolling. The six was coming up and it toppled for a moment, threatening to fall back.

A push, thought Sutton. Just a little push. But with brain power instead of finger power.

The six came up and the two dice lay there, both of them showing sixes.

Sutton drew in a sobbing breath and his heart beat once again and the blood pumped through the veins.

They stood in silence for a moment, staring at one another across the tabletop.

Adams spoke and his voice was quiet and one could not have guessed from any tone he used what he might have felt.

"The visor is over there," he said.

Sutton bowed, ever so slightly, and he felt foolish doing it, like a character out of some incredibly old and bad piece of romantic fiction.

"Destiny," he said, "still is working for me. When it comes to the pinch, destiny is there."

"Your hour will start," said Adams, "as soon as you finish talking."

He turned smartly and walked back to the patio, very stiff and straight.

Now that he had won, Sutton suddenly was weak, and he walked to the visor on legs that seemed to have turned to rubber.

He sat down before the visor and took out the directory that he needed.

INFormation. And the subheading.

Geography, historic, North America.

He found the number and dialed it and the glass lit up.

The robot said: "Can I be of service, sir?"

"Yes," said Sutton, "I would like to know where Wisconsin was."

"Where are you now, sir?"

"I am at the residence of Mr. Christopher Adams."

"The Mr. Adams who is with the Department of Galactic Investigation?"

"The same," said Sutton.

"Then," the robot said, "you are in Wisconsin."

"Bridgeport?" asked Sutton.

"It was on the Wisconsin River, on the north bank, a

matter of seven miles above the junction with the Mississippi."

"But those rivers? I've never heard of them."

"You are near them now, sir. The Wisconsin flows into the Mississippi just below the point where you are now."

Sutton rose shakily and crossed the room, went out on the patio.

Adams was lighting up his pipe.

"You got what you wanted?" he asked.

Sutton nodded.

"Get going, then," said Adams. "Your hour's already started."

Sutton hesitated.

"What is it, Ash?"

"I wonder," said Sutton, "I wonder if you would shake my hand."

"Why, sure," said Adams.

He rose ponderously to his feet and held out his hand.

"I don't know which," said Adams, "but you are either the greatest man or the biggest damn fool that I have ever known."

XXXIII

BRIDGEPORT dreamed in its rock-hemmed niche alongside the swiftly flowing river. The summer sun beat down into the pocket between the tree-mantled cliffs with a fierceness that seemed to squeeze the last hope of life and energy out of everything . . . out of the weather-beaten houses, out of the dust that lay along the street, out of the leaf-wilted shrub and bush and beaten rows of flowers.

The railroad tracks curved around a bluff and entered the town, then curved around another bluff and were gone again, and for the short span of this arc out of somewhere into nowhere they shone in the sun with the burnished sharpness of a whetted knife. Between the tracks and river the railroad station drowsed, a four-square building that had the look of having hunched its shoulders against summer sun and winter cold for so many years that it stood despondent and cringing, waiting for the next whiplash of weather or of fate.

Sutton stood on the station platform and listened to the river, the suck and swish of tiny whirlpools that ran along the shore, the gurgle of water flowing across a hidden, upward-canted log, the soft sigh of watery fingers grasping at the tip of a downward-drooping branch. And above it all, cutting through it all, the real noise of the river . . . the tongue that went talking down the land, the sound made of many other sounds, the deep muted roar that told of power and purpose.

He lifted his head and squinted against the sun to follow the mighty metal span that leaped across the river from the bluff-top, slanting down toward the high-graded road-bed that walked across the gently rising valley on the other shore.

Man leaped rivers on great spans of steel and he never heard the talk of rivers as they rolled down to the sea. Man leaped seas on wings powered by smooth, sleek engines and the thunder of the sea was a sound lost in the empty vault of sky. Man crossed space in metallic cylinders that twisted time and space and hurled Man and his miraculous machines down alleys of conjectural mathematics that were not even dreamed of in this world of Bridgeport, 1977.

Man was in a hurry and he went too far, too fast. So far and fast that he missed many things . . . things that he should have taken time to learn as he went along . . . things that someday in some future age he would take the time to study. Someday Man would come back along the trail again and learn the things he'd missed and wonder why he missed them and think upon the years that were lost for never knowing them.

Sutton stepped down from the platform and found a faint footpath that went down to the river. Carefully, he made his way along it, for it was soft and crumbly and there were stones that one must be careful not to step upon, since they might turn beneath one's foot.

At the end of the footpath he found the old man. The oldster sat perched on a small boulder planted in the mud and he held a cane pole slanted river-wise across his knees. An odoriferous pipe protruded from a two-weeks growth of graying whiskers and an earthenware jug with a corncob for a cork sat beside him, easy to his hand.

Sutton sat down cautiously on the shelving shore beside the boulder and wondered at the coolness of the shade from the trees and undergrowth—a welcome coolness after the fierce splash of sun upon the village just a few rods up the bank.

"Catching anything?" he asked.

"Nope," said the old man.

He puffed away at his pipe and Sutton watched in fascinated silence. One would have sworn, he told himself, that the mop of whiskers was on fire.

"Didn't catch nothing yesterday, either," the old man told him.

He took his pipe out of his mouth with a deliberate, considered motion and spat with studied concentration into the center of a river eddy.

"Didn't catch nothing the day before yesterday," he volunteered.

"You want to catch something, don't you?" Sutton asked.

"Nope," said the old geezer.

He put down a hand and lifted the jug, worked out the corncob cork and wiped the jug's neck carefully with a dirty hand.

"Have a snort," he invited, holding out the jug.

Sutton, remembering the dirty hand, took it, gagging silently. Cautiously, he lifted it and tipped it to his mouth.

The stuff splashed into his mouth and gurgled down his throat and it was liquid fire laced with gall and with a touch of brimstone to give it something extra.

Sutton snatched the jug away and held it by the handle, keeping his mouth wide open to cool it and air out the taste.

The old man took it back and Sutton swabbed at the tears running down his cheeks.

"Ain't aged the way she should be," the old man apologized. "But I ain't got the time to fool around with that."

He took himself a hooker; wiped his mouth with the back of his hand and whooshed out his breath in gusty satisfaction. A butterfly, fluttering past, dropped stone-dead.

The old man put out a foot and pushed at the butterfly.

"Feeble thing," he said.

He put the jug down again and worked the cork in tight.

"Stranger, ain't you?" he asked Sutton. "Don't recall seeing you around."

Sutton nodded. "Looking for some people by the name of Sutton. John H. Sutton."

The old man chuckled. "Old John, eh? Him and me was kids together. Sneakiest little rascal that I ever knew. Ain't worth a tinker's damn, old John ain't. Went off to law school and got him an education. But he didn't make a go of it. Roosting out on a farm up on the ridge, over there across the river."

He shot a look at Sutton. "You ain't no relative of his, are you?"

"Well," said Sutton, "not exactly. Not very close, at least."

"Tomorrow's the Fourth," said the old man, "and I recollect the time that John and me blew up a culvert in

Campbell Hollow, come the Fourth. Found some dynamite a road gang had been using for blasting. John and me, we figured it would make a bigger bang if we confined it, sort of. So we put her in the culvert pipe and lit a long fuse. Mister, it blew that culvert all to hell. I recollect our dads like to took the hide off us for doing it."

Dead ringer, thought Sutton. John H. Sutton is just across the river and tomorrow is the Fourth. July 4, 1977, that's what the letter said.

And I didn't have to ask. The old codger up and told me.

The sun was a furnace blast from the river's surface, but here, underneath the trees, one just caught the edge of the flare of heat. A leaf floated by and there was a grasshopper riding on it. The grasshopper tried to jump ashore, but his jump fell short and the current grabbed him and swallowed him and took him out of sight.

"Never had a chance," said the old man, "that hopper didn't. Wickedest river in these United States, the old Wisconsin is. Can't trust her. Tried to run steamboats on her in the early days, but they couldn't do it, for where there was a channel one day there'd be a sand bar on the next. Current shifts the sand something awful. Government fellow wrote a report on her once. Said the only way you could use the Wisconsin for navigation was to lathe and plaster it."

From far overhead came the rumble of traffic crossing the bridge. A train came by, chuffing and grinding, a long freight that dragged itself up the valley. Long after it had passed, Sutton heard its whistle hooting like a lost voice for some unseen crossing.

"Destiny," said the old man, "sure wasn't working worth a hoot for that hopper, was it?"

Sutton sat bolt upright, stammering. "What was that you said?"

"Don't mind me," the old man told him. "I go around mumbling to myself. Sometimes people hear me and think that I'm crazy."

"But destiny? You said something about destiny."

"Interested in it, lad," said the old man. "Wrote a story about it once. Didn't amount to much. Used to mess around some, writing, in my early days."

Sutton relaxed and lay back.

A dragonfly skimmed the water's surface. Far up the bank, a small fish jumped and left a widening circle in the water.

"About this fishing," said Sutton. "You don't seem to care whether you catch anything or not."

"Rather not," the old man told him. "Catch something and you got to take it off the hook. Then you got to bait up again and throw the hook back in the river. Then you got to clean the fish. It's an awful sight of work."

He took the pipe out of his mouth and spat carefully into the river.

"Ever read Thoreau, son?"

Sutton shook his head, trying to remember. The name struck a chord of memory. There had been a fragment in a book of ancient literature in his college days. All that was left of what was believed to have been an extensive piece of writing.

"You ought to," the old man told him. "He had the right idea, Thoreau did."

Sutton rose and dusted off his trousers.

"Stick around," the old man said. "You ain't bothering me. Hardly at all."

"Got to be getting along," said Sutton.

"Hunt me up some other time," the old man said. "We could talk some more. My name is Cliff, but they call me Old Cliff now. Just ask for Old Cliff. Everybody knows me."

"Someday," Sutton said politely, "I'll do just that."

"Care for another snort before you go?"

"No, thank you," said Sutton, backing off. "No, thank you very much."

"Oh, well," the old man said. He lifted the jug and took a long and gurgling drink. He lowered the jug and whooshed out his breath, but it was not so spectacular this time. There was no butterfly.

Sutton climbed the bank to the blaze of sun again.

"Sure," said the station agent, "the Suttons live just across the river, over in Grant County. Several ways to get there. Which one would you like?"

"The longest one," Sutton told him. "I'm not in any hurry."

The moon was coming up when Sutton climbed the hill to reach the bridge.

He was in no hurry, for he had all night.

XXXIV

THE LAND was wild . . . wilder than anything Sutton had ever seen on the lawn-mowered, trimmed and watered parks of his native Earth. The land tilted upward, as if it rested on a knife edge, and it was littered by great clumps of stone which appeared to have been flung down in god-like anger by a giant hand out of forgotten time. Stark bluffs speared upward, soaring massively, masked by mighty trees that seemed to have strived, at one time, to match the height and dignity of the rocky cliffs. But now they stood defeated, content to be less than the very cliffs, but with a certain dignity and patience learned, no doubt, through their ancient striving.

Summer flowers huddled in the spaces between the strewn rocks or clung close to the mossy root-mounds of the larger trees. A squirrel sat on a limb somewhere and chattered half in anger, half in rapture at the rising sun.

Sutton toiled upward, following the rock-filled ravine from the river road. At times he walked, but more often he went on hands and knees, clawing his way up the slope.

He stopped often and stood with heels dug in and back resting against a tree, wiping the perspiration from his dripping face. In the valley below, the river that had seemed roiled and muddy as he walked along it on the road had assumed a blueness that challenged the very blueness of the sky which it reflected. And the air was crystal clear above it, clearer than the air had ever seemed before. A hawk dived down across the gulf of space between the blueness of the sky and the blueness of the river and it seemed to Sutton that he could see each separate feather in the folded wings.

Once, through the trees, he glimpsed the break in the cliffs ahead and knew that he was at the place that old John Sutton had mentioned in his letter.

The sun was only a couple of hours high and there still was time. There still would be time, for John Sutton had talked to the man only a couple of hours or so and then had gone to dinner.

From there on, with the cleft of the cliff in sight, Sutton took his time. He reached the top and found the boulder that his old ancestor had spoken of and it was appropriate for sitting.

He sat upon it and stared across the valley and was grateful for the shade.

And there was peace, as John Sutton had said there was. Peace and the quieting majesty of the scene before him . . . the strange third-dimensional quality of the space that hung, as if alive, above the river valley. Strangeness, too, the strangeness of expected . . . and unexpected . . . happenings.

He looked at his watch and it was half past nine, so he left the boulder and lay down behind a patch of brush and waited. Almost as he did, there was a soft, smooth swish of motor-noise and a ship came down, a tiny one-man ship, slanting across the trees, to land in the pasture just beyond the fence.

A man got out and leaned against the ship, staring at the sky and trees, as if he were satisfying himself that he had reached his destination.

Sutton chuckled quietly to himself.

Stage setting, he said. Dropping in unexpectedly and with a crippled ship . . . no need to explain your presence. Waiting for a man to come walking up and talk to you. Most natural thing in all the world. You didn't seek him out, he saw you and came to you and of course he talked.

You couldn't come walking up the road and turn in at the gate and knock at the door and say:

"I came to pick up all the scandal and the dirt I can about the Sutton family. I wonder if I might sit down and talk with you."

But you could land in a pasture with a crippled ship and first you'd talk of corn and pasture, of weather and of grass, and finally you'd get around to talking about personal and family matters.

The man had gotten out his wrench now and was tinkering at the ship.

It must almost be time.

Sutton lifted himself on his arms and stared through the close-laced branches of the hazel brush.

John H. Sutton was coming down the hill, a big-bellied man with a trim white beard and an old black hat, and his walk was a waddle with some swagger in it.

XXXV

So THIS is failure, Eva Armour thought. This is how failure feels. Dry in the throat and heavy in the heart and tiredness in the brain.

I am bitter, she told herself, and I have a right to be. Although I am so tired with trying and with failure that the knife edge of bitterness is dulled.

"The psych-tracer in Adams' office has stopped," Herkimer had said and then the plate had gone dead as he cut the visor.

There was no trace of Sutton and the tracer had gone dead.

That meant that Sutton was dead and he could not be dead, for historically he had written a book and as yet he had not written it.

Although history was something that you couldn't trust. It was put together wrong, or copied wrong, or misinterpreted, or improved upon by a man with a misplaced imagination. Truth was so hard to keep, myth and fable so easy to breathe into a life that was more logical and more acceptable than truth.

Half the history of Sutton, Eva knew, must be purely

apocryphal. And yet there were certain truths that must be truths indeed.

` Someone had written a book and it would have had to be Sutton, for no one else could break the language in which his notes were written and the words themselves breathed the very sincerity of the man himself.

Sutton had died, but not on Earth nor in Earth's solar system and not at the age of sixty. He had died on a planet circling some far star and he had not died for many, many years.

These were truths that could not well be twisted. These were truths that had to stand until they were disproved.

And yet the tracer had stopped.

Eva got up from her chair and walked across the room to the window that looked out on the landscaped grounds of the Orion Arms. Fireflies were dotting the bushes with their brief, cold flame and the late moon was coming up behind a cloud that looked like a gentle hill.

So much work, she thought. So many years of planning. Androids who had worn no mark upon their forehead and who had been formed to look exactly like the humans they replaced. And other androids who had marks upon their foreheads, but who had not been the androids made in the laboratories of the eightieth century. Elaborate networks of espionage, waiting for the day Sutton would come home. Years of puzzling over the records of the past, trying to separate the truth from the half-truth and the downright error.

Years of watching and of waiting, parrying the counter-espionage of the Revisionists, laying the groundwork for the day of action. And being careful . . . always careful. For the eightieth century must not know, must not even guess.

But there had been unseen factors.

Morgan had come back and warned Adams that Sutton must be killed.

Two humans had been planted on the asteroid.

Although those two factors could not account entirely for what had happened. There was another factor somewhere.

She stood at the window, looking out at the rising moon, and her brows knit into crinkling lines of thought. But she was too tired. No thought would come.

Except defeat.

Defeat would explain it all.

Sutton might be dead and that would be defeat, utter and complete defeat. Victory for an officialdom that was at once too timid and too vicious to take any active part in the struggle of the book. An officialdom that sought to keep the *status quo*, willing to wipe out centuries of thought to safely maintain its foothold in the galaxy.

Such a defeat, she knew, would be even worse than a defeat by the Revisionists, for if the Revisionists had won, there still would be a book, there still would be the teaching of Man's own destiny. And that, she told herself, was better than no inkling of destiny at all.

Behind her, the visaphone purred, and she spun around, hurried across the room.

A robot said, "Mr. Sutton called. He asked about Wisconsin."

"Wisconsin?"

"It's an old place name," the robot said. "He asked about a place called Bridgeport, Wisconsin."

"As if he were going there?"

"As if he were going there," the robot said.

"Quick," said Eva, "tell me. Where is this Bridgeport?"

"Five or six miles away," said the robot, "and at least four thousand years."

She caught her breath. "In time," she said.

"Yes, miss, in time."

"Tell me exactly," Eva told him, but the robot shook his head.

"I don't know. I couldn't catch it. His mind was all roiled up. He'd just come through a trying experience."

"Then you don't know."

"I wouldn't bother if I were you," the robot told her. "He struck me as a man who knew what he was doing. He'll come out all right."

"You're sure of that?"

"I'm sure of it," the robot said.

Eva snapped the visor off and walked back to the window.

Ash, she thought. Ash, my love, you simply have to be all right. You must know what you're doing. You must come back to us and you must write the book and . . .

Not for me alone, she said. Not for me alone, for I, least of all of them, have a claim on you. But the galaxy has a claim on you, and maybe someday the universe. The little striving lives are waiting for your words and the hope and dignity they spell. And most of all the dignity, she said. Dignity ahead of hope. The dignity of equality—the dignity of the knowledge that all life is on an equal basis, that life is all that matters, that life is the badge of a greater brotherhood than anything the mind of Man has ever spelled out in all its theorizing.

And I, she thought. I have no right to think the way I do, to feel the way I do.

But I can't help it, Ash.

I can't help but love you, Ash.

Someday, she said. Someday.

She stood straight and lonely and the tears came in her eyes and trickled down her cheeks and she did not raise her hand to wipe them off.

Dreams, she said. Broken dreams are bad enough. But the dream that has no hope . . . the dream that is doomed long before it's broken, that's the worst of all.

XXXVI

A DRY stick cracked under Sutton's feet and the man with
the wrench slowly turned around. A swift, smooth smile
spread upon his face and spread out in widening crinkles
to hide the amazement that glittered in his eyes.

"Good afternoon," said Sutton.

John H. Sutton was a speck that had almost climbed
the hill. The sun had passed its zenith and was swinging
toward the west. Down in the river's valley a half-dozen
crows were cawing and it was as if the sound came from
underneath their feet.

The man held out his hand. "Mr. Sutton, isn't it?" he
asked. "The Mr. Sutton, of the eightieth."

"Drop the wrench," said Sutton.

The man pretended not to hear him. "My name is
Dean," he said. "Arnold Dean. I'm from the eighty-
fourth."

"Drop the wrench," said Sutton and Dean dropped it.
Sutton hooked it along the ground with a toe until it
was out of reach.

"That is better," he said. "Now, let's sit down and
talk."

Dean gestured with a thumb. "The old man will be

coming back," he said. "He will get to wondering and he will come back. He had a lot of questions he forgot to ask."

"Not for a while," Sutton told him. "Not until he's eaten and had an after-dinner nap."

Dean grunted and eased himself to a sitting position, back against the ship.

"Random factors," he said. "That's what balls the detail up. You're a random factor, Sutton. It wasn't planned this way."

Sutton sat down easily and picked up the wrench. He weighed it in his hand. Blood, he thought, talking to the wrench. You'll have blood upon one end before the day is out.

"Tell me," said Dean. "Now that you are here, what do you plan to do?"

"Easy," said Sutton. "You're going to talk to me. You're going to tell me something that I need to know."

"Gladly," Dean agreed.

"You said you came from the eighty-fourth. What year?"

"Eighty-three eighty-six," said Dean. "But if I were you, I'd go up a little ways. You'd find more to interest you."

"But you figure I'll never get even so far as that," said Sutton. "You think that you will win."

"Of course I do," said Dean.

Sutton dug into the ground with the wrench.

"A while ago," he said, "I found a man who died very shortly after. He recognized me and he made a sign, with his fingers raised."

Dean spat upon the ground.

"Android," he said. "They worship you, Sutton. They made a religion out of you. Because, you see, you gave

216

them hope to cling to. You gave them something equal, something that made them, in one way, the equal of Man."

"I take it," Sutton said, "you don't believe a thing I wrote."

"Should I?"

"I do," said Sutton.

Dean said nothing.

"You have taken the thing I wrote," said Sutton, evenly, "and you are trying to use it to fashion one more rung in the ladder of Man's vanity. You have missed the point entirely. You have no sense of destiny because you gave destiny no chance."

And he felt foolish even as he said it, for it sounded so much like preaching. So much like what the men of old had said of faith when faith was just a word, before it had become a force to really reckon with. Like the old-time Bible-pounding preachers, who wore cowhide boots and whose iron-gray hair was rumpled and whose flowing beard was stained with tobacco juice.

"I won't lecture you," he said, angry at the smooth way Dean had put him on the defensive. "I won't preach at you. You either accept destiny or you ignore it. So far as I'm concerned I'll not raise a hand to convince any single man. The book I wrote tells you what I know. You can take it or you can leave it . . . it's all the same to me."

"Sutton," said Dean, "you're batting your head against a stone wall. You haven't got a chance. You're fighting humankind. The whole human race against you . . . and nothing's ever stood against the human race. All you have is a pack of measly androids and a few renegade humans . . . the kind of humans that used to swarm to the old cult-worships."

"The empire is built on androids and robots," Sutton

told him. "They can throw you for a loss any time they want to. Without them you couldn't hold a single foot of ground outside the Solar system."

"They will stick with us in the empire business," Dean told him, very confident. "They may fight us on this business of destiny, but they'll stay with us because they can't get along without us. They can't reproduce, you know. And they can't make themselves. They have to have humans to keep their race going, to replace the ones who get knocked off."

He chuckled. "Until one android can create another android, they will stick with us and they will work with us. For if they didn't, that would be racial suicide."

"What I can't understand," said Sutton, "is how you know which ones are fighting you and which are sticking with you."

"That," said Dean, "is the hell of it ... we don't. If we did, we'd make short work of this lousy war. The android who fought you yesterday may shine your shoes tomorrow, and how are you to know? The answer is, you don't."

He picked up a tiny stone and flicked it out on the pasture grass.

"Sutton," he said, "it's enough to drive you nuts. No battles, really. Just guerrilla skirmishes here and there, when one small task force sent out to do a time-fixing job is ambushed by another task force sent out by the other side to intercept them."

"As I intercepted you," said Sutton.

"Huh ..." said Dean, and then he brightened. "Why, sure," he said, "as you intercepted me."

One moment Dean was sitting with his back against the machine, talking as if he meant to keep on talking ... and in the next moment his body was a fluid blaze of motion, jackknifing upward and forward in a lunge toward the wrench that Sutton held.

Sutton moved instinctively, toes tightening their grip upon the ground, leg muscles flexing to drive his body upward, arm starting to jerk the wrench away.

But Dean had the advantage of one long second's start.

Sutton felt the wrench ripped from his grip, saw the flash of it in the sun as Dean swung it upward for the blow.

Dean's lips were moving and even as he tried to duck, even as he tried to throw up his arms to shield his head, Sutton read the words the other's lips were saying.

"So you thought it would be me!"

Pain exploded inside Sutton's head and for one surprised instant he knew that he was falling, the ground rushing upward at his face. Then there was no ground, but only darkness that he fell through for long eternities.

XXXVII

Tricked!

Tricked by a smooth character from five hundred years ahead in time.

Tricked by a letter from six thousand years out of the past.

Tricked, said Sutton, by my own muddle-headedness.

He sat up and held his head in his hands and felt the westering sun against his back, heard the squalling of a catbird in the blackberry patch and the sound of the wind as it ran along the corn rows.

Tricked and trapped, he said.

He took his hands from his head and there in the trampled grass lay the wrench with the blood upon it. Sutton spread out his fingers and blood was on them, too... warm and sticky blood. Gingerly he touched his head with gentle hand and his hair was matted down.

Pattern, he said. It all runs in a pattern.

Here am I and there is the wrench and just beyond the fence is the field of corn that is better than knee-high on this splendid afternoon of July 4, 1977.

The ship is gone and in another hour or so John H. Sutton will come waddling down the hill to ask the questions that he forgot to ask before. And ten years from now he will write a letter and in it he will record his suspicions concerning me and I will be in the farmyard at the very moment pumping me a drink.

Sutton staggered to his feet and stood in the empty afternoon, with the sweep of sky above the horizon of the ridge and the panorama of the winding river far down the slope below.

He touched the wrench with his toe and thought, I could break the pattern. I could take the wrench and then John H. would never find it and with one thing in the pattern changed the end might not be the same.

I read the letter wrong, he thought. I always figured it would be the other man, not me. It never once occurred to me that it was my blood upon the wrench and that I would be the one who would steal the clothes from off the line.

And yet there were certain things that didn't track. He still had his clothes and there would be no need to steal. His ship was still resting on the river's bottom and there was no need to stay.

Yet it had happened once before, for if it had not happened, why had there been the letter? The letter had made him come here and the letter had been written because he had come, so he must have come before. And in that other time he'd stayed . . . and stayed only because he could not get away. This time he would go back, this time he need not stay.

A second chance, he thought. I've been given another chance.

Yet that wasn't right, for if there had been a second time, old John H. would have known about it. And there couldn't be a second time, for this was the very day that

John H. had talked to the man out of the future.

Sutton shook his head.

There had been only one time that this had happened, and this, of course, was it.

Something will happen, he told himself. Something that will not let me go back. Somehow I will be forced to steal the clothes and in the end I'll walk to that farmhouse up there and ask if they need a hand for harvest.

For the pattern was set. It *had* to be set.

Sutton touched the wrench with his toe again, pondering.

Then he turned and went down the hill. Glancing over his shoulder as he plunged into the woods, he saw old John H. coming down the hill.

XXXVIII

FOR THREE DAYS Sutton toiled to free the ship from the tons of sand that the treacherous, swift-running river currents had mounded over it. And admitted, when three days were gone, that it was a hopeless task, for the current piled up the sand as fast as he could clear it.

From there on he concentrated on clearing an opening to the entrance lock, and after another day and many cave-ins, he accomplished his purpose.

Wearily he braced himself against the metal of the ship.

A gamble, he told himself. But I will have to gamble.

For there was no possibility of wrenching the ship free by using the engines. The tubes, he knew, were packed with sand and any attempt to throw in the rockets would simply mean that he and the ship and a good portion of the landscape would evaporate in a flashing puff of atomic fury.

He had lifted a ship from a Cygnian planet and driven it across eleven years of space by the power of mind alone. He had rolled two sixes.

Perhaps, he told himself. Perhaps...

There were tons of sand and he was deathly tired, tired

despite the smooth, efficient functioning of his non-human system of metabolism.

I rolled two sixes, he said.

Once I rolled two sixes and surely that was harder than the task I must do now. Although that called for deftness and this will call for power ... and suppose, just suppose I haven't got the strength.

For it would take strength to lift this buried mass of metal out of the mound of sand. Not the strength of muscles, but the strength of mind.

Of course, he told himself, if he could not lift the ship he still could use the time-mover, shift the ship, lying where it was, forward six thousand years. Although there were hazards he did not like to think about. For in shifting the ship through time, he would be exposing it to every threat and vagary of the river through the whole six thousand years.

He put his hand up to his throat, feeling for the key chain that hung around his neck.

And there was no chain!

Mind dulled by sudden terror, he stood frozen for a moment.

Pockets, he thought, but his hands fumbled with a dread certainty that there was no hope. For he never put the keys in his pockets ... always on their chain around his neck where they would be safe.

He searched, feverishly at first, then with a grim, cold thoroughness.

His pockets held no key.

The chain broke, he thought in frantic desperation. The chain broke and it fell inside my clothes. He patted himself, carefully, from head to foot, and it was not there. He tossed the shirt aside and, sitting down, pulled off his trousers, searching in their folds, turning them inside out.

And there was no key.

On hands and knees, he searched the sands of the river bed, fumbling in the dim light that filtered through the rushing water.

An hour later he gave up.

The shifting, water-driven sand already had closed the trench he had dug to the lock and there was now no point of getting to the lock, for he could not open it when he got there.

His shirt and trousers had vanished with the current.

Wearily, beaten, he turned toward the shore, forcing his way through the stubborn water. His head broke into open air and the first stars of evening were shining in the east.

On shore he sat down with his back against a tree. He took one breath and then another, willed the first heartbeat, then the second and a third ... nursed the human metabolism back into action once again.

The river gurgled at him, deep laughter on its tongue. In the wooded valley a whippoorwill began his measured chugging. Fireflies danced through the blackness of the bushes.

A mosquito stung him and he slapped at it futilely.

A place to sleep, he thought. A hay-loft in a barn, perhaps. And pilfered food from a farmer's garden to fill his empty belly. Then clothes.

At least he knew where he'd get the clothes.

XXXIX

SUNDAYS WERE lonely.

During the rest of the week there was work—physical labor—for a man to do, the endless, trudging round of work that is necessary to extract a living from the soil. Land to plow, crops to be put in and tended and finally harvested, wood to cut, fences to be built and mended, machines to be repaired—things that must be done with bone and muscle, with calloused hand and aching back and the hot sun on one's neck or the whiplash of windy cold biting at one's bones.

For six days a farmer labored and the labor was a thing that dulled one to the aching emptiness of memory and at night, when work was done, sleep was swift and merciful. There were times when the work, not only for its sedative effect but of its very self, became a thing of interest and of satisfaction. The straight line of new-set fence posts became a minor triumph when one glanced back along their length. The harvest field, with its dust upon one's hoes and its smell of sun on golden straw and the clacking of the binder as it went its rounds, became a full-breasted symbolism of plenty and contentment. And there were moments when the pink blush of apple blossoms shining through the silver rain of spring became a wild and pagan paean of the resurrection of the Earth from the frosts of winter.

For six days a man would labor and would not have time to think; on the seventh day he rested and braced himself for the loneliness and the thoughts of desperation that idleness would bring.

Not a loneliness for a people or a world or a way of life, for this world was kindlier and closer to Earth and life and safer—much safer—than the world one had left behind. But a nagging loneliness, an accusing loneliness that talked of a job that waited, a piece of work that now might wait forever, a task that must be done, but now might never be done.

At first there had been hope.

Surely, Sutton thought, they will look for me. Surely they will find a way to reach me.

The thought was a comfort that he hugged close against himself, a peace of mind that he could not bring himself to analyze too closely. For he realized, even as he coddled it, that it was a generalization, that it might not survive too close a scrutiny, that it was fashioned of faith and of wishful thinking and that for all its wealth of comfort it might be a fragile bauble.

The past cannot be changed, he argued with himself, in its entirety. It can be altered—subtly. It can be twisted and it can be dented and it can be whittled down, but by and large it stands. And that is why I'm here, that must be why I'm here, and I'll have to stay until old John H. writes the letter to himself. For the past is in the letter—the letter brought me here and it will keep me here until it's finally written. Up to that point the pattern must necessarily hold, for up to that point in time the past, so far as I and my relation with it are concerned, is a known and revealed past. But the moment the letter is written it becomes an unknown past, it tends to the speculative and there is no known pattern. After the letter's written, so far as I'm concerned anything can happen.

Although he admitted, even as he thought it, that his premise was fallacious. For known or not, revealed or unrevealed, the past would form a pattern. For the past had happened. He was living in a time that already had been set and molded.

Although even in that thought there was a hope, even in the unknownness of the past and the knowledge that by and large what had happened was a thing that stood unchanged, there must be hope. For somewhere, some-when he had written a book. The book existed and there-fore had happened, although so far as he was concerned it had not happened yet. But he had seen two copies of th? book and that meant that in some future age the book was a factor in the pattern of the past.

Sometime, said Sutton, they will find me. Sometime before it is too late.

They will hunt for me and find me. They will have to find me.

They? he asked himself, finally honest with himself.

Herkimer, an android.

Eva Armour, a woman.

They . . . two people.

But not those two alone. Surely not those two alone. Back of them, like a shadowy army, all the other androids and all the robots that Man had ever fashioned. And here and there a human who saw the rightness of the proposi-tion that Man could not, by mere self-assertion, be a spe-cial being; understanding that it was his greater glory to take his place among the other things of life, as a simple thing of life, as a form of life that could lead and teach and be a friend rather than a thing that conquered and ruled and stood as one apart.

They would look for him, of course, but where?

With all of time and all of space to search in, how would they know when and where to look?

The robot at the information center, he remembered, could tell them that he had inquired about and ancient town called Bridgeport. And that would tell them where. But no one could tell them when.

For no one knew about the letter ... absolutely no one. He remembered how the dried and flaky mucilage had showered down across his hands in a white and aged powder when his thumbnail had cracked loose the flap of the envelope. No one, certainly, had seen the contents of that letter since the day it had been written until he, himself, had opened it.

He realized now that he should have gotten word to someone ... word of where and when he was going and what he meant to do. But he had been so confident and it had seemed such a simple thing, such a splendid plan.

A splendid plan in the very directness of its action ... to intercept the Revisionist, to knock him out and take his ship and go forward into time to take his place. It could have been arranged, of that he was certain. There would have been an android somewhere to help fashion his disguise, there would have been papers in the ship and androids from the future to brief him on the things that he would have to know.

A splendid plan ... except it hadn't worked.

I could have told the information robot, Sutton told himself. He certainly was one of us. He would have passed the word along.

He sat with his back against the tree and stared out across the river valley, hazy with the blue of the Indian summer. In the field below him the corn stood in brown and golden shocks, like a village of wigwams that clustered tight and warm against the sure knowledge of the winter's coming. To the west the bluffs of the Mississippi were a purple cloud that crouched close against the land. To the north the golden land swept up in low hill rising on low hill until it reached a misty point where, somewhere, land stopped and sky began, although one could not find the definite dividing point, no clear-cut pencil mark that held the two apart.

A bluejay flashed down across the sky and came to rest upon a sun-washed fence post. It jerked its tail and squalled, scolding anything that might be within its hearing.

A field mouse came out of a corn shock and looked at Sutton for a moment with its beady eyes, then squeaked in sudden fright and whisked into the shock again, its tail looped above its back in frantic alarm.

Simple folk, thought Sutton. The little, simple, furry folk. They would be with me, too, if they could only know. The bluejay and the field mouse, the owl and hawk and squirrel. A brotherhood, he thought . . . the brotherhood of life.

He heard the mouse rustling in the shock and he tried to imagine what life as a mouse might mean. Fear first of all, of course, the ever-present, quivering, overriding fear of other life, of owl and hawk, of mink and fox and skunk. And the fear of Man and cat and dog. And the fear of Man, he said. All things fear Man. Man has made all things to fear him.

Then there would be hunger, or at least the fear and threat of hunger. And the urge to reproduce. There would be the urgency and the happiness of life, the thrill of swiftly moving feet and the sleek contentment of the well-filled belly and the sweetness of sleep . . . and what else? What else might there be to fill a mouse's life?

He crouched in a place of safety and listened and knew that all was well. All was safe and there was food and shelter against the coming cold. For he knew about the cold, not so much from the experience of other winters as from an instinct handed down through many generations of shivering in the cold and dying of the cold.

To his ears came the soft rustlings in the shock as others of his kind moved softly on their business. He smelled the sweetness of the sun-cured grass that had been brought in to fashion nests for warm and easy sleeping. And he smelled, as well, the grains of corn and the succulent weed seeds that would keep their bellies full.

All is well, he thought. All is as it should be. But one must keep watch, one must never lower one's guard, for security is a thing that can be swept away in a single instant. And we are so soft . . . we are so soft and frail, and we make good eating. A paw-step in the dark can spell swift and sure disaster. A whir of wings is the song of death.

He closed his eyes and tucked his feet beneath him and wrapped his tail around him. . . .

Sutton sat with his back against the tree and suddenly, without knowing how or when he had become so, he was rigid with the knowledge of what had happened to him.

He had closed his eyes and tucked his feet beneath him and wrapped his tail about him and he had known the simple fears and the artless, ambitionless contentment of another life . . . of a life that hid in a corn shock from the paw-steps and the wings, that slept in sun-scented grass and felt a vague but vital happiness in the sure and fundamental knowledge that there was food and warmth and shelter.

He had not felt it merely, or known it alone ... he had been the little creature, he had been the mouse that the corn shock sheltered; and at one and the same time he had been Asher Sutton, sitting with his back against a straight-trunked shellbark hickory tree, gazing out across the autumn-painted valley.

There were two of us, said Sutton. I, myself, and I, the mouse. There were two of us at once, each with his separate identity. The mouse, the real mouse, did not know it, for if he had known or guessed I would have known as well, for I was as much the mouse as I was myself.

He sat quiet and still, not a muscle moving, wonder gnawing at him. Wonder and a fear, a fear of a dormant alienness that lay within his brain.

He had brought a ship from Cygni, he had returned from death, he had rolled a six.

Now this!

A man is born and he has a body and a mind that have many functions, some of them complex, and it takes him years to learn those functions, more years to master them. Months before one takes a toddling step, months more before one shapes a word, years before thought and logic become polished tools ... and sometimes, said Sutton, sometimes they never do.

Even then there is a certain guidance, the guidance of experienced mentors ... parents at first and teachers after that and the doctors and the churches and all the men of science and the people that one meets. All the people, all the contacts, all the forces that operate to shape one into a social being capable of using the talents that he holds for the good of himself and the society which guides him and holds him to its path.

Heritage, too, thought Sutton . . . the inbred knowledge and the will to do and think certain things in a certain way. The tradition of what other men have done and the precepts that have been fashioned from the wisdom of the ages.

The normal human has one body and one mind, and Lord knows, Sutton thought, that is enough for any man to get along with. But I, to all intents, have what amounts to a second body and perhaps even a second mind, but for that second body I have no mentors and I have no heritage. I do not know how to use it yet; I'm just taking my first toddling step, I am finding out, slowly, one by one, the things that I may do. Later on, if I live long enough, I may even learn how to do them well.

But there are mistakes that one will make. A child will stumble when it walks at first, and its words to begin with are only the approximation of words and it does not know enough not to burn its finger with matches it has lighted.

"Johnny," he said. "Johnny, talk to me."

"Yes, Ash?"

"Is there more, Johnny?"

"Wait and see," said Johnny. "I cannot tell you. You must wait and see."

XL

THE ANDROID investigator said, "We checked Bridgeport back to the year 2000 and we are convinced nothing ever happened there. It was a small village and it lay off the main trunk of world happenings."

"It wouldn't have to be a big thing," Eva Armour told him. "It could have been a little thing. Just some slight clue. A word out of the context of the future, perhaps. A word that Sutton might have dropped in some unguarded moment and someone else picked up and used. Within a few years a word like that would become a part of the dialect of that community."

"We checked for the little things, miss," the investigator said. "We checked for any aberration, any hint that might point to Sutton's having been in the community. We used approved methods and we covered the field. But we found nothing, absolutely nothing. The place is barren of any leads at all."

"He must have gone there," said Eva. "The robot at the information center talked to him. He asked about Bridgeport. It indicated that he had some interest in the place."

"But it didn't necessarily indicate that he was going there," Herkimer pointed out.

"He went someplace," said Eva. "Where did he go?"

"We threw in as large a force of investigators as was possible without arousing suspicion, both locally and in the future," the investigator told them. "Our men practically fell over one another. We sent them out as book salesmen and scissors grinders and unemployed men looking for work. We canvassed every home for twenty miles around, first at twenty-year intervals, then, when we found nothing, at ten, and finally at five. If there had been any word or any rumor we would have run across it."

"Back to the year 2000, you say," said Herkimer. "Why not to 1999 or 1950?"

"We had to set an arbitrary date somewhere," the investigator told him.

"The Sutton family lived in that locality," said Eva. "I suppose you investigated them just a bit more closely."

"We had men working on the Sutton farm off and on," said the investigator. "As often as the family was in need of any help on the farm one of our men showed up to get himself the job. When the family needed no help, we had men on other farms near by. One of our men bought a tract of timber in that locality and spent ten years at woodcutting ... he could have stretched it out much longer but we were afraid someone would get suspicious.

"We did this from the year 2000 up to 3150, when the last of the family moved from the area."

Eva looked at Herkimer. "The family has been checked all the way?" she asked.

Herkimer nodded. "Right to the day that Asher left for Cygni. There's nothing that would help us."

Eva said, "It seems so hopeless. He is somewhere.

Something happened to him. The future, perhaps."

"That's what I am thinking," Herkimer told her. "The Revisionists may have intercepted him. They may be holding him."

"They couldn't hold him . . . not Asher Sutton," Eva said. "They couldn't hold him if he knew all his powers."

"But he doesn't know them," Herkimer reminded her. "And we couldn't tell him about them or draw them to his attention. He had to find them for himself. He had to be put under pressure and suddenly discover them by natural reaction. He couldn't be taught them, he had to evolve into them."

"We did so well," said Eva. "We were doing so well. We forced Morgan into ill-considered action by conditioning Benton into challenging Sutton, the one quick way to get rid of Asher when Adams failed to fall in with the plan to kill him. And that Benton incident put Asher on his guard without our having to tell him that he should be careful. And now," she said. "And now . . ."

"The book was written," Herkimer told her.

"But it doesn't have to be," said Eva. "You and I may be no more than puppets in some probability world that will pinch out tomorrow."

"We'll cover all key points in the future," Herkimer told her. "We'll redouble our espionage of the Revisionists, check back on every task force of the past. Maybe we'll learn something."

"It's the random factors," Eva said. "You can't be sure, ever. All of time and space for them to happen in. How can we know where to look or turn? Do we have to fight our way through every possible happening to get the thing we want?"

"You forgot one factor," Herkimer said calmly.

"One factor?"

"Yes, Sutton himself. Sutton is somewhere and I have a great faith in him. In him and his destiny. For, you see, he pays attention to his destiny and that will pay off in the end."

XLI

"YOU ARE a strange man, William Jones," John H. Sutton told him. "And a good one, too. I've never had a better hired hand in all the years I've farmed. None of the others would stay more than a year or two, always running off, always going somewhere."

"I have no place to go," said Asher Sutton. "There's no place I want to go. This is as good as any."

And it was better, he told himself, than he had thought it would be, for here were peace and security and a living close to nature that no man of his own age ever had experienced.

They leaned on the pasture bars and watched the twinkling of the house and auto lights from across the river. In the darkness on the slope below them the cattle, turned out after milking, moved about with quiet, soft sounds, cropping a last few mouthfuls of grass before settling down to sleep. A breeze with a touch of coolness in it drifted up the slope and it was fine and soothing after a day of heat.

"We alway get a cool night breeze," said old John H. "No matter how hot the day may be we have easy sleeping."

He sighed. "I wonder sometimes," he said, "how well contented a man should let himself become. I wonder if it may not be a sign of—well, almost sinfulness. For Man is not by nature a contented animal. He is restless and unhappy and it's that same unhappiness that has driven him, like a lash across his back, to his great accomplishments."

"Contentedness," said Asher Sutton, "is an indication of complete adjustment to one's particular environment. It is a thing that is not often found . . . that is too seldom found. Someday Man and other things as well, will know how to achieve it and there will be peace and happiness in all the galaxy."

John H. chuckled. "You take in a lot of territory, William."

"I was taking the long-range view," said Sutton. "Someday Man will be going to the stars."

John H. nodded. "Yes, I suppose they will. But they will go too soon. Before Man goes to the stars he should learn how to live on Earth."

He yawned and said, "I think I will turn in. Getting old, you know, and I need my rest."

"I'm going to walk around a bit, said Sutton.

"You do a lot of walking, William."

"After dark," said Sutton, "the land is different from what it is in daylight. It smells differently. Sweet and fresh and clean, as if it were just washed. You hear things in the quietness you do not hear in daylight. You walk and you are alone with the land and the land belongs to you."

John H. wagged his head. "It's not the land that's different, William. It is you. Sometimes I think you see and . . ." he hesitated, then went on, "almost as if you did not quite belong."

"Sometimes I think I don't," said Sutton.

"Remember this," John H. told him. "You are one of us ... one of the family, seems like. Let me see, how many years now?"

"Ten," said Sutton.

"That's right," said John H. "I can well recall the day you came, but sometimes I forget. Sometimes it seems that you were always here. Sometimes I catch myself thinking you're a Sutton."

He hacked and cleared his throat, spitting in the dust. "I borrowed your typewriter the other day, William," he said. "I had a letter I had to write. It was an important letter and I wanted it done right."

"It's all right," said Sutton. "I'm glad it was some use to you."

"Getting any writing done these days, William?"

"No," said Sutton, "I gave up. I couldn't do it. I lost my notes, you see. I had it all figured out and I had it down on paper, and I thought maybe I could remember it, but I found I couldn't. It's no use trying."

John H.'s voice was a soft, low growl in the darkness. "You in any kind of trouble, William?"

"No," said Sutton. "Not exactly trouble."

"Anything I can do to help?"

"Not a thing," said Sutton.

"Let me know if there is," said the old man. "We'd do anything for you."

"Someday I may go away," said Sutton. "Maybe suddenly. If I do I wish you would forget me, forget I was ever here."

"That's what you wish, lad?"

"Yes, it is," said Sutton.

"We can't forget you, William," said old John H. "We never could do that. But we won't talk about you. If someone comes and asks about you we'll act as if you were never here."

He paused. "Is that the way you want it, William?"

"Yes," said Sutton. "If you don't mind, that's the way I want it."

They stood silent for a moment, facing one another in the dark, then the old man turned around and clumped toward the lighted windows of the house, and Sutton, turning too, leaned his arms on the pasture bars and stared across the river where the faërie lights were blinking in a land of never-never.

Ten years, thought Sutton, and the letter's written. Ten years and the conditions of the past are met. Now the past can get along without me, for I was only staying so that John H. could write the letter...so that he could write it and I could find it in an old trunk six thousand years from now and read it on a nameless asteroid I won by killing a man in a place that will be called the Zag House.

The Zag House, he thought, will be over there across the river, far up the prairie above the ancient town of Prairie du Chien, and the University of North America, with its matchless towers of beauty, will be set on the hills there to the north and Adams' house will be near the confluence of the Wisconsin and Mississippi Rivers. Great ships will climb into the sky from the Iowa prairies and head out for the stars that even now are twinkling overhead . . . and other stars that no man's eye can see unaided.

The Zag House will be over there, far across the river. And that is where someday, six thousand years from now, I will meet a little girl in a checkered apron. As in a storybook, he thought. Boy meets girl and the boy is tow-headed with a cowlick and he's barefooted and the girl twists her apron in her hands and tells him what her name is. . . .

He straightened and gripped the top bar of the pasture gate.

"Eva," he said, "where are you?"

Her hair was copper and her eyes . . . what color were her eyes? I have studied you for twenty years, she had said, and he had kissed her for it, not believing the words she spoke, but ready to believe the unspoken word that lay upon her face and body.

Somewhere she still existed, somewhere in time and space. Somewhere she might be thinking of him as even now he thought of her. If he tried hard enough, he might contact her. Might drive his hunger for her through the folds of space and time and let her know that he still remembered, let her know that somehow, sometime he would come back to her.

But even as he thought of it, he knew that it was hopeless, that he floundered in the grasp of forgotten time as a man may flounder in a running sea. It was not he who would reach out for her, but she or Herkimer or someone else who would reach out to him . . . if anyone ever did.

Ten years, he thought, and they have forgotten me. And is it because they cannot find me, or having found me, cannot reach me; or is it for a purpose, and if that is it, what can the purpose be?

There had been times when he had felt that he was being watched, that nasty touch of cold between the shoulder blades. And there had been the time when someone had run from him when he had been in the woods late of a summer evening hunting for the fence-jumping, cross-eyed heifer that was forever getting lost.

He turned from the pasture bars and crossed the barnyard, making his way in the darkness as a man will walk in a well-remembered room. From the barn came the scent of freshly mown hay and in the row of chicken coops one of the young birds was cheeping sleepily.

Even as he walked, his mind flicked out and touched the disturbed chicken's mind.

Fluttering apprehension of an unknown thing . . . there had been a sound coming on the edge of sleep. And a sound was danger . . . a signal of an unknown danger. Sound and nowhere to go. Darkness and sound. Insecurity.

Sutton pulled back his mind and walked on. Not much stability in a chicken, he thought. A cow was contented and its thought and purpose as slow-moving as its feeding. A dog was alive and friendly, and a cat, no matter how well tamed it might be, still walked the jungle's edge.

I know them all, he thought. I have been each one of them. And there are some that are not quite pleasant. A rat, for example, or a weasel or a bass lying in wait beneath the lily pads. But the skunk . . . the skunk was a pleasant fellow. One could enjoy living as a skunk.

Curiosity or practice? Perhaps curiosity, he admitted, the human penchant for prying into things that were hung with signs: No Trespassing. Keep Out. Private. Do Not Disturb. But practice as well, learning one of the tools of the second body. Learning how to move into another mind and share its every shade of intellectual and emotional reaction.

But there was a line . . . a line he had never crossed, either through innate decency or a fear of being apprehended. He could not decide quite which.

The road was a dusty strip of white that ran along the

ridge, twisting between the deep bowls of darkness where the land fell away into deep hollows. Sutton walked slowly, footfalls muffled by the dust. The land was black and the road was white and the stars were large and soft in the summer night. So different, Sutton thought, from the winter stars. In the winter the stars retreated high into the sky and glowed with a hard and steely light.

Peace and quiet, he told himself. In this corner of the ancient Earth there is peace and quiet, unbroken by the turbulence of twentieth-century living.

From a land like this came the steady men, the men who in a few more generations would ride the ships out to the stars. Here, in the quiet corners of the world, were built the stamina and courage, the depth of character and the deep convictions that would take the engines that more brilliant, less stable men had dreamed and drive them to the farthest rims of the galaxy, there to hold key worlds for the glory and the profit of the race.

The profit, Sutton said.

Ten years, he thought, and the involuntary compact with time has been consummated . . . each condition filled. I am free to go, to go anywhere, any time I choose.

But there was no place to go and no way to get there.

I would like to stay, said Sutton. It is pleasant here.

"Johnny," he said. "Johnny, what are we going to do?"

He felt the stir in his mind, the old dog stir, the wagging tail, the comfort of blankets tucked about a child in his trundle bed.

"It's all right, Ash," said Johnny. "Everything's all right. You needed these ten years."

"You've stayed with me, Johnny."

"I am you," said Johnny. "I came when you were born. I'll stay until you die."

"And then?"

"You'll not need me, Ash. I'll go to something else. Nothing walks alone."

None walks alone, said Sutton, and he said it like a prayer.

And he was not alone.

Someone walked beside him and where he'd come from and how long he'd been there Sutton did not know.

"This is a splendid walk," said the man, whose face was hidden in darkness. "Do you take it often?"

"Almost every night," said Sutton's tongue and his brain said, Steady! Steady!

"It is so quiet," said the man. "So quiet and alone. It is good for thinking. A man could do a lot of thinking, walking nights out here."

Sutton did not answer.

They plodded along, side by side, and even while he fought to keep relaxed, Sutton felt his body tensing.

"You've been doing a lot of thinking, Sutton," said the man. "Ten whole years of thinking."

"You should know," said Sutton. "You've been watching me."

"We've watched," said the man. "And our machines have watched. We got you down on tape and we know a lot about you. A whole lot more than we did ten years ago."

"Ten years ago," said Sutton, "you sent two men to buy me off."

"I know," replied the man. "We have often wondered what became of them."

"That's an easy one," Sutton said. "I killed them."

"They had a proposition."

"I know," said Sutton. "They offered me a planet."

"I knew at the time it wouldn't work," the man declared. "I told Trevor that it wouldn't work."

"I suppose you have another proposition?" Sutton asked. "A slightly higher price?"

"Not exactly," said the man. "We thought this time we'd cut out the bargaining and just let you name your price."

"I'll think about it," Sutton told him. "I'm not too sure I can think up a price."

"As you wish, Sutton," said the man. "We'll be waiting . . . and watching. Just give us the sign when you've made up your mind."

"A sign?"

"Sure. Just write us a note. We'll be looking over your shoulder. Or just say . . . 'Well, I've made up my mind.' We'll be listening and we'll hear."

"Simple," Sutton said. "Simple as all that."

"We made it easy for you," said the man. "Good evening, Mr. Sutton."

Sutton did not see him do it, but he sensed that he had touched his hat . . . if he wore a hat. Then he was gone, turning off the road and going down across the pasture, walking in the dark, heading for the woods that sloped to the river bluffs.

Sutton stood in the dusty road and listened to him go—the soft swish of dew-laden grass brushing on his shoes, the muted pad of his feet walking in the pasture.

Contact at last! After ten years, contact with the people from another time. But the wrong people. Not his people.

The Revisionists had been watching him, even as he had sensed them watching. Watching and waiting, waiting for ten years. But, of course, not ten years of their time, just ten years of his. Machines and watchers would have been sprinkled through those ten years, so that the job could have been done in a year or a month or even in a week if they had wanted to throw enough men and materials into the effort.

But why wait ten years? To soften him up, to make him ready to jump at anything they offered?

To soften him up? He grinned wryly in the dark.

Then suddenly the picture came to him and he stood there stupidly, wondering why he hadn't thought of it much sooner.

They hadn't waited to soften him up . . . they had waited for old John H. to write the letter. For they knew about the letter. They had studied old John H. and they knew he'd write a letter. They had him down on tape and they knew him inside out and they had figured to an eyelash the way his mind would work.

The letter was the key to the whole thing. The letter was the lure that had been used to suck Asher Sutton back into this time. They had lured him, then sealed him off and kept him, kept him as surely as if they'd had him in a cage. They had studied him and they knew him and they had him figured out. They knew what he would do as surely as they had known what old John H. would do.

His mind flicked out and probed cautiously at the brain of the man striding down the hill.

Chickens and cats and dogs and meadow mice—and not one of them suspected, not one of them had known, that another mind than theirs had occupied their brain.

But the brain of a man might be a different matter. Highly trained and sensitive, it might detect outside interference, might sense if it did not actually know the invasion of itself.

The girl won't wait. I've been away too long. Her affections are less than skin-deep and she has no morals, absolutely none, and I'm the one to know. I've been on

*this damn patrol too long. She will be tired of waiting
. . . she was tired of waiting when I was gone three hours.
To hell with her . . . I can get another one. But not like
her . . . not exactly like her. There isn't another one
anywhere quite like her.*

*Whoever said this Sutton guy would be an easy one to
crack was crazy as a loon. God, after ten years in a dump
like this, I'd fall on someone's neck and kiss 'em if they
came back from my own time. Anyone at all . . . friend or
foe, it would make no difference. But what does Sutton
do? Not a God-damn word. Not a single syllable of surprise in any word he spoke. When I first spoke to him
he didn't even break his stride, kept right on walking as
if he knew I'd been there all the time. Cripes, I could use
a drink. Nerve-racking work.*

*Wish I could forget that girl. Wish she would be wait-
ing for me but I know she won't. Wish . . .*

Sutton snapped back his mind, stood quietly in the
road.

And inside himself he felt the shiver of triumph, the
swift backwash of relief and triumph. They didn't know.
In all their ten years of watching they had seen no more
than the superficial things. They had him down on tape,
but they didn't know all that went on within his mind.

A human mind, perhaps. But not his mind. A human
mind they might be able to strip as bare as a sickled field,
might dissect it and analyze it and read the story in it.
But his mind told them only what it wished to tell them,
only enough so that there would be no suspicion that he
was holding back. Ten years ago Adams' gang had tried
to tap his mind and had not even dented it.

The Revisionists had watched ten years and they knew
each motion that he made, many of the things that he
had thought.

But they did not know that he could go to live within the mind of a mouse or a catfish or a man.

For if they had known they would have set up certain safeguards, would have been on the alert against him.

And they weren't. No more alert than the mouse had been.

He glanced back to the road to where the Sutton farmhouse stood upon the hill. For a moment he thought that he could see it, a darker mass against the darkness of the sky, but that, he knew, was no more than pure imagination. He knew that it was there and he had formed a mental image.

One by one, he checked the items in his room. The books, the few scribbled sheets of paper, the razor.

There was nothing there, he knew, that he could not leave behind. Not a thing that would arouse suspicion. Nothing that could be fastened on in some later day and turned into a weapon to be used against him.

He had been prepared against this day, knowing that someday it would come—that someday Herkimer or the Revisionists or an agent from the government would step from behind a tree and walk along beside him.

Knowing? Well, not exactly. Hoping. And ready for the hope.

Long years ago his futile attempt to write the book of destiny without his notes had gone up in smoke. All that remained was a heap of paper ash, mixed these many years with the soil, leached away by the rains, gone as chemical elements into a head of wheat or an ear of corn.

He was ready. Packed and ready. His mind had been packed and ready, he knew now, for these many years.

Softly he stepped off the road and went down across the pasture, following the man who walked toward the river bluffs. His mind flicked out and tracked him through the darkness, using his mind to track him as a hound would use his nose to track a coon.

He overhauled him scant minutes after he had entered the fringe of trees and after that kept a few paces behind him, walking carefully to guard against the suddenly snapping twig, the swish of swaying bushes that could have warned his quarry.

The ship lay within a deep ravine and at a hail it lighted up and a port swung open. Another man stood in the lighted port and stared into the night.

"That you, Gus?" he called.

The other swore at him. "Sure. Who else do you think would be floundering around in these woods at the dead of night?"

"I got to worrying," said the man in the port. "You were gone longer than I thought you would be. Just getting ready to set out and hunt for you."

"You're always worrying," Gus growled at him. "Between you and this outlandish world, I'm fed up. Trevor can find someone else to do this kind of work from here on out."

He scrambled up the steps into the ship. "Get going," he told the other man tersely. "We're getting out of here."

He turned to close the port, but Sutton already had it closed.

Gus took two steps backward, brought up against an anchored chair and stood there, grinning.

"Look at what we got," he said. "Hey, Pinky, look at what followed me back home."

Sutton smiled at them grimly. "If you gentlemen have no objection, I'll hitch a ride with you."

"And if we have objections?" Pinky asked.

"I'm riding this ship," Sutton told him. "With you or

without you. Take your choice."

"This is Sutton," Gus told Pinky. "The Mr. Sutton. Trevor will be glad to see you, Sutton."

Trevor . . . Trevor. That was three times he had heard the name, and somewhere else he had heard it once before. He stood with his back against the closed port and his mind went back to another ship and another two men.

"Trevor," Case had said, or had it been Pringle who had said it? "Trevor? Why, Trevor is the head of the corporation."

"I've been looking forward, all these years," Sutton told him, "to meeting Mr. Trevor. He and I will have a lot to talk about."

"Get her going, Pinky," Gus said. "And send ahead a message. Trevor will want to break out the guard of honor for us. We're bringing Sutton back."

XLII

Trevor picked up a paper clip and flipped it at an inkwell on the desk. The clip landed in the ink.

"Getting pretty good," said Trevor. "Hit it seven times out of every ten. Used to be I missed it seven times out of every ten."

He looked at Sutton, studying him.

"You look like an ordinary man," he said. "I should be able to talk with you and make you understand."

"I haven't any horns," said Sutton, "if that is what you mean."

"Nor," said Trevor, "any halo, either, so far as I'm concerned."

He flipped another paper clip and it missed the inkwell.

"Seven out of ten," said Trevor.

He flipped another one and it was a hit. Ink spouted up and spattered on the desk.

"Sutton," said Trevor, "you know a great deal about destiny. Have you ever thought of it in terms of manifest destiny?"

Sutton shrugged. "You're using an antiquated term. Pure and simple propaganda of the nineteenth century.

There was a certain nation that wore that one threadbare."

"Propaganda," Trevor said. "Let's call it psychology. You say a thing so often and so well that after a time everyone believes it. Even, finally, yourself."

"This manifest destiny," said Sutton. "For the human race, I presume?"

"Naturally," said Trevor. "After all, we're the animals that would know how to use it to the best advantage."

"You pass up a point," declared Sutton. "The humans don't need it. Already they think they are great and right and holy. Certainly, you don't need to propagandize them."

"In the short view, you are right," said Trevor. "But in the short view only."

He stabbed a sudden finger at Sutton. "Once we have the galaxy in hand, what do we do then?"

"Why," said Sutton. "Why, I suppose . . ."

"That's exactly it," said Trevor. "You don't know where you're going. Nor does the human race."

"And manifest destiny?" asked Sutton. "If we had manifest destiny, it would be different?"

Trevor's words were scarcely more than a whisper. "There are other galaxies, Sutton. Greater even than this one. Many other galaxies."

Good Lord! thought Sutton.

He started to speak and then closed his mouth and sat stiffly in his chair.

Trevor's whisper speared at him from across the desk.

"Staggers you, doesn't it?" he said.

Sutton tried to speak aloud, but his voice came out a whisper, too.

"You're mad, Trevor. Absolutely mad."

"The long-range view," said Trevor. "That is what we

need. The absolutely unshakable belief in human destiny, the positive and all-inclusive conviction that Man is meant not only to take over this galaxy alone but all the galaxies, the entire universe."

"You should live long enough," said Sutton, sudden mockery rising to his tongue.

"I won't see it, of course," said Trevor. "And neither will you. Nor will our children's children or their children for many generations."

"It will take a million years," Sutton told him.

"More than a million years," Trevor told him calmly. "You have no idea, no conception of the scope of the universe. In a million years we'll be getting a good start. . . ."

"Then, why, for the love of heaven, do you and I sit here and quibble about it?"

"Logic," said Trevor.

"There is no real logic," Sutton declared, "in planning a million years ahead. A man can plan his own lifetime, if he wishes, and there is some logic in that. Or the life of his children, and there still would be some logic in it . . . and maybe in the life of his grandchildren. But beyond that there can be no logic."

"Sutton," asked Trevor, "did you ever hear of a corporation?"

"Why, yes, of course, but . . ."

"A corporation could plan for a million years," said Trevor. "It could plan very logically."

"A corporation is not a man," said Sutton. "It is not an entity."

"But it is," insisted Trevor. "An entity composed of men and created by men to carry out their wishes. It is a living, operative concept that is handed down from one generation to another to carry out a plan too vast to be accomplished in the lifetime of one man alone."

"Your corporation publishes books, too, doesn't it?" asked Sutton.

Trevor stared at him. "Who told you that?" he snapped.

"A couple of men by the name of Case and Pringle," Sutton said. "They tried to buy my book for your corporation."

"Case and Pringle are out on a mission," Trevor said. "I had expected them back . . ."

"They won't be coming back," said Sutton.

"You killed them," Trevor said, flatly.

"They tried to kill me first," said Sutton. "I'm awfully hard to kill."

"That would have been against my orders, Sutton. I do not want you killed."

"They were on their own," said Sutton. "They were going to sell my carcass to Morgan."

There was no way of telling, Sutton thought, how you hit this man. There was no difference of expression in his eyes, no faintest flicker of change across his face.

"I appreciate your killing them," said Trevor. "It saves me the bother."

He flicked a clip at the inkwell and it was a hit.

"It's logical," he said, "that a corporation should plan a million years ahead. It provides a framework within which a certain project may be carried forward without interruption although the personnel in charge should change from time to time."

"Wait a minute," Sutton told him. "Is there a corporation or are you just posing fables?"

"There is a corporation," Trevor told him, "and I am the man who heads it. Varied interests pooling their resources . . . and there will be more and more of them as time goes on. As soon as we can show something tangible."

"By tangible, you mean destiny for the human race, for the human race alone?"

Trevor nodded. "Then we'll have something to talk about. A commodity to sell. Something to back up our sales talk."

Sutton shook his head. "I can't see what you expect to gain."

"Three things," Trevor told him. "Wealth and power and knowledge. The wealth and power and knowledge of the universe. For Man alone, you understand. For a single race. For people like you and me. And of the three, knowledge perhaps would be the greatest prize of all, for knowledge, added to and compounded, correlated and co-ordinated, would lead to even greater wealth and power . . . and to greater knowledge."

"It is madness," said Sutton. "You and I, Trevor, will be drifting dust, and not only ourselves, but the very era in which we live out this moment will be forgotten before the job is done."

"Remember the corporation."

"I'm remembering the corporation," Sutton said, "but I can't help but think in terms of people. You and I and the other people like us."

"Let's think in terms of people, then," said Trevor, smoothly. "One day the life that runs in you will run in the brain and blood and muscle of a man who shall be part owner of the universe. There will be trillions upon trillions of life forms to serve him, there will be wealth that he cannot count, there will be knowledge of which you and I cannot even dream."

Sutton sat quietly, slumped in his chair.

"You're the only man," said Trevor, "who is standing

in the way. You're the man who is blocking the project for a million years."

"You need destiny," said Sutton, "and destiny is not mine to give away."

"You are a human being, Sutton," Trevor told him, talking evenly. "You are a man. It is the people of your own race that I'm talking to you about."

"Destiny," said Sutton, "belongs to everything that lives. Not to Man alone, but to every form of life."

"It needn't," Trevor told him. "You are the only man who knows. You are the man who can tell the facts. You can make it a manifest destiny for the human race instead of a personal destiny for every crawling, cackling, sniveling thing that has the gift of life."

Sutton didn't answer.

"One word from you," said Trevor, "and the thing is done."

"It can't be done," said Sutton, "this scheme of yours. Think of the sheer time, the thousands of years, even at the rate of speed of the starships of today, to cross intergalactic space. Only from this galaxy to the next . . . not from this galaxy to the ultimate galaxy."

Trevor sighed. "You forget what I said about the compounding of knowledge. Two and two won't make four, my friend. It will make much more than four. In some instances thousands of times more than four."

Sutton shook his head, wearily.

But Trevor was right, he knew. Knowledge and technique would pyramid exactly as he said. Even, once Man had the time to do it, the knowledge in one galaxy alone . . .

"One word from you," Trevor said, "and the time war is at an end. One word and the security of the human race is guaranteed forever. For all the race will need is the knowledge that you can give it."

"It wouldn't be the truth," said Sutton.

"That," said Trevor, "doesn't have a thing to do with it."

"You don't need manifest destiny," said Sutton, "to carry out your project."

"We have to have the human race behind us," Trevor said. "We have to have something that is big enough to capture their imagination. Something important enough to make them pay attention. And manifest destiny, manifest destiny as it applies to the universe, is the thing to turn the trick."

"Twenty years ago," said Sutton, "I would have thrown in with you."

"And now?" asked Trevor.

Sutton shook his head. "Not now. I know more than I did twenty years ago. Twenty years ago I was a human, Trevor. I'm not too sure I'm entirely human any longer."

"I hadn't mentioned the matter of reward," said Trevor. "That goes without saying."

"No, thanks," said Sutton. "I'd like to keep on living."

Trevor flipped a clip at the inkwell and it missed.

"You're slipping," Sutton said. "Your percentage is way off."

Trevor picked up another clip.

"All right," he said. "Go ahead and have your fun. There's a war on and we'll win that war. It's a hellish way to fight, but we're doing it the best we can. No war anywhere, no surface indication of war, for you understand the galaxy is in utter and absolute peace under the rule of benevolent Earthmen. We can win without you, Sutton, but it would be easier with you."

"You're going to turn me loose?" Sutton asked, in mock surprise.

"Why, sure," Trevor told him. "Go on out and beat your head against a stone wall a little longer. In the end, you'll get tired of it. Eventually you'll give up out of sheer exhaustion. You'll come back then and give us the thing we want."

Sutton rose to his feet.

He stood for a moment, indecisive.

"What are you waiting for?" asked Trevor.

"One thing has me puzzled," Sutton told him. "The book, somehow, somewhere, already has been written. It has been a fact for almost five hundred years. How are you going to change that? If I write it now the way you want it written, it will change the human setup. . . ."

Trevor laughed. "We got that one figured out. Let us say that finally, after all of these years, the original of your manuscript is discovered. It can be readily and indisputably identified by certain characteristics which you will very carefully incorporate into it when you write it. It will be found and proclaimed, and what is more, proved . . . and the human race will have its destiny.

"We'll explain the past unpleasantness by very convincing historic evidence of earlier tampering with the manuscript. Even your friends, the androids, will have to believe what we say once we get through with it."

"Clever," Sutton said.

"I think so, too," said Trevor.

XLIII

At the building's entrance a man was waiting for him. He raised his hand in what might have been a brief salute.

"Just a minute, Mr. Sutton."

"Yes, what is it?"

"There'll be a few of us following you, sir. Orders, you know."

"But . . ."

"Nothing personal, sir. We won't interfere with anything you want to do. Just guarding you, sir."

"Guarding me?"

"Certainly, sir. Morgan's crowd, you know. Can't let them pop you off."

"You can't know," Sutton told him, "how deeply I appreciate your interest."

"It's nothing sir," the man told him. "Just part of the day's work. Glad to do it. Don't mention it at all."

He stepped back again and Sutton wheeled and walked down the steps and followed the cinder walk that flanked the avenue.

The sun was near to setting and looking back over his shoulder he saw the tall, straight lines of the gigantic office building in which he had talked to Trevor outlined against the brightness of the western sky. But of anyone who might be following him he did not see a sign.

He had no place to go. He had no idea where to go. But he realized that he couldn't stand around wringing his hands. He'd walk, he told himself, and think, and wait for whatever was going to happen next to happen.

He met other walkers and a few of them stared at him curiously, and now, for the first time, Sutton realized that he still wore the clothing of the twentieth-century farm hand . . . blue denim overalls and cotton shirt, with heavy, serviceable farm shoes on his feet.

But here, he knew, even such an outlandish costume would not arouse undue suspicion. For on Earth, with its visiting dignitaries from far Solar systems, with its Babel of races employed in the different governmental departments, with its exchange students, its diplomats and legislators representing backwoods planets, how a man dressed would arouse but slight curiosity.

By morning, he told himself, he'd have to find some hiding place, some retreat where he could relax and figure out some of the angles in this world of five hundred years ahead.

Either that or locate an android he could trust to put him in touch with the android organization . . . for although he had never been told so, he had no doubt there was android organization. There would have to be to fight a war in time.

He turned off the path that flanked the roadway and took another one, a faint footpath that led out across marshy land toward a range of low hills to the north.

Suddenly now he realized that he was hungry and that he should have dropped into one of the shops in the office building for a bite of food. And then he remembered that he had no money with which to pay for food. A few twentieth-century dollars were in his pockets, but they would be worthless here as a medium of exchange, although quite possibly they might have some value as collector's items.

Dusk came over the land and the frogs began their chorus, first from far away and then, with others joining in, the marsh resounded with their throaty pipings. Sutton walked through a world of faërie sound, and as he walked it almost seemed as if his feet did not touch the ground, but it floated along, driven by the breath of sound that rose to meet the first faint stars of evening shining above the dark heights that lay ahead.

Short hours ago, he thought, he had walked a dusty hilltop road in the twentieth century, scuffing the white dust with his shoes . . . and some of the white dust, he saw, still clung to his shoes. Even as the memory of that hilltop road clung to his memory. Memory and dust, he thought, link us to the past.

He reached the hills and began to climb them and the night was sweet with the smell of pine and the scent of forest flowers.

He came to the top of a slight rise and stood there for a moment, looking out across the velvety softness of the night. Somewhere, near at hand, a cricket was tentatively tuning up his fiddle, and from the marsh came the muted sound of frogs. In the darkness just ahead of him a stream was splashing along its rocky bed and it talked as it went along, talked to the trees and its grassy banks and the nodding flowers that hung their sleepy heads above it.

"I would like to stop," it said. "I would like to stop and talk with you. But I can't, you see. I must hurry on. I have some place I must go. I can't waste a minute. I must hurry on."

Like Man, thought Sutton. For Man is driven like the stream. Man is driven by circumstance and necessity and the bright-eyed ambition of other restless men who will not let him be.

He did not hear a sound, but he felt the great hand close upon his arm and jerk him off the path. Twisting, he sought to free himself of the grasp, and saw the dark blur of the man who had grabbed him. He balled his fist and swung it and it was a sledge-hammer slamming at the dark head, but it never reached its mark. A charging body slammed into his knees and bent them under him, arms wrapped themselves around his legs and he staggered, falling on his face.

He sat up and somewhere off to the right he heard the soft snickering of rapidly firing guns and caught, out of the tail of his eyes, their bright flicker in the night.

Then a hand came out of nowhere and cupped itself around his mouth and nose.

"Powder!" he thought.

And ever as he thought it, he knew no more of dark figures in the woods, nor the cheeping frogs nor the snarling of the guns.

XLIV

Sutton opened his eyes to strangeness and lay quietly on the bed. A breeze came through an open window and the room, decorated with fantastic life-murals, was splashed with brilliant sunlight. The breeze brought in the scent of blooming flowers and in a tree outside a bird was chirping contentedly.

Slowly Sutton let his senses reach out and gather in the facts of the room, the facts of strangeness . . . the unfamiliar furniture, the contour of the room itself, the green and purple monkeys that chased one another along the wavy vine that ran around the border of the walls.

Quietly his mind moved back along the track of time to his final conscious moment. There had been guns flickering in the night and there had been a hand that reached out and cupped his nose.

Drugged, Sutton told himself. Drugged and dragged away.

Before that there had been a cricket and the frogs singing in the marsh and the talking brook that babbled down the hill, hurrying to get wherever it was going.

And before that a man who had sat across a desk from him and told him about a corporation and a dream and plan the corporation held.

Fantastic, Sutton thought. And in the bright light of the room, the very idea was one of utter fantasy . . . that Man should go out, not only to the stars, but to the galaxies.

But there was greatness in it, a very human greatness. There had been a time when it had been fantasy to think that Man could ever lift himself from the bosom of the planet of his birth. And another time when it had been fantasy to think that Man would go beyond the Solar system, out into the dread reaches of nothingness that stretched between the stars.

But there had been strength in Trevor, and conviction as well as strength. A man who knew where he was going and why he was going and what it took to get there.

Manifest destiny, Trevor had said. That is what it takes. That is what it needs.

Man would be great and he'd be a god. The concepts of life and thought that had been born on the Earth would be the basic concepts of the entire universe, of the fragile bubble of space and time that bobbed along on a sea of mystery beyond which no mind could penetrate. And yet, by the time that Man got where he was headed for, he might well be able to penetrate that, too.

A mirror stood in one corner of the room and in it he saw the reflection of the lower half of his body, lying on the bed, naked except for a pair of shorts. He wiggled his toes and watched them in the glass.

And you're the only one who is stopping us, Trevor had told him. You're the one man standing in the way of Man. You're the stumbling block. You are keeping men from being gods.

But all men did not think as Trevor did. All men were not tangled in the blind chauvinism of the human race.

The delegates from the Android Equality League had talked to him one noon, had caught him as he stepped off the elevator on his way to lunch, and had stood ranged before him as if they expected him to attempt escape and were set to cut him off.

One of them had twisted a threadbare cap in his dirty fingers and the woman's hair had dangled and she had folded her hands across her stomach, as determined, stolid women do.

They had been crackpots, certainly. They were fervent crusaders in a cause that held them up to a quiet and devastating scorn. Even the androids were not sympathetic to them, even the androids for whom they were working saw through the human ineffectiveness and the gaudy exhibitionism of their efforts.

For the human race, thought Sutton, cannot even for a moment forget that it is human, cannot achieve the greatness of humility that will unquestioningly accord equality. Even while the League fought for the equality of androids, they could not help but patronize the very ones that they would make equal.

What was it Herkimer had said? Equality not by special dispensation, not by human tolerance. But what was the only way the human race would ever accord equality . . . by dispensation or by overweening tolerance.

And yet that pitiful handful of patronizers had been the only humans he might have turned to for help.

A man who twisted his cap in grimy fingers, an old, officious woman and another man with time heavy on his hands and nothing else to do.

And yet, thought Sutton . . . and yet, there is Eva Armour.

There may be others like her. Somewhere, working with the androids even now, there may be others like her.

He swung his feet out of bed and sat on the bed's edge. A pair of slippers stood on the floor and he worked his feet into them, stood up and walked to the mirror.

A strange face stared back at him, a face he'd never seen before, and for a moment muddy panic surged within his brain.

Then, sudden suspicion blossoming, his hand went up to his forehead and rubbed at the smudge that was there, set obliquely across his brow.

Bending low, with his face close to the mirror, he verified the thought.

The smudge upon his brow was an android identification mark! An identification key and a serial number!

With his fingers he carefully explored his face, located the plastic overcoats that had changed its contours until he was unrecognizable.

He turned around, made his way back to the bed, sat down upon it cautiously and gripped the edge of the mattress with his hands.

Disguised, he told himself. Made into an android. Kidnaped a human, and an android when he woke.

The door clicked and Herkimer said, "Good morning, sir. I trust that you are comfortable."

Sutton jerked erect. "So it was you," he said.

Herkimer nodded happily. "At your service, sir. Is there anything you wish?"

"You didn't have to knock me out," said Sutton.

"We had to work fast, sir," said Herkimer. "We couldn't have you messing up things, stumbling around and asking questions and wanting to know what it was all about. We just drugged you and hauled you off. It was, believe me, sir, much simpler that way."

"There was some shooting," Sutton said. "I heard the guns."

"It seems," Herkimer told him, "that there were a few Revisionists lurking about, and it gets a little complicated, sir, when one tires to tell about it."

"You tangle with those Revisionists?"

"Well, to tell the truth," said Herkimer, "some of them were so rash as to draw their guns. It was most unwise of them, sir. They got the worst of it."

"It won't do us a bit of good," said Sutton, "if the idea was to get me out of the clutches of Trevor's mob. Trevor will have a psych-tracer on me. He knows where I am and this place will be watched three deep."

Herkimer grinned. "It is, sir. His men are practically falling over one another all around the place."

"Then why this get-up?" Sutton demanded angrily. "Why disguise me?"

"Well, sir," explained Herkimer, "it's like this. We figured no human in his right mind ever would want to be taken for an android. So we turned you into one. They'll be looking for a human. It would never occur to them to take a second look at an android when they were looking for a human."

Sutton grunted. "Smart." he said. "I hope it doesn't . . ."

"Oh, they'll get on to it after a while, sir," Herkimer admitted, cheerfully. "But it will give us some time. Time to work out some plans."

He moved swiftly around the room, opening chest drawers and taking out clothing.

"It's very nice, sir," he said, "to have you back again. We tried to find you, but it was no dice. We figured the Revisionists had you cooped up somewhere, so we redoubled our security here and kept a close watch on everything that happened. For the past five weeks we've known every move that Trevor and his gang have made."

"Five weeks!" gasped Sutton. "Did you say five weeks?"

"Certainly, sir. Five weeks. You disappeared just seven weeks ago."

"By my calendar," said Sutton, "it was ten years."

Herkimer wagged his head sagely, unstartled. "Time is the funniest thing, sir. It ties a man in knots."

He laid clothing on the bed. "If you'll get into these, sir, we'll go down for breakfast. Eva is waiting for us. She'll be glad to see you, sir."

XLV

Trevor missed with three clips in a row. He shook his head sadly.

"You're sure of this?" he asked the man across the desk.

The man nodded, tight-lipped.

"It might be android propaganda, you know," said Trevor. "They're clever. That's a thing you never must forget. An android, for all his bowing and his scraping, is just as smart as we are."

"Do you realize what it means?" the man demanded. "It means . . ."

"I can tell you what it means," said Trevor. "From now on we can't be sure which of us are human. There'll be no sure way of knowing who's human and who's an android. You could be an android. I could be . . ."

"Exactly," said the man.

"That's why Sutton was so smug yesterday afternoon," said Trevor. "He sat there, where you are sitting, and I had the impression that he was laughing at me all the time. . . ."

"I don't think Sutton knows," said the man. "It's an android secret. Only a few of them know it. They certainly wouldn't take a chance on any human knowing it."

"Not even Sutton?"

"Not even Sutton," said the man.

"Cradle," said Trevor. "Nice sense of fitness that they have."

"You're going to do something about it, certainly," said the man impatiently.

Trevor put his elbows on the desk and matched careful fingertips.

"Of course I am," he said. "Now listen carefully. This is what we'll do . . ."

XLVI

EVA ARMOUR rose from the table on the patio and held out both her hands in greeting. Sutton pulled her close to him, planted a kiss on her upturned face.

"That," he said, "is for the million times I have thought of you."

She laughed at him, suddenly gay and happy.

"But, Ash, a million times!"

"Tangled time," said Herkimer. "He's been away ten years."

"Oh," said Eva. "Oh, Ash, how horrible!"

He grinned at her. "Not too horrible. I had ten years of rest. Ten years of peace and quiet. Working on a farm, you know. It was a little rough at first, but I was actually sorry when I had to leave."

He held a chair for her, took one for himself between her and Herkimer.

They ate . . . ham and eggs, toast and marmalade, strong, black coffee. It was pleasant on the patio. In the trees above them birds quarreled amiably. In the clover at the edge of the bricks and stones that formed the paving, bees hummed among the blossoms.

"How do you like my place, Ash?" asked Eva.

"It's wonderful," he said, and then, as if the two ideas might be connected in some way, he said, "I saw Trevor yesterday. He took me to the mountaintop and showed me the universe."

Eva drew in her breath sharply, and Sutton looked up quickly from his plate. Herkimer was waiting, with drawn face, with fork poised in midair, halfway to his mouth.

"What's the matter with you two?" he asked. "Don't you trust me?"

And even as he asked the question, he answered it for himself. Of course, they wouldn't trust him. For he was human and he could betray them. He could twist destiny so that it was a thing for the human race alone. And there was no way in which they could be sure that he would not do this.

"Ash," said Eva, "you refused to . . ."

"I left Trevor with an idea that I would be back to talk it over. Nothing that I said or did. He just believes I will. Told me to go out and beat my head against the wall some more."

"You have thought about it, sir?" asked Herkimer.

Sutton shook his head. "No. Not too much. I haven't sat down and mulled it over, if that is what you mean. It would have its points if you were merely human. Sometimes I frankly wonder how much of the human there may be left in me."

"How much of it do you know, Ash?" Eva asked, speaking softly.

Sutton scrubbed a hand across his forehead. "Most of it, I think. I know about the war in time and how and why it's being fought. I know about myself. I have two bodies and two minds, or at least substitute bodies and minds. I know some of the things that I can do. There may be other abilities I do not know about. One grows into them. Each new thing comes hard."

"We couldn't tell you," Eva said. "It would have been so simple if we could have told you. But, to start with, you would not have believed the things we told you. And, when dealing with time, one interferes as little as possible. Just enough to turn an event in the right direction.

"I tried to warn you. Remember, Ash? As near as I could come to warning."

He nodded. "After I killed Benton in the Zag House. You told me you had studied me for twenty years."

"And remember, I was the little girl in the checkered apron. When you were fishing . . ."

He looked at her in surprise. "You knew about that? It wasn't just part of the Zag dream?"

"Identification," said Herkimer. "So that you could identify her as a friend, as someone you had known before and who was close to you. So that you would accept her as a friend."

"But it was a dream."

"A Zag dream" said Herkimer. "The Zag is one of us. His race will benefit if destiny can stand for everyone and not the human race alone."

Sutton said, "Trevor is too confident. Not just pretending to be confident, but really confident. I keep coming back to that crack he made. 'Go out,' he said, 'and butt your head some more'"

"He's counting on you as a human being," Eva said.

Sutton shook his head. "I can't think that's it. He must have some scheme up his sleeve, some maneuver that we won't be able to check."

Herkimer spoke slowly. "I don't like that, sir. The

war's not going too well as it is. If we had to win, we'd be lost right now."

"If we had to win? I don't understand . . ."

"We don't have to win, sir," said Herkimer. "All we have to do is fight a holding action, prevent the Revisionists from destroying the book as you· will write it. From the very first we have not tried to change a thing. We've tried to keep them from being changed."

Sutton nodded. "On his part, Trevor has to win decisively. He must smash the original text, either prevent it from being written as I mean to write it or discredit it so thoroughly that not even an android will believe it."

"You're right, sir," Herkimer told him. "Unless he can do that the humans cannot claim destiny for their own, cannot make other life believe that destiny is reserved for the human race alone."

"And that is all he wants," said Eva. "Not the destiny itself, for no human can have the faith in destiny that, say, for example, an android can. To Trevor it is merely a matter of propaganda . . . to make the human race believe so completely that it is destined that it will not rest until it holds the universe."

"So long," said Herkimer, "as we can keep him from doing that we claim that we are winning. But the issue is so finely balanced that a new approach by either side would score heavily. A new weapon could be a factor that would mean victory or defeat."

"I have a weapon," Sutton said. "A made-to-order weapon that would beat them . . . but there's no way that it can be used."

Neither of them asked the question, but he saw it on their faces and he answered it.

"There's only one such weapon. Only one gun. You can't fight a war with just one gun."

Feet pounded around the corner of the house and when they turned they saw an android running toward them across the patio. Dust stained his clothing and his face was red from running. He came to a stop and faced them, clutching at the table's edge. "They tried to stop me," he panted, the words coming out in gushes. "The place is surrounded. . . ."

"Andrew, you fool," snapped Herkimer. "What do you mean by coming running in like this? They will know . . ."

"They've found out about the cradle," Andrew gasped. "They . . ."

Herkimer came erect in one swift motion. The chair on which he had been sitting tipped over with the violence of his rising and his face was suddenly so white that the identification tattoo on his forehead stood out with a startling clearness.

"They know where . . ."

Andrew shook his head. "Not where. They just found out about it. Just now. We still have time . . ."

"We'll call in all the ships," said Herkimer. "We'll have to pull all the guards off the crisis points. . . ."

"But you can't," gasped Eva. "That's exactly what they would want you to do. That is all that is stopping them. . . ."

"We have to," Herkimer said grimly. "There's no choice. If they destroy the Cradle . . ."

"Herkimer," said Eva, and there was a deadly calm in her unhurried words. "The mark!"

Andrew swung to face her, then took a backward step. Herkimer's hand flashed underneath his coat and Andrew turned to run, heading for the low wall that rimmed the patio.

The knife in Herkimer's hand flashed in the sun and

was suddenly a spinning wheel that tracked the running android. It caught him before he reached the wall and he went down into a heap of huddled clothing.

The knife, Sutton saw, was neatly buried in his neck.

XLVII

"Have you noticed, sir," said Herkimer, "how the little things, the inconsequential, trivial factors, come to play so big a part in any happening?"

He touched the huddled body with his foot.

"Perfect," he said. "Absolutely perfect. Except that before reporting to us he should have smeared some lacquer over his identification mark. Many androids do it, in an attempt to hide the mark, but it's seldom much of a success. After only a short time the mark shows through."

"But, lacquer?" asked Sutton.

"A little code we have," said Herkimer. "A very simple thing. It's the recognition sign for an agent reporting. A password, as it were. It takes a moment only. Some lacquer on your finger and a smear across your forehead."

"So simple a thing," said Eva, "that no one, absolutely no one, would ever notice it."

Sutton nodded. "One of Trevor's men," he said.

Herkimer nodded "Impersonating one of our men. Sent to smoke us out. Sent to start us running, pell-mell, to save the Cradle."

"This Cradle . . ."

"But it means," said Eva, "that Trevor knows about

it. He doesn't know where it is, but he knows about it. And he'll hunt until he finds it and then . . ."

Herkimer's gesture stopped her.

"What is wrong?" asked Sutton.

For there was something wrong, something that was terribly wrong. The whole atmosphere of the place was wrong. The friendliness was gone . . . the trust and friendliness and the oneness of their purpose. Shattered by an android who had run across the patio and talked about a thing that he called a Cradle and died, seconds later, with a knife blade through his throat.

Instinctively Sutton's mind reached out for Herkimer and then he drew it back. It was not an ability, he told himself, that one used upon a friend. It was an ability that one must keep in trust, not to be used curiously or idly, but only where the end result would justify its use.

"What's gone sour?" he asked. "What is the matter with . . ."

"Sir," said Herkimer, "you are a human being and this is an android matter."

For a moment Sutton stood stiff and straight, his mind absorbing the shock of the words that Herkimer had spoken, the black fury boiling ice-cold inside his body.

Then, deliberately, as if he had planned to do it, as if it were an action he had decided upon after long consideration, he balled his fist and swung his arm.

It was a vicious blow, with all his weight and all his strength and anger back of it, and Herkimer went down like an ox beneath a hammer.

"Ash!" cried Eva. "Ash!"

She clutched at his arm, but he shook her off.

Herkimer was sitting up, his hands covering his face, blood dripping down between his fingers.

Sutton spoke to him. "I have not sold destiny. Nor do

I intend to sell it. Although God knows, if I did, it would be no more than the lot of you deserve."

"Ash," said Eva softly. "Ash, we must be sure."

"How can I make you sure?" he asked. "I can only tell you."

"They are your people, Ash," she said. "Your race. Their greatness is your greatness, too. You can't blame Herkimer for thinking . . ."

"They're your people, too," said Sutton. "The taint that applies to me applies to you as well."

She shook her head.

"I'm a special case," she said. "I was orphaned when I was only a few weeks old. The family androids took me over. They raised me. Herkimer was one of them. I'm much more an android, Ash, than I am a human being."

Herkimer was still sitting on the grass, beside the sprawled, dead body of Trevor's agent. He did not take his hands from his face. He made no sign that he was going to. The blood still dripped down between his fingers and trickled down his arms.

Sutton said to Eva, "It was very nice to see you again. And thank you for the breakfast."

He turned on his heel and walked away, across the patio and over the low wall and out into the path that led down to the road.

He heard Eva cry out for him to stop, but he pretended not to hear her.

"I was raised by androids," she had said. And he had been raised by Buster. By Buster, who had taught him how to fight when the kid down the road had given him a licking. Buster, who had whaled him good and proper for the eating of green apples. By Buster, who had gone out, five hundred years before, to homestead a planet.

He walked with the icy fury still running in his blood.

They didn't trust me, he said. They thought I might sell out. After all the years of waiting, after all the years of planning and of thinking.

"What is it, Ash?"

"What's going on, Johnny? What about this?"

"You're a stinker, Ash."

"To hell with you," said Sutton. "You and all the rest of them."

Trevor's men, he knew, must be around the house, watching and waiting. He expected to be stopped. But he wasn't stopped. He didn't see a soul.

XLVIII

SUTTON STEPPED into the visor booth and closed the door behind him. From the rack along the wall, he took out the directory and hunted up the number. He dialed and snapped the toggle and there was a robot in the screen.

"Information," said the robot, his eyes seeking out the forehead of the man who called. Since it was an android, he dropped the customary "sir."

"Information. Records. What can I do for you?"

"Is there any possibility," asked Sutton, "that this call could be tapped?"

"None," said the robot. "Absolutely none. You see . . ."

"I want to see the homestead filings for the year 7990," said Sutton.

"Earth filings?"

Sutton nodded.

"Just a moment," said the robot.

Sutton waited, watching the robot select the proper spool and mount it on the viewer.

"They are arranged alphabetically," said the robot. "What name did you wish?"

"The name begins with S," said Sutton. "Let me see the S's."

The unwinding spool was a blur on the screen. It slowed momentarily at the M's, spun to the P's, then went more slowly.

The S list dragged by.

"Toward the end," said Sutton, and finally, "Hold it."

For there was the entry that he sought.

Sutton, Buster . . .

He read the planet description three times to make sure he had it firmly in his mind.

"That's all," he said. "Thank you very much."

The robot grumbled at him and shut off the screen.

Outside again, Sutton ambled easily across the foyer of the office building he had selected to place his call. On the road outside, he walked up the road, branched off onto a path and found a bench with a pleasant view.

He sat down on the bench and forced himself to relax.

For he was being watched, he knew. Kept under observation, for by this time, certainly, Trevor would know that the android who had walked out of Eva Armour's house could be none other than he. The psych-tracer, long ago, would have told the story, would have traced his movements and pinpointed him for Trevor's men to watch.

Take it easy, he told himself. Dawdle. Loaf. Act as if you didn't have a thing to do, as if you didn't have a thought in mind.

You can't fool them, but you can at least catch them unguarded when you have to move.

And there were many things to do, many things left to think about, although he was satisfied that the course of action he had planned was the course to take.

He took them up, step by step, checking them over for any chance of slip-up.

First, back to Eva's house to get the manuscript notes

he had left on the hunting asteroid, notes that either Eva or Herkimer must have kept through all the years . . . or was it only weeks?

That would be ticklish and embarrassing business at the best. But they were his notes, he told himself. They were his to claim. He had no commitments in this business.

"I have come to get my notes. I suppose you still have them somewhere."

Or, "Remember the attaché case I had? I wonder if you took care of it for me."

Or, "I'm going on a trip. I'd appreciate my notes if you can lay your hands on them."

Or—

But it was no use. However he might say it, whatever he might do, the first step would be to reclaim the notes.

Dawdle up till then, he told himself. Work your way back toward the house until it's almost dark. Then get the notes and after that move fast—so fast that Trevor's gang can't catch up with you.

Second was the ship, the ship that he must steal.

He had spotted it earlier in the day while loafing at the area spaceport. Sleek and small, he knew that it would be a fast job, and the stiff, military bearing of the officer who had been directing the provisioning and re-fueling had been the final tip-off that it was the ship he wanted.

Loafing outside the barrier fence, playing the part of the officer's mind. Ten minutes later, he was on his way, an idly curious, no-good android, he had carefully entered with the information that he needed.

The ship did carry a time warp unit.

It was not taking off until the next morning.

It would be guarded during the night.

Without a doubt, Sutton told himself, one of Trevor's ships, one of the fighting fleetships of the Revisionists.

It would take nerve, he knew, to steal the ship. Nerve and fast footwork and a readiness and the ability to kill.

Saunter out onto the field, as if he were waiting for an incoming ship, mingling with the crowd. Slip out of the crowd and walk across the field, acting as if he had a right to be there. Not run . . . walk. Run only if someone challenged him and made the challenge stick. Run then. Fight. Kill, if necessary. But get the ship.

Get the ship and pile on the speed to the limit of endurance, heading in a direction away from his destination, driving the ship for everything that was in it.

Two years out, or sooner if necessary, he would throw in the time unit, roll himself and the ship a couple of centuries into the past.

Once in the past, he would have to ditch the motors, for undoubtedly they would have built-in recognition signals which could be traced. Unship them and let them travel in the direction he had been going.

Then take over the empty hull with his nonhuman body, swing around and head toward Buster's planet, still piling on the speed, building it up to that fantastic figure that was necessary to jump great interstellar spaces.

Vaguely he wondered how his body, how the drive of his energy-intake body, would compare with the actual motors in the long haul. Better, he decided. Better than the motors. Faster and stronger.

But it would take years, many years of time, for Buster was far out.

He checked. Unshipping the engines would throw off pursuit. The pursuers would follow the recognition signals in the motors, would spend long days in overhauling them before they discovered their mistake.

Check.

The time roll would unhook the contact of Trevor's psych-tracers, for they could not operate through time.

Check.

By the time other tracers could be set in other times to find him he would be so far out that the tracers would go insane trying to catch up on the time lag of his whereabouts—if, in fact, they could ever find it in the vastness of the outer reaches of the galaxy.

Check.

If it works, he thought. If it only works. If there isn't some sort of slip-up, some kind of unseen factor.

A squirrel skipped across the grass, sat up on its haunches and took a long look at him. Then, deciding that he was not dangerous, it started a busy search in the grass for imaginary buried treasure.

Cut loose, thought Sutton. Cut loose from everything that holds me. Cut loose and get the job done. Forget Trevor and his Revisionists, forget Herkimer and the androids. Get the book written.

Trevor wants to buy me. And the androids do not trust me. And Morgan, if he had the chance, would kill me.

The androids do not trust me.

That's foolish, he told himself.

Childish.

And yet, they did not trust him. You are human, Eva had told him. The humans are your people. You are a member of the race.

He shook his head, bewildered by the situation.

There was one thing that stood out clearly. One thing he had to do. One obligation that was his and one that must be fulfilled or all else would be with utterly no meaning.

There is a thing called destiny.

The knowledge of that destiny has been granted me. Not as a human being, not as a member of the human race, but as an instrument to transmit that knowledge to all other thinking life.

I must write a book to do it.

I must make that book as clear and forceful and as honest as I can.

Having done that, I have discharged my responsibility.

Having done that, there is no further claim upon me.

A footstep sounded on the path back of the bench and Sutton turned around.

"Mr. Sutton, isn't it?" said the man.

Sutton nodded.

"Sit down, Trevor," he said. "I've been expecting you."

XLIX

"You didn't stay long with your friends," said Trevor.

Sutton shook his head. "We had a disagreement."

"Something about this Cradle business?"

"You might call it that," said Sutton, "It goes a good deal deeper. The fundamental prejudices rooted between androids and humans."

"Herkimer killed an android who brought him a message about the Cradle," Trevor said.

"He thought it was someone that you sent. Someone masquerading as an android. That is why he killed him."

Trevor pursed his mouth sanctimoniously ."Too bad," he said. "Too bad. Mind telling me how he recognized the . . . might we call it the deception?"

"That is something," Sutton said, "that I'm not telling you."

Trevor labored at acting unconcerned. "The main point is," he said, "that it didn't work."

"You mean the androids didn't run helter-skelter for the Cradle and show you where it was."

Trevor nodded. "There was another angle to it, too. They might have pulled some of their guards off the crisis points. That would have helped us some."

"Double-barreled," said Sutton.

"Oh, most assuredly," said Trevor. "Nothing like getting the other fellow square behind the eight-ball."

He squinted at Sutton's face.

"Since when," he asked, "and why did you desert the human race?"

Sutton put his hand up to his face, felt the hardness of the plastic that had remodeled his features into those of another person.

"It was Herkimer's idea," he declared. "He thought it would make me hard to spot. You wouldn't be looking for an android, you know."

Trevor nodded agreement. "It would have helped," he said. "It would have fooled us for a while, but when you walked away and the tracer followed you, we knew who you were."

The squirrel came hopping across the grass, sat down in front of them and looked them over.

"Sutton," Trevor asked, "how much do you know about this Cradle business?"

"Nothing," Sutton told him. "They told me I was a human and it was an android matter."

"You can see from that how important it must be."

"I think I can," said Sutton.

"You can guess, just from the name, what it might be."

"That's not too hard to do," said Sutton.

"Because we needed a greater force of humans," said Trevor, "we made the first androids a thousand years ago. We needed them to fill out the too-thin ranks of mankind. We made them as close to humans as we could. They could do everything the humans could except one thing."

"They can't reproduce," said Sutton. "I wonder, Trevor, if it had been possible, if we would have given that power to them, too. For if we had, they would have been true humans. There would have been no difference between a man whose ancestors were made in a laboratory and those whose ancestors stemmed back to the primal ocean. The androids would have been a self-continuing race, and they wouldn't have been androids. They would have been humans. We would have been adding to our population by chemical as well as biological means."

"I dont' know," said Trevor. "Honestly, I don't. Of course, the wonder is that we could make them at all, that we could produce life in the laboratory. Think of the sheer intellectual ability and the technical skill that went into it. For centuries men had tried to find out what life was, had run down one blind alley after another, bumping into stone wall after stone wall. Failing in a scientific answer, many of them turned back to the divine source, to a mythical answer, to the belief that it was a matter of divine intervention. The idea is perfectly expressed by du Noüy, who wrote back in the twentieth century."

"We gave the androids one thing we do not have ourselves," said Sutton, calmly.

Trevor stared at him, suddenly hard, suddenly suspicious.

"You . . ."

"We gave them inferiority," said Sutton. "We made them less than human. We supplied them with a reason to fight us. We denied them something they have to fight to get . . . equality. We furnished them with a motive Man lost long ago. Man no longer needs to prove he is as good as anyone else, that he is the greatest animal in his world or in his galaxy."

"They're equal now," said Trevor, bitterly. "The androids have been reproducing themselves . . . chemically, not biologically, for a long time now."

"We could have expected it," said Sutton. "We should have suspected it long ago."

"I suppose we should have," Trevor admitted. "We gave them the same brains we have ourselves. We gave them, or we tried to give them, a human perspective."

"And we put a mark upon their foreheads," Sutton told him.

Trevor made an angry motion with his hand.

"That little matter is being taken care of now," he said. "When the androids make another android they don't bother to put a mark upon his head."

Sutton started and then settled back as the thunder hit him . . . thunder that rolled and rumbled in his brain, a growing, painful, roaring thunder that shut out everything.

He had said a weapon. He had said there was a weapon. . . .

"They could make themselves better than they were originally," said Trevor. "They could improve upon the model. They could build a super-race, a mutant race, call it what you will. . . ."

Only one weapon, he had said. And you can't fight with just one cannon.

Sutton put a hand up to his forehead, rubbed hard against his brow.

"Sure," said Trevor. "You can go nuts thinking about it. I have. You can conjure up all sorts of possibilities. They could push us out. The new pushing out the old."

"The race would be human still," said Sutton.

"We built slowly, Sutton," Trevor said. "The old race. The biological race. We came up from the dawn of Man, we came up from chipped flints and fist ax, from the cave and the treetop nest. We've built too slowly and painfully and bloodily to have our heritage taken from us by something to which that slowness and the pain and blood would mean not a thing at all."

One gun, Sutton thought. But he had been wrong. There were a thousand guns, a million guns, wheeling into line. A million guns to save destiny for all life that was or would be. Now or a million billion years from now.

"I suppose," he said, shakily, "that you feel now I should throw in with you."

"I want you," said Trevor, "to find out for me where the Cradle is."

"So you can smash it," Sutton said.

"So I can save humanity," said Trevor. "The old humanity. The real humanity."

"You feel," said Sutton, "that all humans should stick together now."

"If you have a streak of the human in you," said Trevor, "you will be with us now."

"There was a time," said Sutton, "back on Earth, before men went to the stars, that the human race was the most important thing the mind of Man could know. That isn't true any longer, Trevor. There are other races just as great."

"Each race," said Trevor, "is loyal to its own. The human race must be loyal unto itself."

"I am going to be traitor," Sutton said. "I may be wrong, but I still think that destiny is greater than humanity."

"You mean that you refuse to help us?"

"Not only that," said Sutton. "I am going to fight you. I'm telling you this now so that you will know. If you want to kill me, Trevor, now's the time to do it. Because if you don't do it now, it will be too late."

"I wouldn't kill you for all the world," said Trevor. "Because I need the words you wrote. Despite you and the androids, Sutton, we'll read them the way we want them read. And so will all the other slimy, crawling things you admire so much. There's nothing in God's world that can stand before the human race, that can match the human race. . . ."

Sutton saw the loathing that was on Trevor's face.

"I'm leaving you to yourself, Sutton," Trevor told him. "Your name will go down as the blackest blot in all of human history. The syllables of your name will be a sound that the last human will gag upon if he tries to speak it. Sutton will become a common noun with which one man will insult another. . . ."

He called Sutton a name that was a fighting word and Sutton did not stir upon the bench.

Trevor stood up and started to walk away and then turned back. His voice was not much larger than a whisper, but it cut into Sutton's brain like a whetted knife.

"Go and wash your face," he said. "Wash off the plastic and the mark. But you'll never be human again, Sutton. You'll never dare to call yourself a man again."

He turned on his heel and walked away, and staring at his back, Sutton saw the back of humanity turned upon him forevermore.

Somewhere in his brain, as if it were from far away, he seemed to hear the sound of a slamming door.

L

THERE WAS one lamp lighted, in a corner of the room. The attaché case lay on a table underneath the lamp and Eva Armour was standing beside a chair, as if she had been expecting him.

"You came back," said Eva, "to get your notes. I have them ready for you."

He stood just inside the door and shook his head.

"Not yet," he said. "Later I will need the notes. Not yet."

And there it was, he thought, the thing he had worried about that afternoon, the thing that he had tried to find the words to say.

"I told you about a weapon at breakfast this morning," he said. "You must remember what I said about it. I said there was only one weapon. I said you can't fight a war with just one gun."

Eva nodded, face drawn in the lamplight. "I remember, Ash."

"There are a million of them," said Ash. "As many as you want."

He moved slowly across the room until he stood face to face with her.

"I am on your side," he told her, simply. "I saw Trevor this afternoon. He cursed me for all humanity."

Slowly she put up a hand and he felt it slide across his face, the palm cool and smooth. Her fingers tightened in his hair and she shook his head gently, tenderly.

"Ash," she said, "you washed your face. You are Ash again."

He nodded. "I wanted to be human again," he told her.

"Trevor told you about the Cradle, Ash?"

"I'd guessed some of it," Sutton said. "He told me the rest. About the androids that wear no mark."

"We use them as spies," she said, as if it was quite a natural thing to say. "We have some of them in Trevor's headquarters. He thinks that they are human."

"Herkimer?" he asked.

"He isn't here, Ash. He wouldn't be here, after what happened out on the patio."

"Of course," said Sutton. "Of course he wouldn't. Eva, we humans are such heels."

"Sit down," she told him. "That chair over there. You talk so funny that you scare me."

He sat down.

"Tell me what happened," she demanded.

He didn't tell her. He said, "I thought of Herkimer this afternoon. When Trevor was talking with me. I hit him this morning and I would hit him tomorrow morning if he said the same thing to me. It's something in the human blood, Eva. We fought our way up. With fist ax and club and gun and atom bomb and . . ."

"Shut up," cried Eva. "Keep still, can't you?"

He looked up at her in astonishment.

"Human, you say," she said. "And what is Herkimer if he isn't human? He is a human, made by humans. A robot can make another robot and they're still robots, aren't they? A human makes another human and both of them are humans."

Sutton mumbled, confused. "Trevor is afraid the androids will take over. That there will be no more humans. No more original, biological humans . . ."

"Ash," she said, "you are bothering yourself over something that a thousand generations from now will not have been solved. What's the use of it?"

He shook his head. "I guess there is no use. It keeps stirring around in my head. There's no rest for me. Once it was so clear-cut and simple. I would write a book and the galaxy would read it and accept it and everything would be just fine."

"It still can be that way," she said. "After a while, after a long while. But to do it we have to stop Trevor. He is blinded by the same tangled semantics that blind you."

"Herkimer said one weapon would do it," Sutton said. "One weapon would be the balance that was needed. Eva, the androids have gone a long way in their research, haven't they? Chemical, I mean. The study of the human body. They would have to, to do what they have done."

She nodded. "A long way, Ash."

"They have a scanner, then . . . a machine that could take a person apart, molecule by molecule, record it almost atom for atom. Make a blueprint for another body."

"We've done that very thing," said Eva. "We've duplicated men in Trevor's organization. Kidnaped them and blueprinted them and made a duplicate . . . sent him back the duplicate and placed the other under benevolent detention. It's only been through tricks like that that we've been able to hold our own at all."

"You could duplicate me?" asked Sutton.

"Certainly, Ash, but . . ."

"A different face, of course," said Sutton. "But a duplicate brain and . . . well, a few other things."

Eva nodded. "Your special abilities," she said.

"I can get into another mind," said Sutton. "Not mere telepathy, but the actual power to be another person, to be that other mind, to see and know and feel the same things that the other mind may see or know or feel. I don't know how it's done, but it must be something in the brain structure. If you duplicated my brain, the abilities should go along with the duplication. Not all of the duplicates would have it, maybe, not all of them could use it, but there would be some of them that could."

She gasped. "Ash, you would mean . . ."

"You would know everything," said Sutton, "that Trevor thinks. Every word and thought that passes through his mind. Because one of you would be Trevor. And the same thing with every other person who has anything to do with the war in time. You would know as soon as they know what they're going to do. You could plan to meet any threat they might be considering. You could block them at everything they tried."

"It would be stalemate," Eva said, "and that is exactly what we want. A strategy of stalemate, Ash. They wouldn't know how they were being blocked and many times they would not know who was blocking them. It would seem to them that luck was permanently against them . . . that destiny was against them."

"Trevor, himself, gave me the idea," Sutton said. "He told me to go out and butt my head against a wall for a while. He told me that finally I would get tired of doing it. He said that after a while I would give up."

"Ten years," said Eva. "Ten years should do the job. But if ten won't, why, then, a hundred. Or a thousand if it takes that long. We have all the time there is."

"Finally," said Sutton, "they would give up. Literally throw up their hands and quit. It would be such a futile thing. Never winning. Always fighting hard and never winning."

They sat in the room with its one little oasis of light that stood guard against the darkness that pressed in upon them and there was no triumph in them, for this was not a thing of triumph. This was a matter of necessity and not one of conquest. This was Man fighting himself and winning and losing at the same time.

"You can arrange this scanning soon?" asked Sutton.

Eva nodded. "Tomorrow, Ash?"

She looked at him, queerly. "What's your hurry?"

"I am leaving," Sutton said. "Running away to a refuge that I thought of. That is, if you'll lend me a ship."

"Any ship you want."

"It would be more convenient that way," he told her. "Otherwise, I'd have to steal one."

She did not ask the question that he had expected and he went on, "I have to write the book."

"There are plenty of places, Ash, where you could write the book. Safe places. Places that could be arranged to be foolproof safe."

He shook his head.

"There's an old robot," he said. "He's the only folks I have. When I was on Cygni, he went out to one of the star systems at the very edge and filed a homestead. I am going there."

"I understand," she said, speaking very gravely.

"There's just one thing," said Sutton. "I keep remembering a little girl who came and spoke to me when I was fishing. I know that she was a person conditioned in my mind. I know she was put there for a purpose, but it makes no difference. I keep thinking of her."

He looked at Eva and saw how the lamplight turned her hair into a copper glory.

"I don't know if I'll ever be in love," said Sutton. "I can't tell you for sure if I love you, Eva. But I wish you would go with me out to Buster's planet."

She shook her head. "Ash, I must stay here, for a while at least. I've worked for years on this thing. I must see it through."

Her eyes were misty in the lamplight. "Perhaps sometime, Ash, if you still want me. Perhaps a little later I can come."

Sutton said, simply, "I'll always want you, Eva."

He reached out a hand and tenderly touched the copper curl that dropped against her forehead.

"I know that you'll never come," he said. "If it had been just a little different . . . if we had been two ordinary people living ordinary lives."

"There's a greatness in you, Ash," she told him. "You will be a god to many people."

He stood silently and felt the loneliness of eternity closing in upon him. There was no greatness, as she had said, only the loneliness and bitterness of a man who stood alone and would stand alone forever.

LI

Sutton floated in a sea of light and from far away he heard the humming of the machines at work, little busy machines that were dissecting him with their tiny fingers of probing light and clicking shutters and the sensitive paper that ran like a streak of burnished silver through the holders. Dissecting and weighing, probing and measuring . . . missing nothing, adding nothing. A faithful record not of himself alone but of every particle of him, of every cell and molecule, of every branching nerve and muscle fiber.

And from somewhere else, also far away, from a place beyond the sea of light that held him, a voice said one word and kept repeating it:

Traitor.

Traitor.

Traitor.

One word without an exclamation point. A voice that had no emphasis. One flat word.

First there was one voice crying it and then another joined and then there was a crowd and finally it was a roaring mob and the sound and word built up until it was a world of voices that were crying out the word.

Crying out the word until there was no longer any meaning in it, until it had lost its meaning and became a sound many times repeated.

Sutton tried to answer and there was no answer nor any way to answer. He had no voice, for he had no lips or tongue or throat. He was an entity that floated in the sea of light and the word kept on, never changing . . . never stopping.

But back of the word, a background to the word, there were other words unspoken.

We are the ones who clicked the flints together and built the first fire of Man's own making. We are the ones who drove the beasts from out the caves and took them for ourselves, in which to shape the first pattern of a human culture. We are the ones who painted the colorful bison on the hidden walls, working in the light of lamps with moss for wicks and fat for oil. We are the ones who tilled the soil and tamed the seed to grow beneath our hand. We are the ones who built great cities that our own kind might live together and accomplish the greatness that a handful could not even try. We are the ones who dreamed of stars. We are the ones who broke the atom to the harness of our minds.

It is our heritage you spend. It is our traditions that you give away to things that we have made, that we have fashioned with the deftness of our hands and the sharpness of our minds.

The machines clicked on and the voice kept on with the one word it was saying.

But there was another voice, deep within the undefinable being that was Asher Sutton, a faint voice . . .

It said no word, for there was no word that framed the thought it said.

Sutton answered it. "Thank you, Johnny," he said. "Thank you very much."

And was astonished that he could answer Johnny when he could not answer all the others.

The machines went on with their clicking.

LII

THE SILVERY ship roared down the launching ramp, slammed into the upcurve and hurled itself into the sky, a breath of fire that blazed against the blue.

"He doesn't know," said Herkimer, "that we arranged it for him. He does not know we managed him to the last, that we sent Buster out many years ago to establish refuge for him, knowing that someday he might need that refuge."

"Herkimer," said Eva. "Herkimer . . ."

Her voice choked. "He asked me to go with him, Herkimer. He said he needed me. And I couldn't go. And I couldn't explain."

She kept her head tilted, watching the tiny pinpoint of fire that was fleeing spaceward.

"He had to keep on thinking," Eva said, "that there were some humans he had helped, that there were some humans who still believed in him."

Herkimer nodded. "It was the only thing to do, Eva. It was what you had to do. We took enough from him, enough of his humanity. We could not take it all."

She put her hands up to her face and huddled her shoulders and stood there, an android woman crying out her heart.

CLIFFORD D. SIMAK has been writing science-fiction for more than thirty years. His stories have appeared in almost all the science-fiction magazines, past and present, and he is rated among the top authors in the field.

Mr. Simak was born in Millville, Wisconsin, and now lives in Minnesota.

BEST-SELLING
Science Fiction
and
Fantasy

Stories
⊱ of ⊰
Swords and Sorcery